A Burden of Love

A BURDEN OF LOVE

Copyright © 2023 by Heather Hataley

All rights reserved. No part of this book may be reproduced or used in any manner without written permission of the copyright owner except for the use of quotations in a book review.

This book is a work of fiction. Names, characters, places, and incidents either are the product of the authors imagination or are used fictitiously. Any resemblance to actual persons, living or dead, events, or locales is entirely coincidental.

Cover & Interior Design by Stone Ridge Books

ISBN 978-1-7777973-2-4 (paperback)
ISBN 978-1-7777973-3-1 (ebook)

10 9 8 7 6 5 4 3 2 1

HEATHER HATALEY

A Burden of Love

ALSO BY HEATHER HATALEY

A Collection of Scars

To James

Visit www.heatherhataley.com to sign up for the email newsletter to receive extra content and updates sent straight to your inbox.

Prologue

The wedding ceremony would take place that evening at the back of the palace on the very patio where Yonah and Naris spent so much of their time. The very patio where Yonah had first seen Naris' violent temper. Until then, however, she had no intention of leaving her room for fear of running into one of their guests.

The guests – the masters – were already watching her with suspicion. Their first impressions of her were lukewarm, at best.

The bedroom door opened, causing the cat sitting on Yonah's lap to stir, and a woman several years older than Yonah's twenty swept in, carrying a small tray of food. "I brought you something to get you through until dinner." She set the tray on a table. "Have you been hiding here all day?"

The woman's name was Praha and she had been serving Yonah since Naris brought her to the palace.

"I didn't want to talk to anyone," Yonah replied. Not even Naris. She didn't want to let anything she said put any thoughts of backing out into Naris' head. It would be best for her to stay out of everyone's way until the ceremony, at which point any objections or second thoughts would have to be public and potentially reputation-ruining choices.

She pulled Saza the cat back onto her lap.

Praha pursed her lips. "Both you and the master. I'm surprised you even bothered to invite these people. It's clear that—" She stopped suddenly.

Yonah finished the thought. "That Naris doesn't like them, and none of them like me."

With a shrug, Praha said, "We all know what happened the last time there was a gathering here."

Naris had tried so hard to prove to Yonah that she would be accepted by the masters as his guest, despite the collar she wore that marked her as a slave. His attempts to convince the masters had been futile, so much so that one master – Zanith – had assaulted Yonah and received a swift punch to the face from Naris.

"He wants to be the head of one of the most respected families in the upper class," Yonah replied. "Even if that means spending time with people he doesn't like."

Praha shook her head and sighed. "Let's do your hair first." She opened a drawer and removed a brush, pins, and an orange ribbon. She then picked up a chair and placed it in front of the full-length mirror that hung from one of the bedroom walls. "Sit."

Yonah stood from the chaise she had been reclined in—Saza landed gracefully on the floor and sprang onto the bed, where she curled up into a little black ball—and sat in front of Praha. As Praha braided her hair, Yonah took a moment to take in her reflection.

Her long dark hair was unkempt after the previous night. She had dull brown eyes, a square chin, and a forehead lined with wrinkles that made her look older than she was. Her eyes rested on the pink scar in the centre of her bottom lip. Naris had done that to her.

Her gaze drifted to the scar on her right arm. A member of the Guard had done that to her.

The farther along into the dressing process Yonah went, the more her nerves shook. She watched her transformation in the mirror as Praha did her hair and applied her makeup. From slave to master she went, although she was still wearing the copper collar that marked her enslavement.

Slavery was the new justice system institutionalized by President Althu, the man who had taken over Harasa after the coup. It was enforced by a group of men and women who policed the country known as the Guard. Yonah had been enslaved when she and her two siblings were found living on the streets—orphans were enslaved until their twentieth birthday.

Yonah kept sliding the palms of her hands down the tops of her thighs as if wiping her nerves away. Her chest felt too small for her pounding heart. She exhaled loudly through rounded lips.

Praha gave Yonah a sideways glance through the mirror before them. "Why are you marrying him?"

It wasn't the first time Praha had questioned Yonah's motives for marrying their shared master. Each time, Yonah replied with as vague a response as she could give.

"Because," Yonah said. "It will make things easier."

"That's not true," Praha said, sounding bored. "You know that. I know that."

"Maybe I can tell you once I'm free."

"But that's just it, Yonah." Praha's eyes were alight with a challenge. "You won't be free after you marry Naris. Never."

Yes. That was the sacrifice she was making.

IN ORDER TO make their entrances to the ceremony, Yonah and Naris would ride in separate carriages from the front of the estate to the back, at which point they would walk up the vineyard to the rear courtyard. A new gravel path had been built for the occasion.

Praha walked down to the front of the palace with Yonah, staying a few steps behind her. When she stepped through the front doors, Yonah saw her friend Seidon stroking one of the horses' long faces. As the stable master, he was very familiar with each animal. When he noticed Yonah's arrival, he turned to face her. His age-lined face opened into one of surprised awe. The look sent a wave of embarrassed gratitude through Yonah.

"Yonah," the aging stable master said. He gave her a tight-lipped smile. "You look very grown up."

"Do I look like a master?"

"Besides the collar?" Seidon looked her over. "You look like a lady."

Maybe that would be enough for the masters to accept her as their own.

"You'd best hop in," Seidon said, nodding his head towards the second carriage. "Master Naris hasn't come down yet, and you shouldn't see each other before it all starts."

Seidon opened the carriage door for Yonah and took her hand to help her inside. Praha helped make sure Yonah's dress and floor-length veil were tucked inside before the door was shut.

Inside the velvet-lined carriage, Yonah sat in a hushed silence that made her feel suddenly very alone. The linen curtains were drawn across the windows so Yonah and Naris wouldn't see each other until the ceremony began.

Yonah ran her fingertips over the orange satin edge of her otherwise white sheer veil. It was fastened to her head with a silver circlet that sat on top. She could feel the gems that hung from the top edge of the veil bump against her forehead every time she moved.

There was a brisk voice outside the carriage. Yonah paused for a moment, knowing she should wait until the ceremony, but she drew the curtain back ever so slightly and peeked outside.

She only caught a glimpse of him as he strode out of her sightline. He was a lean and powerful blur of navy and white.

Yonah sat back in her seat and brought her hand to the copper ring around her neck. That would be off soon. She would be married to a master and released from her servitude. Then the real work could begin.

Her nerves gnawed at her skin from the inside. Just as Yonah wished she could stand up and walk around to shake them away, the carriage started to move.

It was happening.

Yonah knew they were driving around the outside of the estate to the back, but with the curtains closed, she could only imagine what the view might look like from this new path. She pressed her white dress flat against her body and adjusted the skirt over her legs. Naris would be upset if anything about her outfit wasn't perfect, with so many of the other masters watching.

The carriage came to a stop. Yonah waited for any other movement, sounds, or signals as to what was happening.

Gentle violin music came floating through the air, accompanied by a guitar. Although the song had a soothing quality, it marked the start of the ceremony, which set Yonah's breath shaking.

There came the gentle snap of a carriage door opening and closing. Naris was making his way down the aisle, among the guests, to the patio.

After a few moments, the door to her own carriage opened, and Yonah stepped out.

She blinked at the bright sunlight. Hundreds of faces turned to look at her. The sudden attention made Yonah want to shrink back into the safety of the carriage for a brief moment, but she steeled herself, pulled her chest upwards, held her head high, and took up her space. She would not be a blushing and timid bride; she would not be the shame-faced slave they had all met months ago.

She was more than that.

Naris was standing on the patio, a couple steps higher than the guests. His figure was imposing in his navy jacket laced with silver decoration. But he was always imposing, always taking up space, always exuding the confidence of a predator. Yonah noticed that his fingers were shimmering with rings. He didn't normally wear jewelry. Neither did Yonah, but she wore several armlets, bangles, and large hoop earrings with deep blue stones hanging in the centre.

Through all the pomp and performance, Yonah saw sincerity in Naris' golden-brown eyes. He looked at her with love. It was a flawed loved, but it was love, nonetheless.

That look brought both serenity and guilt to Yonah.

She was walking down the aisle, around the large stone fountain. She wasn't sure where to put her hands and hoped she didn't look too awkward.

There was a variety of expressions on the guests in attendance. Many were stoically watchful. Some appeared to be genuinely enjoying themselves. Others narrowed their eyes in judgment at Yonah.

As Yonah started up the steps to the top of the patio, Naris grinned. He held his hand out to assist her. When she took it, she felt it shaking ever so slightly. She looked at Naris' face in search of anything that revealed nervousness or fear, but she saw only his mask of confidence.

A magistrate dressed in a cream-coloured robe cleared his throat and began to speak. Yonah didn't listen very closely to the magistrate. She was too busy trying to keep her face calm.

Then Naris was reciting his vows while he fastened a long white beaded necklace around Yonah's neck. He carefully maneuvered around her veil and ensured the necklace was straight as he pulled away.

The magistrate handed Yonah a similar necklace in black beads and asked her to repeat after him.

She tried not to let her voice shake. "I, Yonah, do wed thee, Naris. In marriage, I bind my body with your body, my mind with your mind, and my spirit with your spirit. We are both one and two beings. As one, we stand by each other, support each other, care for each other, and love each other. This I swear to do."

Yonah placed the necklace over Naris' head and laid it gently on his shoulders. Their eyes caught, tangled in a moment suspended in time. Yonah's breath stopped as she looked at Naris' handsome face and charming smile. She knew, more so than anyone, how fast that face could turn.

She stepped away, returning to her place.

They were instructed to clasp hands and walk once around the magistrate, to symbolize their parallel journey through life together. As they turned, Yonah's foot got caught up in her long veil, and she tripped. There was a moment of weightlessness as Yonah lost her footing, followed by the sudden stability of Naris grabbing her elbows and holding her steady.

She searched Naris' eyes for any displeasure, but there was only care there. Embarrassed for her lack of grace in front of the masters, Yonah rushed through the rest of the circle, neglecting to retrieve Naris' hand, and returned to her place in front of the magistrate, casting her eyes down with self-loathing. Naris followed and took Yonah's hand in his own.

"With these promises you have sworn today," the magistrate said, "you bind yourself together in matrimony in the eyes of your community and the government of Harasa." The magistrate frowned briefly at Yonah. "As you are now partners in life, you, Yonah, are immediately free from your servitude to Naris and the government of Harasa."

Yonah's heart swelled with anticipation. She tried to keep her face impassive, mindful of the watchful masters.

The magistrate took a step back and nodded to a Guard. The Guard, the body that policed all of Harasa in the search for orphaned children, criminals, disabled people, and rebels to enslave, dressed in their black clothes and red sashes, had plagued Yonah ever since the coup ten years ago.

This Guard carried a long tool with two wooden handles and a rounded metal end. He pulled the handles apart, and the rounded end opened like the mouth of a beast.

Yonah fought her panic as the Guard came towards her with the tool and wrapped the metal ends around her rounded copper collar. She glanced at Naris, but while he wore a nervous expression, he didn't look alarmed.

There came a thick crack and movement from Yonah's collar that made her squint her eyes shut. She wished she hadn't. The masters were watching her. She forced her eyes open again. It seemed her collar wasn't quite broken. The Guard adjusted the tool's hold on the collar and pressed the handles together again.

This time, the collar broke and clattered to the stone patio. Yonah's eyes followed its fall. As she stared at the now useless metal next to her feet, her hand went up to her throat. Her bare neck, unburdened by that awful mark of slavery. She was free.

Yonah looked up at Naris. He didn't smile as before, but his face was clear. He nodded once slowly at Yonah as if to say, 'I promised you I would set you free. I held up my end of the agreement.'

And now he expected Yonah to hold up her end.

The magistrate stepped forward. "I present to you Naris and Yonah Muran."

They both reached for the other's hand and turned to face their guests. There was polite applause.

Yonah felt as if she could float away. She was a free woman. All of these people had witnessed her release. She was one of their peers now.

She was a master.

THE NEWLYWEDS LED their guests into the feasting hall. The long tables were already set with mountains of food. Every glass was filled with wine that Naris' vineyard had produced. A dozen slaves stood around the perimeter of the hall, waiting for their service to be required.

While Yonah had never been entirely accepted by the slaves on Naris' estate, the divide between her and them was even greater now that she had so ceremoniously had her own slave collar removed. She could order them to do as she bid, make demands of them, and punish them as she saw fit.

The weight of her newly gained power sent a shudder through Yonah.

She and Naris strode to the opposite end of the hall where there was a raised dais on which sat the head table. In normal circumstances, the newlyweds would be seated there with their families, but as neither Yonah nor Naris had any family left, it would be just the two of them.

Once at their table, Yonah removed her veil from her head, folded it and wrapped it around her shoulders like a shawl, and replaced the circlet back on her head. She forced herself to sit up tall in her chair next to Naris to match his confidence.

As they ate, guests took their turn to move towards the head table and congratulate the couple on their nuptials.

A man slightly older than Yonah and Naris with a sun-tanned face came forwards. At the man's arrival, Naris stood up and stepped off the dais to meet him, arms open wide.

"Kejal," Naris said, unable to contain a grin.

The two men embraced. Yonah smoothed out her dress as she stood up, taking a moment to compose herself. The last time she had seen Kejal was the night she had tried to escape from his estate with her ill sister Sayzia.

Kejal had left Sayzia to die in the cold.

Yonah twisted her face into as pleasant an expression as she could and moved to meet the men on the floor. Upon noticing Yonah's arrival, Kejal bowed his head to her and said, "Congratulations, Yonah. I wish you and Naris all the happiness in the world."

She tilted her head slightly downwards. "Thank you, Master Kejal."

"You don't need to be so formal with Kejal, my dear," Naris said. "He's like family."

"Of course," she replied serenely.

Later, when their guest Zanith came to congratulate them, Naris was much cooler.

"I offer my congratulations to you both," Zanith said. He was so tall that he did not need to look up as much as the other guests to make eye contact with the newlyweds. There was impish laughter in his eyes.

Yonah did not bother trying to hide her displeasure at having to speak to this man. She remembered how he had cornered her, his husky voice in her ear, his grip on her wrist, his hand across her face.

"Thank you, Master Zanith," Naris said. "We hope you enjoy your stay here at Vaha."

"Oh, I already am," Zenith said with a sneer. "The guests are full of gossip and speculation over you two and your…arrangement."

Yonah could feel the anger emanating from Naris. She rested a hand on his clenched fist, which released slightly.

"I figure I'll start a pool on how long you two will last," Zanith continued. His eyes gleamed mischievously. "And how it will end."

Fueled by a residual hatred for the man and a small amount of arrogance gained from her new status, Yonah said, "No marriage is perfect, Master Zanith. But since Naris and I are, fortunately, completely unlike you, I don't think there'll be much to worry about."

The insult induced a mere scoff from Zanith.

"Perhaps your pool should be based on when the next time you will be removed from a master's home," Yonah added. "It could be sooner than you think."

"I see the wedding ceremony and the removal of your collar has tricked you into thinking you have power over me."

"Only when you are in our home," Yonah said. Her insides were shaking violently. Never before had she been so outspoken with a master.

With a bored look on his face, Zanith looked to Naris. "You married a slave, Naris. We all saw. Just a slave." Without bothering to bow his head, Zanith turned and went back to his table.

Yonah and Naris sat in heavy silence. Keeping her head forward, Yonah reached for her wine glass and sipped. Naris was still. She wanted to check that he wasn't upset with her, but she did not want to apologize for speaking to Zanith as she did. She knew Naris disliked him just as much as she did.

"I'm sorry if I affected the business in any way," she said. "And I am not sorry for what I said."

Naris finally turned his head to look at her. Yonah returned his look, fiercely connecting with his penetrating gaze. Countless times before this, they had locked wills this way.

Naris began to laugh softly, his shoulders shaking. Yonah gasped in surprise, then joined him in his laughter.

"I'm not sorry you said those things either," Naris said. He took Yonah's hand and kissed it, keeping his eyes firmly on her. Her heart fluttered, and, for a moment, she felt like she and Naris were truly life partners, just as the magistrate had said.

There was dancing and more wine, and the guests' lively chatter turned to raucous laughter. Yonah was sure it was the wine talking when they cheered her and Naris out of the hall as they headed back to his room.

Once they were in the privacy of Naris' room, Naris undressed Yonah and she – playing the part of loving wife – undressed him. They fell onto the bed and stayed up pleasuring each other until the wine made them too fatigued for any more activity, and fell asleep, a tangle of legs and sheets.

Chapter One
Two Years Later

She felt Naris lean across the bed and kiss her tenderly on her temple. The gentle touch sent warmth through Yonah. The corners of her mouth curled slightly upwards. Naris chuckled softly.

"So, you are awake," he said, nuzzling his forehead against her head.

"I'm still sleeping," Yonah replied with a moan.

Naris gave her thigh a squeeze. The bed shifted slightly as he rolled out of bed. "I'll see you later, Sleepyhead."

The only reply Yonah gave was one more soft moan before letting sleep take over once more.

It wasn't long before she was awake for the day. Yonah sat up in the bed with a wide-mouthed yawn. She used to love mornings. They had been times of tranquil solitude. Now, they were a painful start to the day. She got so little sleep these days.

Yonah threw a robe over her naked body and made her way to her own bedroom to change. While she spent every night in Naris' room—she honestly felt comfortable enough there to consider it *their* room—her personal items were still housed in the bedroom she had lived in since first arriving at Vaha. It may not have been convenient for little day-to-day tasks such as this, but it gave Yonah privacy when she needed it.

Praha was waiting in Yonah's room for her arrival. She handed Yonah an envelope whose wax seal hosted the image of a deer.

"Good morning, Master Yonah," the woman said briskly.

"Good morning, Praha." Yonah's tone was lighter than Praha's. "You've intercepted something?"

"It's for you."

Yonah read the sender's address and saw that the letter was from her acquaintance in Kelab, a man named Beneri. They had met shortly after Yonah and Naris' marriage on a tour of the city. Yonah ripped open the seal, removed the letter, and began to read.

Greetings to you, Yonah,

Even though it is still spring, I am already melting from the heat. But you are in the plains, where it isn't as hot as it is here in the desert region. I try to spend most of my days visiting Master Lania or Master Noran. They have pools at their city houses where you can fully submerge yourself in water! They might be getting annoyed with my spending so much time at their homes with little reciprocation. I'll have to host an event soon, so they don't tell others not to spend time with me.

The reason for my writing is to pass on this news that I heard. Slavery has been recently abolished in Jalid! Peacefully, too! The government surrendered to the protesters and lobbyists and signed an agreement stating that slavery would no longer be permitted in the county.

There is a rumour that some of the Jalid rebels are moving south into Harasa to try their hand at abolishing slavery here, too. I haven't heard if there is any real reason to believe that to be true.

When are you coming back to visit? I know your husband doesn't particularly enjoy my company, but I would be happy to host you two for a couple nights if you needed.

Your friend,

Beneri

Yonah read the second paragraph again. Slavery had been abolished in Jalid. She wondered if any slaves taken from Harasa would be trying to make their way back home or if it was better to stay in Jalid. Her sister, Sayzia, might have been freed from slavery if only she were still alive.

"What does it say?" Praha asked, interrupting Yonah's thoughts.

"Jalid has abolished slavery." Yonah passed the letter to Praha, whose eyes moved swiftly over the page.

"What was President Althu's response?"

President Althu had been the military minister for the Harasan government when he and his followers staged a coup and placed him in charge of the country, at which point he instituted the Slavery Act of Harasa.

Yonah shook her head. "I don't know. I imagine he'll feel a lot more pressure from the rebellion to do the same in Harasa, though." She started for her wardrobe and opened the doors. "Last night was successful?" A group of slave escapees had been brought to Vaha on their way to Modeef, the country south of Harasa. Since Yonah's marriage to Naris, she had placed Vaha on the rebels' map as one of many safehouses that could be used to move escapees.

"Yes. Seidon will send them out tonight."

"Good. And everything is ready for the midday meal?"

A short burst of air escaped Praha's nostril in a brief, silent chuckle. "From one kind of business to another, right? Yes, everything's ready."

Dressed in a plain but elegant skirt and shirt, Yonah first made her way to the back patio where she and Naris would be taking lunch with some potential clients. A round table and cushioned chairs had been brought out, and a couple of slaves were setting the table with dinnerware. When they noticed Yonah's arrival, the slaves bowed their heads slightly to her and sent looks of disdain her way.

Her relationship with the majority of the slaves at Vaha had never been cordial, but with Yonah's elevation in status, any hope of reconciliation was lost. She was worse than a master. She was a traitor.

Better the slaves think that than know the truth.

Yonah then went back inside and upstairs to Naris' office. She listened briefly at the closed door to hear if anyone was inside, but at the sound of silence, she knocked softly and entered.

Naris was sitting at his desk, bent over his ledgers. He looked up at Yonah's appearance, and a smile widened his tightly cropped bearded face.

"Good morning, my dear." He leaned back in his chair and beckoned Yonah towards him. She walked around the desk, bent over, and kissed him.

Kissing Naris was easy now. It was part of Yonah's duties as a spouse and part of the deal she had made with Naris upon their engagement: to be his and his alone, to be loving, to be obedient.

There were some kisses that reminded Yonah of the days she had found herself falling for Naris, kisses that were soft and full and made Yonah forget.

This was a usual kiss, from which Yonah pulled away easily, despite the reminder of Naris' dark side tugging at her. "Good morning," she said with a smile. "The patio is nearly set for our guests."

"Perfect. If we can convince them to make a purchase, new markets in the south might open up for us."

"We might have to expand soon."

Naris' eyes sparkled with excitement. "Wouldn't that be wonderful?" He took Yonah's hand. "And wouldn't it be wonderful if we could expand not just the business, but our own little family, too."

Yonah forced a smile onto her face and said, "I'm sure that will happen soon enough."

"I might bring someone in to take a look at you. It's been over two years, and still no child. And I'd hate to have to adopt."

"I don't think we should worry yet," Yonah said, placing her hand on Naris' shoulder. "We'll give it a little more time."

"You want to be a mother, right?" Naris asked. "I know you and I would be much better parents to our children than mine were to me. I know we could love them and give them everything they wanted."

Yonah kissed Naris' head. "You will make a great father."

He cradled her cheeks in his hands. "And you will make a great mother."

She tried to focus on the joys motherhood would have brought her, so Naris wouldn't see the fear in her eyes.

They shared a luxurious lunch with their visitors, a couple of women from the southern border of Harasa. Naris was charming and charismatic, Yonah thoughtful and gracious, and a contract was signed.

As they finished the meal, one of the women said, "Your grounds are beautiful. I'd love to see more."

Yonah pricked to attention.

"We can give you a tour," said Naris. "Yonah knows all the best spots, maybe even better than I do now."

"Before we go," Yonah said, "I'd like to find a scarf for the sun." She looked at their guests. "Do either of you need something for shade?"

The guests informed Yonah that they were fine for the walk, and Yonah went inside. She bolted to her bedroom and rang the call bell. She grabbed her orange scarf, wrapped it around her head and neck, and waited impatiently for Praha.

The moment Praha entered, Yonah hissed at her, "You must move the escapees. We're taking the visitors on a tour of the grounds, and we might end up at the stable."

"Move them where?" Praha's eyes were wide.

"The treehouse. No, the passage. You remember the way in, yes?"

"Yes, but that won't be easy to get to."

"I'll stall them. We'll go to the front first and take the other side around. I have to go; they're waiting for me."

They walked together from Yonah's room to the entrance hall, then Yonah went ahead to the back patio, trying to quell her shaking insides.

"Thank you for waiting," she said. "Why don't we start out front?"

One of the guests said, "I'd like to go down that way, if you don't mind." She pointed down the back path beyond the fountain.

"Uh..." Yonah glanced at Naris. There was a look of perplexed curiosity on his face. "Alright," Yonah said. If they went too fast through the vineyard to the open plain, the stable would be in view, and Praha and the escapees might be seen. "Let's take a closer look at the fountain, since we're here."

The small party went down the few patio steps to the dirt path and came closer to the looming stone fountain. Its arcing spray wafted a refreshing mist over their heads, providing a slight reprieve from the sun.

"When I have spare time, I like to sit here and think," Yonah said.

"Is it too cool to be here during the winter?"

Yonah forced herself not to look down the vineyard to the plain but to look at their guests. "On some days, yes, it gets too chilly to really enjoy this spot, but those days are few."

"Come, Yonah," Naris interrupted. "Let's show them something more interesting than this."

Yonah fumed at Naris' impatience but held her face in its calm position. "Why don't you tell them a little bit about the history of the vineyard?"

"Yes. We'll walk." Naris started down the dirt path to the back of the estate at a faster pace than Yonah would have liked. He spoke of how his great-great-grandfather developed the vineyard, and his mother and father had started expanding their circle of clients.

As inconspicuously as she could, Yonah pulled ahead of the group until she was at the edge of the vineyard and able to look across the plain to the stable in the near distance. She could see Praha leading a line of six people of varying ages away from the stable and towards the side of the palace.

"The treehouse!" Yonah said loudly, hoping Praha might hear how near they were and know to hurry.

"What?" asked Naris. He and their two guests were nearing the edge of the vineyard. Yonah rushed in front of them to block their way.

"We should visit your treehouse." If Yonah could keep them in the vineyard for just a few moments more, Praha and the escapees might be able to outrun their line of vision.

"A treehouse?" asked one of the women.

"That's whimsical."

Naris furrowed his brow. He and Yonah didn't normally include the treehouse on their estate tour. It had been one of his private havens as a child. "Why don't we take them to the stable, Yonah?"

"Oh, of course, if you ladies don't hold any interest in seeing the treehouse, then we will move on," Yonah said hurriedly. "I just thought it might be something different to explore."

"You've certainly piqued my interest," said one of the guests.

As they emerged from the vineyard, Yonah glanced once more towards the stable. She couldn't see Praha and the escapees. She could only assume that they had found success in reaching the palace's secret entrance.

They came upon the treehouse, a gift Naris' grandfather made for his children that Naris had inherited in his childhood. After looking at it briefly, Naris insisted they move on to the stable. Yonah didn't argue but hoped that Seidon had enough time to remove any evidence of the stable's recent guests.

As they came upon the stable, Saza, the black cat, came sidling out. Yonah scooped up the animal and felt the vibrations of her purr on her arm. It had a calming effect on her trembling insides.

"Do you need to see the inside?" Yonah asked.

"Yes, Yonah," Naris said, a tinge of annoyance in his voice. "Show them inside."

Yonah flashed a tight-lipped smile and led the way through the open doorway. "Hello, Seidon," she called.

There didn't look to be anything out of place in the stable. It was empty but for the stable master and one horse. The stable master was cleaning out one of the horse's shoes. He looked up at the party with his lined face and brown eyes. The copper collar around his neck shimmered slightly at his movement.

"Good afternoon, Master Yonah. Master Naris." The aging man stood up and bowed his head once.

"We've just come to take a look around," Naris said, strolling through the building. Yonah watched his roving eyes.

"How is everything here?" she asked Seidon. "Are all the other horses out?"

The man looked pointedly at Yonah. "Yes, they're all out."

The escapees were gone. The tension in Yonah's shoulders seeped away, and she breathed easier.

"May we see them?" asked one of the guests.

"Follow me," Seidon replied. He started for the back doorway with his perpetual limp—the reason he had been enslaved for life—when Naris said, "Has someone been sleeping in here?"

Everyone turned to Naris, who was looking at a patch of hay in the corner of one of the stalls. It was patted down in a circle, like a nest. The mark was too small to have come from a horse, even a foal.

"I did last night, Master," Seidon answered. "I was worried for one of the horses, but she pulled through. She's fit and fine today."

Naris nodded in acknowledgement of the answer, though there was a thoughtful look on his face. "I'm pleased you take so much care with them," he said.

The rest of the tour was uneventful. The guests seemed to take much pleasure from seeing the horses and the rest of the grounds. Although Yonah and Naris offered them a bed for the night, the women insisted they continue their journey. Yonah and Naris bid the new clients goodbye and watched as their carriage glided across the plain.

Naris leaned in close to Yonah, a dark fire in his eyes. "Never offer to show the treehouse to guests again. It's unprofessional."

"I just thought–"

"Never again."

He stormed back into the palace. Yonah watched him go like one gratefully watched storm clouds blow away.

Chapter Two

After giving Naris a moment to, presumably, return to his office on the second floor, Yonah sauntered back into the palace and headed straight for the library, the entrance to which was also on the second floor. As the library was normally kept locked, Yonah used her key—something she had finally acquired upon marrying Naris—to open the door and step inside.

The library was Yonah's favourite room in all of Vaha. It was a massive room filled with free-standing shelves connected by the second-floor walkway. It was lit by a monumental skylight. A cozy reading nook sat in the centre of the room. The far wall was checkered with imposing portraits of Naris' ancestors.

Yonah strode straight to the life-size portrait of Naris' great-grandmother, the mind behind the construction of Vaha itself. Yonah tugged on a small golden handle sticking out the side of the portrait frame. There was a clunking noise and the portrait shifted on the wall. Yonah swung the picture away from the wall to reveal a doorway.

She had discovered the passageways long before she and Naris were even engaged to be married. Yonah knew that Naris also used the passages himself. Although Naris was aware that Yonah knew of the passages' existence, Yonah wasn't sure if he knew to what extent, which was partly why she didn't normally keep the slaves within them.

Knowing the passage routes so well, Yonah didn't bother to bring a light with her. She maneuvered the stone path to the opposite side of the palace, where she knew the escapees would be anxiously waiting for news.

She heard them whispering as she drew closer and then the sudden lack of sound when they realized she was there, too.

"It's alright," she whispered. "I'm the reason you have a place to sleep tonight."

No one among the escaped slaves had a light either. A voice from the darkness asked Yonah, "Is everything alright?"

"Yes," she replied. "There was a minor issue, but nothing came of it. I'll take you back to the stable."

"Maybe we should stay here?" someone else asked.

"My husband knows about these passageways, so I wouldn't recommend it."

As there was no response to this statement, Yonah shrugged past the bodies towards the hidden doorway that would lead them outside. Her hand fumbled along the wall until she found the seam of the door and, eventually, a latch. Upon pulling the latch, the door popped loose, and Yonah slowly pressed it partially open and peeked outside.

A small path ran along the side of the palace, nestled between the pale, grey brick building and a green row in the vineyard. Yonah looked left and right along the row and saw that it was empty for now. She stepped out from the passage and motioned for the escapees to follow her.

Once the half-dozen escapees were outside, Yonah ensured the secret door was properly shut. With Yonah in the lead, they started the journey through the vineyard back to the stables.

They couldn't be seen by the slaves of Vaha. Nobody at the estate knew about them except three people: Yonah, Seidon, and Praha. If anybody else saw the escapees, there was no way for Yonah to be sure that word wouldn't get to Naris that his home was being used as an escape route for slaves. Yonah knew her luck in keeping her contribution to the rebellion a secret would run out at some point, but that didn't mean she didn't dread that moment with a panic-inducing terror.

She had the escapees press as deeply as they could into the vines as they walked while Yonah walked openly in the row. She often looked over her shoulder to check for a worker but saw no one.

They came upon the edge of the vineyard. It was a clear shot to the stable that sat on a sloping hill. After one more check to see if anybody was out, Yonah said, "Go. Hurry!"

The escapees bolted from the vineyard towards the stable. Yonah watched them go, anxiety twisting her stomach. She checked the edges of the vineyard, but no one emerged from the vines. Even if they did, there was nothing Yonah could do at this point to stop them from seeing the escapees.

She watched them file into the stable where she knew Seidon would be waiting. As the last escapee disappeared into the building, Yonah let out a sigh of relief and started back to the palace.

She went, first, to her bedroom. Praha was waiting for her there.

The slave woman opened her mouth to speak, but Yonah quickly said, "They're all back, safely. Everything's fine. Thank you for your help." She went to a glass pitcher of water on the small table in the centre of the room, poured two glasses, and gulped one down. She set the glass down. "I wish we could just keep them in the passageways."

"How often does Master Naris use them?" asked Praha.

Yonah shook her head. "I don't know."

"I could try to find out."

"Don't bother." Yonah handed the second glass of water to Praha, who held it without drinking. "The most likely entrances he would use are in his office and bedroom. The point of the passages is the privacy they provide. We can't keep track of his movement."

Praha didn't respond, though her face turned inward in thought.

"I'm going to town," Yonah said, striding over to the bedroom door. "If the master asks, I took a horse, not a carriage. He might not like that, but that's too bad."

Yonah made her way back down the stairs, through the back door, past the back fountain, beyond the vineyard, and up the slope to the stable.

There were cries of surprise when she stepped inside and a general withdrawal, but when the escapees finally saw her face, they relaxed.

"Where's Seidon?" she asked them.

"Outside," one of them said.

Yonah continued through the room to the back door that led to the corral. Seidon was standing outside the corral with his hands on the fence and his eyes on the horses.

"Seidon," Yonah called. He turned.

"That was a scare, eh?" he said without any humour.

"Thank you for cleaning up after the escapees. Naris didn't suspect anything."

"Except that someone had been sleeping here."

"Which you took care of nicely."

The man grunted in reply.

"I'm taking a horse to town," Yonah said.

"You can take Meadow."

Meadow was the horse on which Yonah learned to ride. When she had arrived at Vaha, she was scared of the horses and riding them. She had to ride with Naris whenever they went to town together. She knew that as a master—and a member of the rebellion—she would need to learn how to ride. Naris taught her. Yonah had fond memories of afternoons on the grounds with him, some of her truly carefree memories at Vaha.

Yonah nimbly mounted the horse, gave a nod to Seidon, and set off to town.

Where riding had previously frightened Yonah, now she found power in the activity. She was as fast as the wind, as mighty as the horse between her legs, and as wild as the surrounding nature.

The town of Kirash sent a sense of warm comfort through Yonah each time she arrived there. It was alive, pulsing, moving, loud noises, bright colours. When Yonah dismounted and led her horse off the main road through the residential streets, Kirash became hushed, slow, and relaxed.

Yonah arrived at a small square filled with vendors selling their wares along the perimeter. Several children, some of whom Yonah was sure were orphans constantly on the lookout for the Guard, lazed around the well at the centre of the square. A row of trees on one side cast a little shade from the bright sun.

Yonah crossed the square and tied Meadow to a post. She stepped up to a stall with a table covered in candles of various colours and sizes. A man taller and older than Yonah was standing behind the table. His kind eyes rested on Yonah, waiting on her to speak.

"What's your finest scent?" she asked.

"Hello, Yonah," the man said.

"I prefer roses." When she had been first taught the code, she had been told to always reply the same way, no matter what the man said.

"What do you need today?"

Yonah spoke quietly. "I need more potion. And I have news."

The man nodded for Yonah to come around the table to the door into the building behind him. When Yonah stepped inside, it was dark. As her eyes adjusted to the light, she saw the hallway that led to the small kitchen at the back of the building. A trapdoor in the kitchen floor was open. When Yonah peeked down, she could see the soft light from a single candle moving in the secret room.

"Vitora," the man called down into the cellar.

"Yes, Loni, what is it?" came a firm woman's voice.

"Yonah is here."

"I need some more of my potion," Yonah added.

There came a shuffling sound from below. Yonah knew Vitora, Loni's wife, was moving the innumerable objects in the room to find a bottle of Yonah's potion. Soon, Vitora was climbing up the ladder. Once her head emerged above ground, she held a deep blue bottle just a little smaller than a bottle of wine up into the air. Yonah took it. Vitora climbed out of the cellar, closed the trapdoor, and covered it with the rolled-up rug.

"Ten ora," Vitora said, holding out her hand.

Yonah pulled a small drawstring bag from her pocket and handed the appropriate number of coins over to Vitora.

"Is that all?" the woman asked as she pocketed the coins, dozens of bracelets on her arms jangling against each other.

"I also have some news."

"Then sit." The woman turned to her husband. "Loni, mind the stall."

"Yes, dear," said Loni, and he started for the door to the square.

Vitora went to the kitchen counter and pulled two cups from a cupboard. "Cold tea?"

"Thank you," Yonah replied, sitting at the small wooden kitchen table.

Vitora poured two cups of tea and joined Yonah at the table. "Firstly, how are you?"

Yonah's meetings with Vitora always started out this way. When she initially joined this branch of the rebellion, the woman described their group as something of a family. Yonah had yet to meet any other members of the rebellion, however. She only knew Vitora and Loni and had brought Praha and Seidon into her own operation, with Vitora's permission, of course.

"I'm fine. We had a bit of a scare today with the escapees."

"How so?"

"We had business guests. They wanted a tour of the estate."

Vitora nodded thoughtfully. "Perhaps we should avoid bringing in escapees when you have guests."

"I can have them moved within the estate upon a guest's arrival," Yonah said.

"Where can you possibly move them?"

Yonah smiled softly. "Vaha has its secrets."

Vitora shook her head, not finding any humour in Yonah's answer. "I don't want to take unnecessary risks when we have other safe houses, Yonah. For now, we avoid your safe house when you have guests. Even if it is just for an afternoon visit."

"We have many visitors, Vitora. That will make us miss out on too many opportunities to help the slaves."

"You are more valuable than just a safe house," Vitora said briskly. "I need you to get Naris closer to the capital. Now, you said you have news."

Fuming slightly at Vitora's decision to let fewer escapees through her safe house, Yonah shifted in her seat and said, "Slavery has been peacefully abolished in Jalid, and word has it that some of the rebels are moving into Harasa to help abolish slavery here."

Vitora's face was impassive at this massive piece of news. Her eyes were cast downwards as she registered the information. "You heard this from your friend in Kelab?"

"I did."

"Where did he hear it from?"

"I don't know."

"How likely is this information to be true?"

"The abolishment of slavery in Jalid is not a rumour," Yonah said. "Whether there are people coming to Harasa or not is less clear."

Vitora nodded. "Thank you."

"What are you going to do?" Yonah asked.

"That's not your concern. You're going to Kelab soon, yes?"

Yonah nodded.

"Remember your mission. Befriend the masters and politicians in the capital. Give Naris more reasons to return there more often. Learn everything you can about Althu. And find out where your friend gets his information from."

"Will I have more escapees soon?"

Vitora stood and set her cup on the counter. "Besides the group expected on the thirty-third day of the season? We'll talk when you get back from Kelab."

Sensing the implicated dismissal, Yonah, too, stood up, reaching for her newly purchased potion.

"And Yonah," Vitora said, making Yonah pause. "Be sure your husband never finds out about that." She motioned to the blue bottle in Yonah's hand.

"I know." Having already faced Naris' wrath before, Yonah knew that Naris would find this offense unforgivable. What she didn't know was what sort of punishment he would deem appropriate.

SHE HAD ONE last errand in Kirash before returning to the palace. Yonah continued to the west side of town, where there stood a large pub and inn called The White Stallion. She entered the clay-packed building.

The White Stallion was almost always moderately busy, and today was no different. Yonah scanned the large room spotted with tables for an empty space. Only a few moments after she had sat down, a woman wearing a slave collar stood next to her.

"Can I get you a drink?" asked the woman.

"Wine, please," Yonah replied.

The woman retreated behind the bar at the side of the room. Yonah looked around the room. There was a collection of people, free and enslaved, stopping for a moment of rest here. Before she had married Naris and regained her own freedom, Yonah had visited this pub.

The woman – her name was Meerha – returned to Yonah's table and set a cup in front of her.

"Your brother says hello," Meerha said.

"He wasn't able to come out here?" Yonah asked, taking a sip of her drink.

"Apparently, their visits to port have been quite brief lately."

Yonah's little brother, Obi, was a slave for a captain from the island nation just west of Harasa. When they made port in Basee, the city west of Kirash, Obi would check in with a musician there, who would then pass his message on to Meerha in Kirash. Sometimes Obi would even come to Kirash to see Yonah in person, though those occasions were rare. Yonah hadn't yet been able to find the courage to go back to Basee, as the first time she had done so had resulted in her scarred lip.

"Does he say anything else?" Yonah asked.

"They made port in Jalid. Everything was a mess. There's no shortage of workers, but there is a shortage of cash, which means employers are having a tough time meeting their old work demands. Apparently, there are some adjustments to be made with slavery being abolished there."

Yonah listened greedily to the news. To hear that Jalid was struggling was disheartening, but she hoped the country could get back on its feet to show Harasans they could do it, too.

Meerha also relayed information on Obi's visit to the island nation west of Harasa. They stayed there for a prolonged period and Obi was able to meet his good friend's family.

"Is there anything you'd like me to tell him?" Meerha asked.

Yonah told Meerha that she and Naris were going to Kelab soon but that her life was otherwise quiet. Obi didn't know that she was helping with the rebellion. It was safer for him that way. And safer for the rebellion.

"And how are you?" Yonah asked Meerha.

The woman shrugged. "Same old. I like it when Tolga comes to town." Tolga was the musician in Basee that helped Obi and Yonah communicate. He was also Meerha's sweetheart.

"Why doesn't he come to Kirash to stay?"

Meerha sighed. "We've had that argument many times. He says the money is in Basee. I don't know if he just likes his independence. Besides, it's hard to plan a future with someone when one of you is enslaved for life."

Yonah tried not to turn her attention to Meerha's maimed hand. She had been born with it and, according to the Slavery Act of Harasa, would be enslaved for life because of it.

"The rebellion will change that," Yonah said with conviction.

"I hope so."

Chapter Three

"Yonah." Naris said her name quietly, gently.

They sat upright on the bed, Yonah's legs wrapped around Naris' hips. Their clothes were strewn on the floor. The sheet was tangled around them. It was dark in the room but for the moonlight.

Naris had been rushed earlier. When he and Yonah had been playing chess—as they had done since they had met—a gleam appeared in his eye and he suddenly swiped his hand across the board, knocking the pieces to the ground, closed the space between him and Yonah in a split second with a playful smile lighting his face, and pressed his mouth to hers.

She was safe, she reminded herself.

Although Naris' suddenness startled her, Yonah forced herself to return the kisses and eventually relaxed into the activity.

Now she was on top of him, his arms wrapped protectively around her waist, his wonder-filled eyes gazing up at her.

"Yes, Naris," she whispered back.

"You know I love you."

He said it to her often. Sometimes he said it because it was true, and it was a moment of happiness he wished to share with Yonah. But Yonah thought that sometimes Naris said it to remind himself how important it was to love, to prevent himself from being anything like his parents. It was as much a reminder to him as it was to Yonah.

Yonah placed her hand on his cheek, the coarseness of his trim and shaped beard scratching her palm. "I know."

"Do you love me?" His golden-brown eyes gaped open so that Yonah could see into his soul. She didn't used to understand what she saw when they were still new to each other, but now Yonah could easily make sense of those eyes. There would always be a part of Naris that was afraid he was unlovable because that was what his childhood experience taught him. Yonah saw that part of him clearly looking up at her now.

Seeing that broken piece of Naris' soul always made Yonah's insides twist. She wanted to comfort him, to let him know that his parents were wrong, to show him what true family meant.

But she was betraying him at this very moment. She was abusing his love. She was abusing it for a purpose greater than them, yes, but it was abuse all the same.

And even though part of Naris just wanted to be loved, that didn't change the fact that another part of him was a monster that happily hurt Yonah and the slaves.

Yonah wondered how Naris bore to look at her scarred lip every day, to touch his lips to hers in love where he had once brought a blade to them in punishment. She wondered if, every time they made love, he remembered what it felt like to force her to do so their very first time. Yonah remembered, although she tried to forget when she had to fulfill her wifely duties.

Right now, his eyes begged her to tell him that she loved him. She could do that. Part of her did love him. She hated herself for it, but she couldn't deny the fact that just as much as she hated his temper and violent tendencies, she loved his vulnerability and gentle touch. Just as much as she despised his politics, she loved his thirst for life, laughter, and love. Just as much as she was afraid of the day he discovered her betrayal, she was happy to help him with the everyday work of running the vineyard and keeping the palace.

If only everything was different.

"Yonah?"

Had he yet learned to understand what he saw through her eyes?

Yonah cupped Naris' face in her two hands and planted a soft kiss on his forehead, then his nose, and finally one on his lips that made her chest swell.

"I love you," she said.

He stroked her cheek with his fingertips, his eyes still on hers. "I want to build a life with you."

"I do, too."

"Why haven't we gotten pregnant yet? Why is it so hard?"

Yonah wrapped her fingers around Naris' hand. "I don't know, my love." But she knew.

"We'll keep trying," Yonah added.

"I want us to be parents together. Good parents that love their children and show them what happiness is."

"I know."

Sadness bled into Naris' eyes. Longing. Yonah understood the feeling.

She longed for family, too. She wanted children of her own, too.

But not in this world. Not with the way things were.

Yonah kissed Naris once more. "We've done what we can tonight. Let's go to sleep."

With a melancholy nod, Naris untangled himself from Yonah and they lay down next to each other, fingers entwined. The position reminded Yonah of her time living on the streets with her brother and sister when she took their hands in hers for their, or her own, comfort.

The sudden memory brought stinging tears to her eyes. Her body stiffened as she tried to stop them from pouring onto her pillow.

Naris' gentle hand found her wet face. "I'm sorry to make you cry. I never want to make you feel a bad thing ever again."

He meant that only as long as she played by his rules. Yonah took Naris' hand from her face and held it in front of her. She curled up in a tight ball, closed her eyes, and pretended to fall asleep.

She did fall asleep for a few hours. When she awoke, it was still dark outside. Naris had rolled over in the bed and was snoring gently.

As silently as she could, Yonah slipped out of bed, wrapped a robe around herself, and padded out into the darkness of the palace halls. She had made this walk in the night countless times before; she didn't need the assistance of light to find her way.

Once alone in her own bedroom, Yonah started for the dresser. A soft meow came from the bed. Saza was nestled between the pillows.

Yonah retrieved the deep blue bottle from a drawer and wrenched the cork out of the mouth. She poured a half cup's worth into a glass and downed the clear liquid, potent with the scent of herbs. Yonah grimaced at the taste. No matter how many times she took it, the potion never tasted any better.

The first time Yonah had a potion such as this was the night Naris had first taken her to bed. She had barely registered drinking it at the time, but the kind older woman who had given it to her had been clear about what it was for.

"So there will be no child."

As much as Yonah wanted a family of her own, especially since her sister Sayzia had died and her brother Obi said he didn't need rescuing, she knew she could not have any children with Naris. She knew that she would love them with her whole heart and that they could be used against her. It was best that Naris think one of them was infertile, that they were unlucky. Then the only person she would have to worry about when she was eventually caught was herself.

Yonah stashed the bottle back into the drawer, hiding it among her clothing, then made her way down to the main floor of the palace and out the back door.

It was a cool spring night with a breeze brushing through the vineyard bushes. The shadows cast by the plants locked Yonah in a darkness that rendered even her own flesh invisible to herself.

She silently walked through the vineyard and emerged onto the plain. She could see the stable sitting atop the slight hill. There came the faintest light from one of its windows.

When she arrived at the closed door of the stable, Yonah gave a soft patterned knock: *quick slow, quick slow*. She stepped inside.

One of the horses gave a low nicker, but the animals were otherwise quiet. Yonah stood in the entranceway for a moment to let her eyes adjust to the lighting inside, then she slowly walked down the centre of the room, peeking into the stalls and glancing to the rafters. There was no sign of human activity in here. It seemed that Seidon had successfully led the escapees away to their next handler.

Yonah heaved a sigh that marked her being able to relax for the first time in a few days and started back for the palace. As she walked beneath high ceilings and through empty halls, she thought that she must be the only person awake at this time, but if she wasn't, there was no way she could ever know of another person being awake here—she lived in a different world from the slaves.

Quietly as she could, Yonah slipped back into bed next to Naris, who rolled over and mumbled, "Where did you go?"

"Just for a drink of water. Go back to sleep."

Naris did as he was told, not before he took Yonah's hand in his own. He always liked to fall asleep holding her hand.

Chapter Four

A strange sense of dread filled Yonah's chest as she looked up at Master Puru's silver-coated palace. The last time she had been here, she had been a slave. The last time she had been here, she and Naris had first met, and Naris had purchased her from Master Puru to take her home with him to Vaha.

Now, she returned to Puruha three years later, not only free from slavery but as a master.

Master Puru himself was standing in front of his palace, waiting to greet Naris and Yonah. He was a large, round man whose head looked too little for his body.

"Master Naris!" Puru exclaimed. "It's good to see you again. I don't think I've seen you since your wedding." His gaze turned to Yonah, who bristled under his attention. "Master Yonah. It is a pleasure to see you."

"And you, as well, Master Puru," Yonah said politely. He didn't remember at the wedding and certainly didn't remember now that Yonah had been his slave for four years of her youth.

"I'll have you shown to your room," Puru said. He gestured to one of the slaves lined up behind him—a young woman Yonah didn't recognize—and Naris and Yonah followed the slave into the palace.

As they walked through the winding halls of Puruha, Yonah tried to hide the awe she felt at its sparkle and embellishment. Save for her last week as Puru's slave, Yonah had only ever worked outside the palace and had never had a proper chance to explore its interior. The decoration style within Puruha was far less refined than that of Vaha. Its wealth was boasted loudly through jewels, silver-encrusted walls, and crystal chandeliers. Everything glittered.

Their room was familiar to Yonah for two reasons; it was purposely decorated similarly to Naris' own room at Vaha, and Yonah had spent several evenings playing chess with Naris in this very room upon their first meeting. This time, however, she would not be expected to leave the room in the middle of the night to return to the slaves' quarters.

As soon as the slave who had brought them to their chamber left, Naris took Yonah in his arms and said, "This is where I first began to court you." He took Yonah's hand and led her to the game table. "This is where we played our first game of chess." He pointed to the balcony doors. "That's where I asked you if you would like to come live with me." He took her to the closed bedroom door and looked deeply into Yonah's eyes. "And this is where we first kissed."

His eyes held onto Yonah's with a tenderness that made her unable to look away.

Naris was right. This was the place where they first met. It was also where Yonah first became a slave, where she learned what true loneliness was, and where she nursed her best friend to his death during the sickness that ravaged the continent.

"There are a lot of memories here," Yonah finally said, a little breathlessly.

As Master Puru's only visitors, they had dinner with him in a small but lavishly decorated dining room. Yonah tried to calm her nerves as she sat down across from Naris. She would recognize the slaves working here, and even though she had only worked indoors for a week before Naris whisked her away to Vaha, there was a strong possibility that they would recognize her, too.

Yonah's suspicions were confirmed when a young woman just a few years younger than her swept into the room. When her pale brown eyes rested on Yonah, the woman froze for a brief moment. Something between shock and confusion ran across her face before she pulled herself together and continued towards the table to set down a platter of food.

Of course, they couldn't speak to each other, not in front of Naris and Puru. Yonah hoped she would have a chance to talk to the slave woman, but that was not likely to happen in the near future.

There was a painful quietness between Yonah and the woman as the woman served their table. There were unasked questions, untold explanations. The unsaid words burned the air between them whenever the woman came close to Yonah.

"Master Yonah," Puru said as he chewed on a piece of dried fruit. "How do you spend your time these days now that you're…"

No longer a slave.

"Married?"

Yonah put on her most regal smile. "I help Master Naris with the wine business where I can. I correspond with our clients and organize meetings with them. I oversee the workers to ensure they're properly looking after the plants. I'm helping my husband free up some of his time for leisure."

Puru nodded as he swallowed. "Master Naris, are you finding your new wife's work effective?"

"Very much so," Naris replied. "She's the one who set up this entire journey to Kelab."

Puru raised an eyebrow. "You give her much control over yourself?"

Yonah tried to ignore the fact that Puru was now talking about her as if she wasn't there.

"Don't all wives have control over their husbands?" Naris asked in a joking tone.

A snort rumbled in Yonah's throat at the thought of Naris ever letting her control him. She quickly tried to turn the sound into polite laughter that would convince her husband that she found his joke funny.

"It was Naris' business first," Yonah said. "I just want to assist him in any way he'll have me."

Puru leaned towards Naris with a conspiratorial look. "I suppose that's where the leisure time comes especially handy, eh?"

As the large man started to chuckle at his crude joke, Yonah's face burned. She turned her eyes down to her meal and pursed her lips, trying to keep herself together in a regal manner. It was true what Zanith had said to her and Naris at their wedding; she would always be a slave in the masters' eyes.

Yonah's eyes shifted over to Naris, who was already watching her. The look on his face was one of careful attentiveness.

"Master Puru," Naris said. "You've just disrespected my wife and a fellow master by speaking of her so vulgarly. I would appreciate it if you would apologize."

The stillness that filled the room was suffocating. Puru blinked in bewilderment. Yonah waited intently for his response. Even the slaves that were serving them had frozen mid-work.

Puru realized his slaves were watching him and sent them a glare that propelled them back to work. He flashed a smile at Naris.

"Master Naris, I didn't mean anything by it."

"That may be," Naris replied. "But it was offensive, nonetheless. Please apologize."

Yonah knew what the possible outcomes of this conversation were. If Puru apologized, they would move forward on good terms, no harm done. If Puru refused, however, Naris would take Yonah and leave immediately, severing all ties, losing a client, and providing more fodder for the gossipers and more reason for his business advisor to hate Yonah.

Puru stiffly turned towards Yonah. "Master Yonah, please accept my apology for speaking of you with disrespect. It won't happen again."

Maintaining her cool demeanor, Yonah said, "Thank you."

The tense energy in the room relaxed as Naris asked, "Do you have plans to go to the city anytime soon, Master Puru?"

Puru was a little hesitant with his answer, to begin with, but was soon his jovial self as he explained to Naris how he hadn't been to Kelab in a very long time but would like to go soon. Yonah picked at her food, wishing she could leave the room without appearing rude.

Eventually, the dinner portion of the evening was finished, and the three masters rose from their seats. Puru offered to show Naris and

Yonah to his games room, but they both declined and retreated to their bedroom.

As Naris began to change out of his dinner attire and into lounge wear, Yonah slipped one of her earrings from her ear into her pocket. She stood in front of a dresser, unmoving, steeling herself. Naris didn't notice her hesitation.

"I can't find my earring," Yonah finally said, keeping her eyes on the dresser's surface. "It must have fallen out."

"We can have one of the slaves look for it," Naris said with a shrug.

"I'd like to go look for it myself."

Naris gave Yonah a perplexed look. "The slaves can do it. It's their job."

"I'll just be a few minutes," Yonah said, walking over to Naris and gently taking his hand.

He sighed, but his face softened. "Do you need me to come with you?"

"Of course not," Yonah said with a smile. "I'll be right back."

Naris gave Yonah's hand a squeeze before letting her go. Yonah made her way back to the small dining room, her chest tightening with nerves.

The dining room was dark and empty, the table cleared of all traces of supper. The candles that lined the centre of the table and perched in wall sconces still smoked from their freshly snuffed wicks. Yonah paused in the dark room, resting her hand on one of the chair backs. She didn't particularly want to go looking for that slave woman; she must think of Yonah as a traitor. But that was why Yonah wanted to see her, to assure her that she hadn't changed on a moral level, only changed her status.

For what purpose, though? Yonah asked herself. She didn't know whether it was for her own pride, to address a sense of shame she had buried deep within, or to maintain a network of allies.

With a forced sense of determination, Yonah stepped back into the dimly lit hall. She vaguely remembered the way to the basement where the indoor slaves slept. In her time as Master Puru's slave, she had barely gotten a chance to get to know the interior of the palace, so she had a little trouble finding the way tonight.

She soon found the inconspicuous door that led to the basement stairs. Yonah hesitated in front of it, then gave a loud knock. She thought it best not to barge into the slaves' quarters. That was their space where they were free of the masters for a time, even the ones who claimed to be on their side.

The door opened slowly, and a teenage girl peered out at Yonah. The girl lowered her eyes. "How may I be of service, Master?"

"I was wondering if I could speak to Mila."

There was confusion in the girl's expression as she stammered, "You'd like Mila to see you here?"

"If she's not too busy."

"Of course, Master," the girl said, shaking her head as if to shake away her hesitancy to obey a master's orders. "I'll find her."

The door closed, and Yonah waited. A minute later, she heard the click of the door opening once again, and the slave woman who had been serving at dinner stepped into the hallway.

While she had been undoubtedly in teenagerhood when Yonah was here last, this slave had grown into a woman since.

"You must be nearing your release date," Yonah said. Those enslaved because of their orphanhood were released upon their twentieth birthday.

"Next season," Mila replied. Her eyes paused on Yonah's bare neck, where there once had been a copper slave collar, much like the one Mila wore.

The two women stood in silence for a moment. Yonah didn't know how to begin, or even what she wanted to say to Mila. They had known each other for only a short time.

Mila spoke first. "Is there something you would like me to help you with?"

"No," Yonah said quickly, shaking her head. "No, I don't want anything." She started playing with her wedding beads. Spouses didn't customarily wear their wedding necklaces every day, but Yonah often wore them when she dressed up for dinners with other masters. "I suppose I just wanted to see how you were doing."

"Not as well as you," Mila said. Yonah couldn't quite tell if there was disdain in her voice or not.

"Well." Yonah let the sentence fade away into nothing. "I'm not— It's not like I'm a real master. I'm still—"

She couldn't explain. Not without putting her mission in jeopardy. But beyond that, she couldn't quite believe she was still the same person she was before marrying Naris. The fact was that she now had slaves of her own; she let them serve her and she gave them orders. Yes, she was far kinder to them than Naris, but she was their master all the same.

Yonah tried for a different topic. "I suppose Lari was released?"

Mila nodded.

"Good. I'm glad for her. I don't suppose you know any of the outdoor slaves?" She wanted to ask about Zabira and the others that had survived the sickness.

"Sorry," Mila replied. "I don't."

"That's alright." It was likely that, in nearly three years, everyone she knew had long since fulfilled their terms of enslavement and moved on with their lives. If she hadn't married Naris, she would have moved on like them.

Mila cut into Yonah's thoughts. "How did you become a master?"

"My master fell in love with me, and I married him."

"Why?" Bewilderment settled on the young woman's face.

"I have my reasons." Yonah finally let her hands fall away from her necklace. "I'd better leave you to your work." She knew full well that even though the masters were settling in for the night, the slaves downstairs still had work to do before they could sleep. "Thank you for letting me speak with you."

"I can't deny a master."

The statement sent a chill through Yonah's insides, causing her body to freeze and her breathing to stop.

Chapter Five

Yonah and Naris arrived in Kelab by train. Yonah watched the cream and brown buildings glide past the window with a heaviness in her chest. Although this wasn't her first time back in her home city, unease, melancholy, and longing tugged at her just the same.

The train station was in a wealthy part of the city. Yonah knew that even though the station was a tall, strong, and well-kept brick building, there were many parts of Kelab that had been left in rubble after the coup over ten years ago.

As they stepped onto the platform, Naris instructed some workers—not slaves—to gather their luggage. They hailed a carriage and waited for their luggage to be loaded. Yonah watched travellers bustle back and forth between the carriages and the station. Some were masters who travelled with their own slaves, and others were free folk carrying well-worn leather cases and keeping their heads down. Guards wearing their black uniforms with red sashes scattered the area, clearly armed and carefully watching for any signs of trouble. Yonah tried to ignore their presence.

"Let's go, my dear," Naris said, cutting into Yonah's thoughts. He was gazing at her expectantly.

Yonah nodded to her husband and, taking the hand he had extended to her, stepped up into the carriage.

They stayed at a hotel whenever they went to Kelab. Some masters had second houses in the city, but Naris' family's wealth was new enough that they hadn't had the chance to purchase one for themselves.

"We'll buy a house here soon," Naris said, glaring out the carriage window. "Then we won't appear so middle class."

Yonah had grown up in a middle-class household with a father who was a university professor. That was before the coup, before all schools were closed, before her family fell into near poverty, before her parents were killed, before she was separated from her brother and sister.

Upon their arrival at the hotel, their luggage was brought to their rooms and they each changed from their travel clothes into something clean. Naris flopped down onto one of the massive beds and said, "Well, I suppose we have an engagement tonight?"

"Of course." Yonah sat in a spindly, cushioned armchair near the window where the breeze could brush over her. "We're going to Master Lania's. She's having a large party."

Although Naris didn't audibly groan, he might as well have with the face he made. "Is it going to be fun?"

"Well, my friend Beneri tells me she has a swimming pool. Does that sound fun to you?"

Naris rolled onto his side and propped himself up on one elbow. "Only if it's just you and me in it."

Yonah smirked playfully at him. "I don't think that's what's going to happen."

"I'm growing less interested."

"It will be good for the business, Naris. We'll both have plenty of opportunity to meet new people and potentially expand our sales to southern clients."

"I know," Naris sighed, lying back down. "You're right about that." He furrowed his brow at Yonah. "Is your friend going to be there?"

She shrugged. "I don't see why not."

"I don't like him."

"I know. Why not?"

"Because he steals your attention away from me."

Even as her master, Naris never liked for Yonah to have relationships beyond their own.

"I hear that absence makes the heart grow fonder," Yonah replied coyly.

"And he's gossipy and tactless," Naris grumbled. "I wish he wouldn't try so hard."

Yonah couldn't disagree that her friend did thrive on talking about the other masters and putting his nose where it didn't belong, but that was what made him a useful ally in gathering information on the rebellion. And he was also the only person living in Kelab that Yonah could call a friend. "Well, it's a good thing you'll only see him for as long as we're in the city."

Naris rolled his eyes. "Less than that would be better."

WHEN YONAH STEPPED out of the carriage at Master Lania's house, she could hear rambunctious laughter and shouting inside. She glanced nervously at Naris, who chuckled and said, "Aren't you looking forward to talking to all those people?"

"Not all of them," Yonah replied. "Some of them won't be happy to see me there at all."

A dark look clouded Naris' face. "Then I will let them know how I feel about that."

Yonah wrapped her hand around Naris' arm. "Behave. I'll let you know if I need any help."

They started up the steps to the massive front doors. "If anyone misbehaves towards you, I get to misbehave towards them. It's only fair."

Master Lania's house was a multi-level, cream-coloured building trimmed with gold paint and decorative carvings. Two slaves were manning the front doors, which they opened for Yonah and Naris. A wave of noise knocked into Yonah as the party came into view. The long room was golden: the dishware, the rug, the portrait frames, the chandelier, and of course, the glow from the dozens of candles and lamps that lit the room.

It felt as though there were more people crammed into the room than there were at Yonah's wedding. She didn't recognize the majority of the guests and immediately felt herself trying to grow small and inconspicuous. The fact that several of them stared at the scar on her lip didn't help.

Yonah leaned into Naris to say into his ear, "Do you recognize anyone here?"

"Not many," he replied. "We should start with a friend so they can make introductions for us."

Yonah nodded in agreement and let Naris lead the way through the crowd. She thought she could hear music coming from another room, but it was overpowered by the chatter in the main hall.

A woman with ears lined with piercings and wearing a dress that matched the decor stepped in Naris' path. "Master Yonah," she said to him in greeting. "It's a pleasure to finally meet you in person."

"I'm Master Naris," he said. "You've been corresponding with my wife, Master Yonah." He gently tugged Yonah forward.

The woman, Master Lania, let her mouth open into a round 'o' shape but quickly recovered and said, "My apologies. Master Yonah," She took Yonah's hand in both of hers, and her eyes stopped briefly on her lip. "It's lovely to meet you. Your friend, Master Beneri, says nothing but good things about you."

"I am pleased to meet you as well," Yonah said politely. She felt Naris' impatience next to her. "This is my husband, Master Naris. He runs our vineyard."

"Master Beneri says good things about your wine, too," Lania said.

"Anything good he says about it is true," Naris replied.

Lania chuckled. "But only the good things, yes?"

Naris joined in the laughter. "You understand me!"

"Why don't I introduce you to some of my friends?" Lania stepped between Yonah and Naris and took their elbows. The three of them slowly wove through the party. Yonah took in the colours of the guests' outfits, the sparkle of their jewelry, and their dispositions as they noticed her.

For the most part, Yonah felt more ignored than disliked as they made their way through the crowd.

Master Lania eventually tapped a guest's shoulder. When he turned around, Lania introduced him to Yonah and Naris. Yonah squared her shoulders and lengthened her neck, bare but for her wedding beads.

They spoke with the man of nothing that particularly interested Yonah, not even of the vineyard, though not for lack of effort on hers and Naris' part. The man was eventually pulled away by another guest, leaving Naris and Yonah to each other's company.

"We can't expect to make any real connections with just one conversation," Naris said, mostly to himself. "I hate this format for a gathering." Both he and Yonah were more familiar with dinner events at which Naris preferred to stay in his seat and let fellow partiers come to him. That only worked, however, because his family was well-known north of Kelab. Here, they were strangers and, as a result, inconsequential.

"I thought I heard music," Yonah said. "Why don't we see what that's about?"

"You go." Naris' eyes shifted around the room. "I need a drink."

As Naris disappeared into the crowd, Yonah worked through the room in the direction she thought she had heard music. Her intuition was proven correct when the sound of several stringed instruments came slinking towards her. She stepped through a large doorway into a room just as packed as the main hall. There were couples dancing in the centre, clasping hands and spinning in and away from each other. Some of the dancers moved around the dance space more than others. Yonah watched mesmerized by their movement.

Someone tapped her shoulder and Yonah turned to find her friend Beneri standing next to her. She grinned as she took in his lanky frame and nearly completely shaved head.

Beneri's green eyes flashed. "Am I happy to see you! We have much to discuss. Where did your husband run off to?"

"He's in search of a drink. He likely won't find anything up to his standards. Only his own wine will do."

"He's a proud man." Beneri presented his arm to Yonah. She wrapped her hand around the crook of his elbow. "Let's find somewhere to chat." He noticed her empty hands. "And we'll find you a drink, too!"

As they shuffled to a doorway at the other side of the music room, Beneri asked about Yonah's trip to the city. In the next room, there sat a glass table lined with golden cups. Yonah and Beneri each took one and continued through another door that brought them back to the main hall. They walked up a staircase that lined the wall, stepped through a glass-paned door at the back of the building, and found themselves on a balcony overlooking a small courtyard with a pool. The water was illuminated by lamplight. A few guests were sitting on the pool's rocky edge with their legs floating in the water, but no one had yet dared to fully submerge themselves. The pool reminded Yonah of her time as a slave at Master Puru's palace, where part of her daily work was to maintain the pools of water in the courtyard.

"Have you tried the wine?" Beneri asked, resting his elbow on the balcony railing. He and Yonah were the only people there.

Yonah took a sip and let the liquid sit in her mouth for a moment while she explored the flavours, comparing it to the wine Naris produced. After swallowing, she looked into the cup. "It's very good. We don't make red wine, though."

"Are you allowed to appreciate other wines?" Beneri asked with a cheeky smile.

Even though there were some people who didn't know that Yonah had once been Naris' slave, they still spoke to her as if Naris was the one who was really in charge of her. She wasn't sure if it was because they assumed she was the lower-class spouse who had married up into Naris' status or because Naris had always been very independent and opinionated.

"Naris isn't my master," Yonah replied. Not anymore. "I can do what I want." That was partially true. To accentuate her statement, she took a large gulp of her wine.

"Good to know," Beneri said with a smirk. "Now, to business. There have been confirmed sightings of rebels from Jalid here in Kelab. They've already joined the protesters here."

"The slave trade is really done in Jalid?" The notion made Yonah feel as if she was about to float away.

"Yes, and the rebels want to abolish it in Harasa, too."

"Do they have a headquarters yet?"

"Not that I know of. Beyond being at the protests, they're being very secretive."

Yonah said thoughtfully, "They're likely spending their time getting a clearer picture of what's happening down here before they make a move. They'll know who to contact among the free folk when they're ready. Where are you getting this information from?"

Coyness lit up Beneri's face. "You know I can't tell you that, Yonah."

Yonah sighed. "Well, is it another master? A low class rebel? A politician?"

"Ah, speaking of politicians," Beneri replied, "there is a new minister in Kelab, and she is at this party right now." He beamed slightly as he spoke. "Minister Hara."

Yonah was trying to wrap her mind around the implication of this news. "What's her involvement in Althu's government? Why is she here?"

"Her father was a minister, but he's grown so sick that she's taking over his responsibilities."

"It doesn't seem likely that she's sympathetic to the slaves if she's at a party full of masters," Yonah said.

"We're at a party full of masters," Beneri replied. "Who's to say she doesn't have an ulterior motive like us?"

"So, you haven't met her."

"I, unfortunately, have yet to be granted an introduction."

Yonah pursed her lips. "That's a problem."

A voice came from behind her. "Yonah." She turned and saw Naris standing in the doorway, two cups in his hands. He sent an annoyed glance in Beneri's direction. "I've been looking for you."

"Master Beneri and I decided to find somewhere a little quieter to chat." Yonah kept her voice breezy, even though she wasn't sure if Naris had heard any of their conversation. No, he couldn't have. They were too quiet.

Naris walked over and handed Yonah one of the cups in his hand. "I thought we were here to network with new masters. Unless Master Beneri here would like to invest in the Muran brand?"

"I'd be happy to make a modest order, Master Naris," Beneri said.

"I'll be sure to send someone to retrieve your order," Naris replied a little sharply. Yonah could feel him growing agitated.

"Naris, did you see the pool?" she tried.

Naris briefly glanced over the balcony railing at the shimmering water below. "Wonderful."

Yonah bristled at his grumpiness. "Let's take a closer look together. Excuse us, Master Beneri."

Beneri nodded once in respect at their departure. As soon as they stepped back into the house, Yonah said calmly to Naris, "What is the matter?"

"I told you. I don't like that man."

"He barely spoke to you."

"Yes, he was busy speaking with you while I was left alone to look like a country idiot among these snobby Kelabians."

Yonah wanted very much to argue the fact that Naris was the one who rejected her suggestion to look around the party together, but she crushed the impulse and plastered her most pleasant expression on her face. "Let's stay together, then. I hear there's a new politician here. Imagine if we made a good impression on her. Imagine having regular orders with all of Harasa's highest-ranking politicians."

"How are we going to get an introduction with someone so high-profile?"

Yonah took Naris' arm and kissed his cheek, creating the image of the perfect husband and wife partnership. "We'll figure it out."

Chapter Six

They stood at the top of the stairs, gazing down at the party. Master Lania was talking animatedly to a group of masters in the middle of the room. The two masters Naris had just filled an order with upon their visit to Vaha were entering the house. They would have to speak to them at some point tonight.

But Yonah could not find the woman that might be Minister Hara. If she was in this room, she wasn't dressed in formal political attire.

"I don't know what she looks like," Yonah admitted to Naris, keeping her eyes on the crowd.

Naris was silent for a moment. When he finally spoke, the words shocked Yonah. "Does Master Beneri?"

"I'm not sure," Yonah replied, trying to keep her voice neutral. She turned around just in time to see Beneri sneaking behind them towards the stairs. "Master Beneri." He stopped. "Do you know what Minister Hara looks like?"

Beneri nodded. He peered over the railing to the party below. "She's not in this room. She's tall. Taller than me. And wearing a circlet."

Beneri towered over Yonah. A woman taller than him would certainly stand out.

"Thank you, Master Beneri. Let's go, Naris."

As Yonah and Naris passed Beneri, he muttered softly to Yonah, "Good luck." They descended the stairs into the thick of the party and veered into the wine room. A quick glance around the room told them that the politician wasn't there, so they continued to the music room.

Minister Hara was dancing. She was impossible to miss as her head stood above everyone else. A dainty silver circlet sat atop her white braided hair. While she looked as though she had forgotten where she was in her dancing, the man she was dancing with looked mildly frightened at the large woman with boundless energy.

"You need to dance with her," Yonah said.

Naris' eyes widened. "Dance with that? She'll crush me."

"Don't be rude."

"You dance with her!"

Yonah watched the minister for a moment. The man with her looked as if he regretted agreeing to dance with her. "Fine," Yonah said.

Naris' eyes zipped over to Yonah. "I was only joking."

The song came to an end, and applause filled the room. Minister Hara's dance partner nodded shakily to her before scrambling away, leaving the woman in search of a new partner. No one appeared to be clamouring for the newly vacated position, however.

As a new song began, Yonah shoved through the crowd to the open dance floor and swept across the room to stand in front of the politician. "Would you care to dance?" she asked.

The woman blinked down at Yonah with a little surprise, then smiled.

"I would be happy to."

The two women took each other's hands and began to twist and step around each other. Yonah felt immediately grateful that she had invested in dancing lessons after marrying Naris.

Minister Hara stood nearly a foot taller than Yonah. Her shoulders were broader, her arms longer, and everything about her felt more powerful. She whipped Yonah around with more gusto than Yonah had ever experienced before, but Yonah refused to let herself grow intimidated by it. She, instead, flexed her arms and core in preparation for the minister's strong movements and followed along with confidence.

They were marching around the perimeter of the dance floor, hands still clasped, bobbing up and down. Yonah saw mirth in Minister Hara's eyes. When she glanced quickly at the onlookers, she saw surprise and awe. She was certainly making an impression of her own here in the south.

The song came to an end, and Yonah and the minister bowed slightly to each other.

"Thank you very much," Minister Hara said breathlessly. Her cheeks were rosy from exertion.

A new song began. Yonah liked this dance. "Would you care for another?"

Perplexed pleasure crept onto the minister's face. "Are you sure? Most people can barely last a single dance with me."

"I suppose I'm not most people."

The minister smiled and nodded. She and Yonah squared off and joined in the dance. This one called for more slow stomping and clapping than spinning and twisting, giving Yonah the chance to speak.

"I'm Master Yonah, by the way."

"Minister Hara. But you probably knew that already."

Sensing that this woman would appreciate the honesty, Yonah said, "Yes, I did. I hear you're new to the city. I'm visiting with my husband."

"Your husband?"

Yonah searched for Naris in the crowd. "The man in the navy jacket over there."

Hara looked to where Yonah motioned. "He's handsome."

"I think so."

They circled around each other, pausing to clap.

Hara asked, "And what brings you to town?"

"We have a vineyard up north," Yonah replied, "and we're looking to expand our clientele."

"I'm from an estate south of Basee. Is your vineyard around there?"

"We're near Kirash!" Kirash was just west of Vaha, and Basee was just west of Kirash, along the coast.

"What's your estate called?" Hara asked.

"Vaha. Naris is from the Muran family."

Recognition lit up Hara's eyes. "I've heard of you. You're the slave he married."

Yonah's chest clenched. "That's common knowledge up north, but people around here don't know about that."

"Is it a secret?" Hara's question was genuine.

"Well, it's not advertised."

Hara nodded in understanding.

They were silent for a few moments. The song was growing faster.

"Are you in love with him, then?" Hara asked suddenly.

"Of course," Yonah said without missing a beat. "Why do you ask?"

"I'm just curious as to why a slave would marry her master."

Yonah paused, focusing on the pattern of their stomping feet before asking carefully, "What other reason would there be?"

"I don't know," Hara replied. She and Yonah turned around, then faced each other again, clapping loudly. "I've never been a slave."

Yonah suddenly realized how precarious her current position was. All the power lay with this politician, regardless of whether she was sympathetic to the rebellion or not. Yonah could not be the first one to hint at the cause, but she couldn't let this opportunity slip away.

"Will you be attending Master Beneri's event later this week?" Yonah asked. "I'd be happy to bring some samples from our vineyard for you to try."

The song came to an end, and the women stood facing each other, a light shimmer of sweat glistening on their brows.

"Yes, I'll be there," Hara said. "And I will gladly try your samples." She nodded her head slightly to Yonah. "Thank you for the dances."

Yonah bowed her head deeply. "It was lovely meeting you, Minister."

Hara suddenly left the dance floor, moving gracefully. People scrambled to get out of her way as she walked towards them.

Ignoring the strange looks she was receiving from the partygoers, Yonah found Naris in the crowd.

"Well?" he asked. "How did it go?"

"She said we could bring her some samples at Master Beneri's party."

Naris grimaced. "We're going to Master Beneri's house?"

"Of course. He's my friend. Didn't you hear me? We're bringing samples to her."

"Yes, that's good news." Naris' tone didn't reflect his words. "Let's go. I'm tired of this."

Beneri emerged from the crowd and placed a hand on Yonah's arm. "Did I just see you dancing with Minister Hara? You were amazing! Nobody could keep their eyes off you!"

Yonah couldn't help but smile proudly. "Just doing what I can for my husband's business." Ever the perfect wife.

Naris was frowning. "Yonah, please. Let's go."

"Of course," Yonah answered, keeping her voice light. She turned to Beneri. "I'll see you at your party, if not sooner."

Naris mumbled, "Not sooner."

"Feel free to come over anytime," Beneri said to her. "Master Naris, you are welcome also."

When Naris didn't answer promptly, Yonah glared at him until he said, "Thank you, Master Beneri." He gave Yonah an 'are-you-happy-now?' look, and she nodded in response.

They made their way to the front of the house, where they found a carriage that took them back to their hotel.

Once in their room, Yonah said, "I'm taking a bath."

"Perhaps I'll join you," Naris replied coyly.

Yonah smirked back at him. "I'll leave that up to you." She wished he wouldn't.

Naris did not end up joining Yonah in the bath. In fact, when Yonah returned to the main bedroom, he was sitting in a chair at the window, his face even darker than it had been at the party.

"Is everything alright?" Yonah asked.

Naris turned his head towards her. He stared for a moment, trying very hard to read her. Then his face brightened, and he flashed his charming smile. "Of course. Come here." He stood and met Yonah and began to undress her. Yonah played along and let Naris take her to bed to perform her wifely duties. That seemed to brighten Naris' mood, and he promptly fell asleep.

Yonah lay awake thinking of her conversation with the minister, trying to puzzle out where her morals lay, but she couldn't come to any conclusions without further information. Despite that undetermined factor, Yonah considered the evening an overall success.

She slid out of bed and went to one of her cases. She dug around inside in search of a small bottle. When she was packing, Yonah had divided her anti-pregnancy potion into three small bottles so she could carry them more discreetly.

She couldn't find a bottle, however. Panic rose in Yonah's chest as her search grew more frantic. She pulled everything out of the case. No bottles. She searched her other cases. No bottles.

"You idiot," she hissed at herself. She must have divided up the potion and forgotten to actually put it into a case. She would have to buy some tomorrow, preferably in the morning. The potion lost its effectiveness the longer she waited.

She recalled Naris' sudden change of mood during her bath. It was certainly possible that he had gone snooping through her things and found the bottles. Why he wouldn't have said anything, however, was a mystery to Yonah. Perhaps she simply forgot to pack the potion after all.

Fuming, Yonah climbed back into bed and willed herself to sleep.

Chapter Seven

The deeper into the city Yonah walked, the smaller the houses grew. She went from the large houses, the hotels, and the high-end shops to moderately-sized homes and thriving marketplaces. She recognized these streets from her childhood: the fruit stall with the best mangoes, the back alley where she used to play with her school friends, the baker who had helped Yonah and her siblings while they were living on the streets.

During her other sparse visits to Kelab with Naris, Yonah had tried and failed to walk up to the bakery and greet the man who had provided her with bread every day. She supposed she was afraid of what he would think of her now that she was a master. Her father had protested the slave trade from the moment Althu put the slavery act into place. Her father had died protesting.

She couldn't face the potential that the baker would think she was betraying her father's memory.

Yonah continued down the road until she stood in front of a square, two-storey house. The wooden shutters had been painted red where they used to be blue, but the house otherwise looked just as it had when Yonah and her family lived there. She had dubbed it 'the big house' before she worked at and visited and lived in palaces and mansions.

Deeper into the city she went. Some of the houses were crumbling here, abandoned and derelict. They were growing smaller, too. There were more apartments squashed together, more families crammed into one home, more people in smaller places.

The small house. It was a three-room apartment on the ground floor. Yonah stood in front of it, letting old memories wash over her. She remembered the dirt-packed floor, how all three children had shared a bedroom, her father taking over their education, her mother singing while she cooked, the night their friends carried her father's body inside, the day her mother's blood pooled on their bedroom floor. As hard as her parents tried to make this house just as much of a home as the old one, the memories of tragedy that it possessed far outweighed any good it might have carried.

Although the memories were from long ago, Yonah still felt a sickening sense of loneliness at the thought of her family. All that was left of them was her brother Obi and herself. She hoped that maybe one day she would be able to see Obi under safer circumstances, but for now, she couldn't count on it.

The tour into the past over, Yonah snapped herself out of her melancholy and made her way to the nearest market. Although she didn't entirely blend in wearing her most modest clothes that had been gifted to her when she was a slave, she didn't stick out as she would have if she had worn her bejewelled outfits that were now part of her daily wardrobe.

She wandered through the market, taking note of the sellers' wares. There were plenty of food stalls, some clothing, trinkets, and things that had clearly been taken from larger houses. As she walked past a shaded side street, Yonah saw a stall tucked inside with a blanket lined with bottles, jars, and bowls. A sign sat on the blanket next to an elderly man that read 'Apothecary'. Yonah slipped into the dark street and knelt in front of the man.

"I'm looking for an anti-pregnancy potion," Yonah said softly.

With a calm expression, the man picked up a bottle and held it up for Yonah to see. "Twenty-five ora."

"I only pay ten ora for a larger bottle with my other vendor," Yonah said.

"And yet, I'm sure you can afford twenty-five." The man waved his free hand towards Yonah's person. "You're dressed far too lavishly to be shopping around here."

She could afford the elevated price. This man lived in poverty. Yonah silently dug out the appropriate number of coins from her purse and handed them to the man. He passed the bottle to her.

"Come back soon," he said with a smile.

Yonah didn't respond as she tucked the bottle into an interior pocket of her jacket and stood up.

For the following two days, Yonah and Naris spent their time going to tea houses, meals, and small gatherings, all to network with prominent masters who also happened to be in Kelab in the hopes of expanding the vineyard's clientele. With each meeting, Yonah tried to gauge each master's thoughts on the slavery act, the local protesters, and the arrival of rebels from Jalid.

One afternoon, the two of them were able to take a leisurely walk through a wealthy neighbourhood. Yonah noticed how much more greenery and landscaping there was in this area, a stark contrast to the rubble buildings in the poorer neighbourhoods.

"Perhaps we could buy a house around here," said Naris, looking from one large house to the next. "Which ones do you like?"

All the houses had clay exteriors, although they were painted in a variety of colours. Some had beautiful balconies. Others were home to massive windows.

"They're all beautiful in their own way."

Naris chuckled. "You never like to give a straight answer."

Yonah opened her mouth to protest, then stopped herself. She couldn't stop one corner of her mouth from turning upwards. "You might be right."

"It keeps me entertained, though," Naris said.

"You always found our conversations entertaining." Yonah thought back to the first time Naris had ordered her to his room for a private audience, back when she was still a slave in Puru's household.

"It's part of what made me fall in love with you."

Yonah felt herself blush.

"And what else?" she found herself asking before she could stop herself.

"Everything felt comfortable with you," Naris replied. "It was like you and I had been best friends since childhood, even though we only met a few years ago."

Yonah's heart unwittingly and, perhaps, foolishly swelled with pleasure.

The street opened into a large park lined with windowed shops. The park was crowded with people that didn't look as though they belonged in a wealthy neighbourhood.

Naris didn't seem to notice. He asked, "What made you fall in love with me?"

Yonah wasn't sure if what she felt for Naris was truly love or the proper kind of love that came with a real relationship. She wasn't sure if it was what her parents had shared or if it was something more toxic and twisted. But she certainly felt something for Naris, something that made her see him as more than an unfeeling master.

"Your vulnerability," she said. "It showed me that we had something in common." They both just wanted to be loved by their family.

Naris looked down at his feet. "I never told anybody about my childhood except for Kejal. And you."

"And you still hide yourself when we're out in public."

"What do you mean?"

The crowd was building. There was an excited anticipation buzzing through the park. Yonah knew what this was.

"You put on airs. Your charm. You look like you have all the answers." She nervously watched the crowd while she spoke, feeling more on edge as they tried walking past.

"I can't let masters think I don't know what I'm doing."

"And I'm in on that secret," Yonah said.

Naris took her hand. "I'm glad I can share my secrets with you."

His secret-sharing could never be reciprocated.

Someone began shouting from the centre of the park. It was a woman, her head elevated above the others. All eyes were on her.

"The government knows what we want and refuses to act on our wishes! Althu and his ministers see us not as citizens of Harasa but as a threat to their wasteful lifestyles. They've turned the wealthy on the poor as a means of distraction! As a means of control!"

"Oh no," Naris muttered. "What have we stumbled upon?"

"We should go," Yonah said. It wouldn't be long until the Guard arrived to break up the protesters.

"Their homes and streets are well looked after," the woman continued. "Meanwhile, I live in a hovel that's half fallen down because I don't matter to the government!"

Cries of encouragement came from the crowd.

Still holding onto Yonah's hand, Naris led Yonah along the edge of the park in search of an exit.

"You there!" the woman cried. "I know you can hear me! If we're not your slaves, you pretend we're invisible! You're the reason the slavery act lives on!"

Yonah couldn't help but turn her gaze to the woman. She was pointing right at them, her eyes ablaze with hatred.

A nearby protester grabbed Yonah's arm. "She's speaking to you. What do you have to say for yourself?"

"Unhand my wife immediately!" Naris yelled.

"Just because I'm poor doesn't mean I'm your slave," the protester said with a sneer.

"And just because you're free doesn't mean you can go around manhandling women," Naris replied with just as much venom.

"So, if he was your slave," someone else said, "you wouldn't mind ordering him around?"

"Slaves are meant to obey, aren't they?" said Naris.

The protesters started to jostle Naris and Yonah as they shouted angrily. Naris clung tightly to Yonah's hand and tried to push through the bodies. Even though they held on tightly to each other, Yonah couldn't see Naris through the bodies surrounding her. Panic welled inside her as contorted faces just inches from her shouted and shoved her.

There came a new kind of shouting from the distance, and everyone turned to look. A dozen Guards on horseback had ridden into the park. Some of the protesters ran at the sight of them. Many stood their ground and turned their energy towards the Guards.

A gunshot went off, and there was panicked screaming. The protesters were beginning to lose their nerve. Yonah slipped between them and crashed into Naris. They ran for safety.

As soon as they stepped back onto a street just outside the park, they slowed to a brisk walk. Naris looked angrily over his shoulder at the chaos behind them.

"Those bastards," he said. "How dare they harass you."

"They're angry, Naris."

"Well, now, I'm angry. I hope they're all arrested as rebels and sent to the labour camp."

"That would only fuel their cause."

Naris turned his blazing eyes on Yonah, stopping suddenly. "Do you think I was in the wrong back there?"

"Of course not."

"Because if someone is hurting you, I will do everything in my power to stop them."

"And I appreciate that."

"Nothing matters to me more than you, Yonah. Not a thing."

Yonah looked deeply into his eyes. "I know that."

Chapter Eight

On their fourth evening in the city, they dressed up once more to go to Beneri's house for another large party.

Naris was smoothing out the creases on a pale blue tunic. "You know, we've had so much success with all our meetings this week; we don't really need to go to Master Beneri's tonight."

Besides getting a chance to visit with her friend once more before returning home to Vaha, Yonah needed to be at that party to talk to Minister Hara.

"We've been very fortunate," she said. "Signing on a new client with the promise of two more." She kissed Naris' cheek. "You're a huge success."

She was about to return to the mirror when Naris gently took her hand. "*We* are," he said. "You've done so much to make our time here a success."

Yonah's heart warmed at Naris' compliment. She pressed her lips together in an attempt not to smile too widely. Naris stepped closer to her, his lips hovering over hers.

"I love you," he said.

She hated that his closeness could still make her feel so warm. But he could never know that. "I love you, too."

They kissed. Softly. It was a still kiss where each of them tried to hold on to a single moment among an infinite number of moments. It was a kiss that made Yonah forget, letting gentleness and love take over.

Their eyes held each other as their lips parted. Yonah loved his golden-brown eyes.

"We're still going to that party tonight," she said with a smirk.

Naris chuckled. "Of course, my dear."

Beneri's house was a little smaller than Master Lania's, but what he lacked in size he made up for with spectacle. Fire breathers greeted the guests from either side of the path leading to the front door, sending an uncomfortable heat their way. Inside, live peacocks stood above the guests on perches that appeared to have been made specially for this occasion. Contortionists wove through the crowd in various positions: on their hands, rolling like a wheel, upside down. And, of course, there was an immense amount of food and drink in which the guests partook.

"It's like a zoo in here," Naris said, his nose wrinkled in disgust.

"I think it's fun," Yonah replied.

Naris gave Yonah a wide-eyed look. "We might need to refine your tastes, my dear, so we don't embarrass ourselves in front of the other masters."

Yonah took a calming breath. "Should we find Minister Hara?"

"Yes, let's." Naris pointed to the slave tasked with carrying their box of sample wines. The slave followed Naris and Yonah through the party as they searched for the minister. She was surrounded by a group of women who all laughed loudly with her.

Yonah boldly led the way towards the group and said, "My apologies for interrupting." She ignored the disgruntled faces of the group. "Minister Hara, Master Naris and I have brought our samples, just as we discussed at Master Lania's house."

"Wonderful!" the minister said brightly. "Let's find a spot where we can properly enjoy them."

The three of them eventually found themselves in a study, sitting on plush chaises with the selection of wines between them on a small end table, the noise of the party dulled by the closed door.

"How long have you been in the business?" Minister Hara asked while Naris opened the first small bottle.

"I've been in charge for a few years," Naris replied, "but my great-great-grandfather started the vineyard years ago."

"I must have, at some point, tasted your family's wine, then," Hara said, "since my family's estate is so near yours."

"Well, if you haven't," Naris said as he poured three glasses and handed one to the minister, "we're about to remedy that."

They each took a sip. Naris and Yonah watched the minister closely as her eyes brightened with pleasure. Yonah could feel excitement swelling from Naris' direction.

"That's very lovely," Hara said. "Quite refreshing."

"That's our bestseller," Naris said. "And our original recipe."

"It's delicious."

"Now, try this one." Naris began to open a bottle whose contents Yonah was very intimate with. "It's named for Yonah's mother."

Hara asked Yonah, "Why's that?"

"When I first tried it," she replied, "when the recipe was new, it reminded me of her."

"Intriguing," Hara said playfully. She took the glass Naris held out to her and took a sip. Her eyebrows shot upwards. "That's a surprise! But a good one! Yonah, how does this remind you of your mother?"

"It smells like her cooking." Yonah shot a glance at Naris. He didn't always like it when she spoke of her family, especially to members of the upper class.

"That's a lovely memory." Hara smiled kindly at Yonah. "Have you seen your mother recently?"

"No, she died a long time ago." Perhaps this was her moment. She said the words before she could talk herself out of doing so. "She was killed by a member of the Guard."

Naris choked loudly on his wine, spitting some back into his glass. Yonah and Hara both watched him in surprise. He smiled quickly and waved their shock away. "My apologies, masters. I just swallowed poorly. Although this recipe isn't as popular as our original, those who enjoy it are quite loyal."

Although Naris was trying to steer the conversation away from Yonah's brazen mention of her past, what had been said couldn't be unheard. Minister Hara knew that Yonah had a negative history with the nation's enforcement service, one that couldn't be forgotten or forgiven.

What the minister thought of this information, Yonah couldn't tell. Her pleasant demeanour never wavered as she continued to politely taste-test the samples. Naris, Yonah could tell, was furious at her for having brought up such a political topic. An angry heat rose from him so hot that Yonah half-expected him to burst into flames.

"Well, Master Naris, Master Yonah," Minister Hara said as she stood up.

"Why don't you send an order form to my family's estate upon your return to Vaha?"

Naris hastily stood up. Yonah followed suit. "I can take your requests now if you prefer," he said. "And I could send your order straight here to Kelab."

"You're very kind, Master Naris, but I want to spend the rest of this evening enjoying the party." The minister rested her hand on the doorknob. "Thank you for allowing me to experience your product. You should be very proud of it." She opened the door, letting in the noise of the guests, and stepped out into the crowd.

Naris suddenly whipped around to face Yonah and hissed into her face, "What did you say that about your mother for?"

Yonah steadily held his gaze. "She asked me a question, so I answered it."

"You made a political statement in front of a national minister!"

"I stated a fact. That is not a political statement. Besides, she wants to make an order. We were successful tonight."

Naris' eyes widened into appalled indignation. His nostrils flared, and he pursed his lips. Without a word, he stormed out of the study, slamming the door shut behind him. Yonah fell into the seat she had just vacated and let her legs splay ungracefully in front of her.

The study door creaked open, and a red-haired man peeked inside. Yonah sat upright and brought her legs together.

"Yonah," said Zanith. "I just saw your husband rush out of here. He looked upset." He stepped inside and closed the door. "Trouble in paradise?"

"Hello, Zanith," Yonah replied, returning the lack of title attached to his name. "I didn't know you were in the city."

"Yes, well, I thought it might be entertaining to see what kind of gaudy event Master Beneri put on."

Yonah tried not to let her face show her distaste for Zanith's rudeness towards her friend. Her face twitched, and the man chuckled.

"Oh, yes. He's a friend of yours, isn't he? The only master who could possibly think of someone like you as a friend."

"What do you want, Zanith?"

Zanith was standing in front of her now. Looming. A mild panic set into Yonah's bones, and she stood up.

"I just wanted to check in." He slowly lifted his hand up to Yonah's face and started to tuck a strand of her hair behind her ear. Yonah's skin prickled all over, and she lunged away. "And to remind you that you're still nothing. You're just a slave dressed up in a master's clothing."

"Do not touch me," Yonah said in a biting tone. She glanced at the door over Zanith's shoulder. "Get out."

"Remember, Yonah, this isn't your home. You don't get to tell me what to do."

"And you don't get to do anything to me that I don't want you to." Yonah started for the door, but Zanith's hand latched onto her wrist, stopping her in her tracks.

"You'll always be just a slave, Yonah." Zanith's voice was cool and steely. "And masters can do whatever they want to slaves."

Her heart was trembling. She grimaced. "It seems I need to remind you that the last time you tried to do whatever you wanted with me, my husband knocked you to the ground."

"Your husband's not here."

"The laws of Harasa recognize me as a master. If you do anything to me, you will be punished." Her voice was starting to shake. With rage, with fear, Yonah didn't know.

The door opened, sending a whoosh of fresh air into the room that cooled the perspiration on Yonah's skin. Beneri looked inside.

"Master Yonah, I've been looking for you." He narrowed his eyes at the red-headed man clutching Yonah's wrist. "Master Zanith. Can I help you?"

Zanith's fingers peeled off Yonah's wrist. "No, thank you, Master Beneri. Yonah and I were just catching up."

"I'm sure," Beneri replied dryly. "Well, I need to speak with Master Yonah right now, if you don't mind."

"Of course." Zanith started for the door, not without giving Yonah a look that sent a chill over her neck and arms.

Beneri watched Zanith go down the hallway, then whispered to Yonah, "Are you alright?"

Yonah pursed her lip, refusing to let herself cry. Her eyes were growing hot with tears, but she would not let them fall. "I hate that man."

"I don't know who invited him. It certainly wasn't me."

Yonah waved the topic away with her hand, desperate to forget the ugly feeling that pricked at her skin. "He's gone now. Do you need to talk to me?"

"The minister is talking about leaving, and I wanted to ask if you've had a chance to talk to her."

Yonah snapped to attention. "She's leaving? Why?"

"She says she needs to go to parliament tomorrow early in the morning. Wants to get a good night's sleep."

"We only spoke about the stupid wine!"

"I could host another party in a few days..."

"Naris and I are going back to Vaha tomorrow," Yonah said. "I need to speak to Minister Hara tonight."

Yonah bolted out the door with Beneri hot on her heels. As she shoved her way through the crowd, she ignored the looks of shock she received from the guests. She just needed to get to the minister before she left for the night.

When Yonah stepped outside, flames erupted into the air, causing her to gasp in surprise. At the bottom of the front steps, Minister Hara was just climbing into a carriage.

Chapter Nine

"Minister, wait!" Yonah cried out. She felt several pairs of eyes on her as she flitted down the steps towards the carriage.

The minister had paused with one foot in the carriage, watching Yonah in bewilderment.

"Minister Hara," Yonah gasped. "My apologies." She glanced around at the various slaves and masters that were watching them. "Would it possible for us to speak in private before you leave?"

"Is this urgent?"

"Well, I'm leaving the city tomorrow."

After a moment's pause, the minister removed her foot from the carriage and said, "Take a walk with me."

Yonah sighed with relief as she fell into step with the tall woman. She waited for them to be several houses down the street before speaking.

"Minister, I wanted to apologize for mentioning the Guard in that manner. I know it's not tasteful to speak of such things at a social event."

"Think nothing of it," Hara replied. She and Yonah continued walking down the street. The sounds of the party were fading behind them as they walked deeper into the still streets of the city. "Master Yonah, why did you marry Master Naris?"

Yonah looked at Hara's face to gauge the meaning behind her question, but the minister showed no signs of what she was truly asking.

"Because I love him."

"I find that hard to believe."

"We came from very different worlds, yes. It doesn't surprise me that people think of us as an odd couple."

"Because it would make sense for a slave to marry a master if she had other intentions." Hara stopped walking suddenly and gave Yonah a hard look. Yonah had seen Naris look at her in a similar way many times before when he was trying to read her. "Using one's opportunities," Hara continued, "is a great way to make change. Stepping into my father's position in parliament was my opportunity."

"What kind of change?"

"Yonah, I've just told you that I want to use my position as a minister for President Althu to make a change in this country."

The first move. The sign Yonah was looking for.

"I didn't marry Naris just for love." Saying the words out loud sent a thrill through Yonah. It was both terrifying and freeing to admit the true motivation behind her actions.

A tiny smirk tugged at Hara's lip. "It's nice to meet an ally."

Yonah tried not to grin too dumbly, to maintain her composure.

"Were you sent to make contact with me?" Hara asked as she started slowly walking again.

"I've been instructed to make contacts in Kelab, if possible, preferably within the government."

"May I ask, instructed by whom?"

Yonah said, "By the person I answer to."

"It's good of you to be shrewd," Hara said with a nod. "So, you've made contact with me. What do you want?"

"I'll need further instruction before I can answer that." Yonah glanced back towards the way they had come. "We should probably get you back."

Hara sighed as she looked towards Beneri's house, a soft and faraway glow of light.

The two women turned and made their way back to the minister's carriage.

"If I need to contact you from Vaha, I can send a letter to Beneri, and he can forward it to you," Yonah said. "I assume you'll be in the city for the foreseeable future."

Hara furrowed her brow at Yonah. "Master Beneri is an ally?"

"Yes. He's the one who told me that you were around and that I should talk to you."

"You never really know a person," Hara said with a dry chuckle. "We all have secrets."

Yonah only nodded solemnly in response. She kept many secrets.

"You leave for Vaha tomorrow?" Hara asked.

"Yes."

"Then I'm sure I'll hear from you soon."

The unmistakable sound of galloping hooves filled the air, causing anyone outside to turn their heads. An open wagon drawn by two horses was coming towards them. Two Guards sat at the front of the wagon, and two in the back.

Yonah tried to remain calm as the Guards dismounted in front of Beneri's house. There was no reason for them to be there for her. But they were certainly here to arrest somebody. They rarely made nighttime calls like this.

Everyone backed away from the Guards as they threaded through the party guests and up the steps to the house. They didn't bother knocking but went inside.

"I'd better go," the minister muttered. "Before this turns into a scandal." She stepped towards her carriage, and a slave opened the door for her.

"Thank you for your apology, Master Yonah," the minister said loudly.

Yonah bowed her head.

Minister Hara stepped into the carriage, which rocked gently at her weight. The door was shut behind her, and the carriage rolled away. As Yonah watched it go, her chest swelled with excitement.

She hesitated outside the house, not wanting to spend any more time near the Guards than she had to.

Naris came out of the house, paused at the top of the steps, found Yonah, and strode over to her. "Yonah, where have you been?"

"I was just talking to the minister," Yonah replied calmly. "I wanted to apologize for what I said."

Naris gave Yonah a begrudging look. "That was very good of you. I'm glad you caught her before she left."

"So am I."

"Did you see the Guards arrive?"

Yonah nodded solemnly.

"There's far too much political activity here in the city for my liking," Naris grumbled.

They could hear the arrested master before they saw him.

"You've got the wrong man! I'm nothing but a loyal citizen to the country!"

The Guards emerged from the house, two of them holding the master in question. His face was panic-stricken. He twisted and writhed against the clutches of his captors.

They dragged the master down the steps and to the wagon. His wrists were shackled, and he was pulled into the wagon bed, where he sat looking very undignified. "You will regret this!" he shouted. "The ministers will not stand for this!"

One of the Guards leaned down to the man and shouted, "Shut up!"

The master stopped yelling, his mouth hanging open in shock.

The Guards took their posts in the wagon and rode off into the night. The farther they went, the more Yonah felt like she could breathe again.

"Are you alright?" Naris asked her.

She nodded. "I'm fine. Let's go."

"Yes, that certainly put a damper on the party."

Yonah wished she could say goodbye to Beneri, but she wanted to leave the scene as fast as she could, and he was still in the house. She and Naris hired a carriage and returned to their hotel. Yonah was exhausted when they arrived at their room, and both she and Naris began to get ready for bed. She noticed a soft scowl on Naris' face as he removed his dress clothes.

"Are you happy we're going back home tomorrow?" she asked sweetly.

"Yes." His voice was sullen.

"We live a quieter life in Vaha, but there's much more freedom to it, isn't there?" Yonah started removing her earrings and jewelry. She added, "And free of the politics of Kelab."

Naris suddenly disappeared into the other room in their apartment. Yonah stared at the spot he had vacated, dumbfounded. Just as suddenly as he had gone, Naris returned.

He cradled the three small bottles of potion Yonah thought she had forgotten to pack in one arm and held the bottle she had bought earlier that week in his other hand. His face was fiercely dark.

A fear Yonah hadn't felt for a long time spread through her body and limbs, jumping agitatedly from nerve to nerve.

"I see you've been going through my things," she said.

"So, you admit that this is yours?"

"I've been having headaches–"

"Don't lie to me about what this is." Naris' voice had risen in volume. He tossed the three small bottles onto the bed. "This." He looked at the remaining bottle in his hand, his face crumpling. "This is the reason we don't have a family." His face turned up to Yonah, and he stormed towards her. "You're the reason we don't have a family!"

He lifted the bottle above his head as he closed in on Yonah. She instinctively brought her arms above her to ease the blow. Naris stopped just in front of her, his arm still raised. Rage and disbelief swirled through his golden-brown eyes.

They were frozen. How many times had the pair of them been caught suspended in time, lost in their own little world, on the precipice of something new?

Rage overtook the disbelief in Naris' eyes. With his teeth bared, he whirled around and threw the bottle into the wall, where it shattered, spilling its clear contents onto the wall and floor. Yonah shrieked at the sound and quickly backed away from Naris while his gaze was still away from her.

"Why?" he said with a snarl. He whipped around to face Yonah, who had backed against the far wall. He filled the space between them with two long steps and clamped his hands on her shoulders. "Why are you doing this?"

"I-I-I," Yonah stammered, desperately searching for a story to tell him. "I'm afraid! I'm afraid I'll be a terrible mother."

Naris' rage cooled, though he still breathed heavily. "I think you're lying to me."

Yonah remained silent.

"You think I'll be a terrible father." Naris looked as if he were watching a nightmare unfold before his eyes. "How could you think so little of me?"

"No, Naris, I'm sure you'll be a wonderful father," Yonah said quickly.

"Then why won't you bear my children?" Naris shook her once.

Yonah closed her eyes and flinched, expecting more pain than was being doled out. "I told you, I'm afraid I'll be a bad mother."

"So, you won't even try? Yonah. Yonah. Look at me."

He grabbed her chin and turned her face towards his. Yonah opened her eyes to Naris' pained expression.

"Yonah," he said. "You've been lying to me."

He had no idea how much she was lying to him.

"You told me I could trust you," he continued.

"I'm sorry," she whispered. There was some truth to that sentence. She was sorry she was taking advantage of him. She was sorry that he would never get to prove to himself that he would be a caring and compassionate father.

Naris thrust her chin away, making Yonah's neck crack at the sudden movement. He stormed out of the room once again.

Rubbing the back of her neck, Yonah looked to the doorway Naris had gone through. She slowly walked over and peered through it. Naris was lying on a chaise, his eyes clamped shut beneath furrowed brows.

As quietly as she could, Yonah took the blanket from the bed, padded over to Naris, and covered him. He sent a soft glare in her direction but otherwise made no note of her action. Yonah returned to the bedroom and went to sleep.

Chapter Ten

The return trip to Vaha was quiet. Although Naris' fury at Yonah had cooled even by the next morning, he barely spoke to her at all. He continued to take her hand to assist her in and out of carriages and train cars, but he did so without looking at her.

The silent treatment filled Yonah with a sense of unease, but she took the time to recover from their busy schedule in the city. As she sat alone in the train car (Naris had said he was going to find something to drink and hadn't returned for nearly an hour), Yonah delighted in the fact that she had successfully made contact with a rebel sympathizer within the government.

Even though the trip to Kelab had been a success, Yonah couldn't help but feel a sense of coming home as the white palace of Vaha came into view across the plain.

Once the carriage had stopped in front of the palace and Yonah and Naris disembarked, Naris said to one of the slaves that came out to meet them, "Search Master Yonah's room. Remove any medications you find in there."

It wasn't at all surprising that Naris would have Yonah's room searched, but it felt violating all the same. With clenched fists, she started towards the back of the palace.

"Where are you going?" Naris demanded. It was the first time he had spoken directly to Yonah in days.

Yonah glared unwaveringly at Naris and said, "For a walk."

"You have no right to be angry with me, Yonah."

But she was angry, which was why she kept walking without responding. If this were a normal marriage, she wouldn't be afraid for her future children's safety. If this were a normal marriage, she would be able to have a genuine conversation with her husband about these things. If this were a normal marriage, she would be married to someone filled with joy like her brother, steady like her sister, loyal like her mother, and just like her father.

She came upon the stable where Seidon was tending to the horses in the corral. They met each other from either side of the fence.

"Welcome back," Seidon said. Yonah could see him gauging the stormy look on her face. "Everything alright?"

The reason for her and Naris' argument was perhaps too intimate to share with a middle-aged man, Yonah thought.

"Naris is upset with me," she said.

Alarm flashed across Seidon's eyes. "Did he hurt you?"

"No. I think he was going to." She remembered how Naris had drawn his hand with the bottle above their heads. "But he didn't."

"He won't hurt another master, I suppose."

"I have more rights, now." If Yonah were to tell a magistrate that her husband had attacked her, there would be an investigation at the very least.

"Why's he upset with you?" Seidon asked. "Something to do with the cause?"

"Nothing to do with that," Yonah replied, waving the question away with her hand.

Seidon gazed at her with his watchful eyes. Yonah felt herself pulling inward, away from him. "Will you talk to Praha about it?" he finally asked.

"Maybe."

Seidon's eyes rested on Yonah for a while longer while she adamantly looked away towards the horses. They grazed on the sparse grass in their coral. One lazily galloped around the perimeter.

"Can I take one of the horses out?" Yonah asked suddenly.

Seidon's eyebrows shot up in surprise. "You going somewhere?"

"Nowhere particular. Just away from here."

"You've never gone for a ride for the sake of a ride before," Seidon said with a shrug as he started toward the stable. Yonah followed without replying to his statement. She wasn't a great rider, which was why she kept the activity only to running errands. But today, she needed to fly away.

Within a few minutes, Yonah was atop a light brown gelding named River, tying her hair back with a string.

"Where will you go?" Seidon asked.

Yonah shrugged, feeling oddly obstinate.

"You don't get reckless out there just because you're in a mood," Seidon said sternly.

Yonah tried to hold back the glare she wanted to send the stable master. The point of this ride was to go where she could do whatever she wanted.

"I'll be safe," she said, not sure if she really meant it, kicked the gelding into motion, and galloped away at a speed that sent the wind whistling through her ears.

She went past Naris' childhood treehouse, beyond the lines of the estate, deep into the emptiness of the plains. Storm clouds billowed angry and grey in the distance. The wind chilled her skin, rippling it with goosebumps. At the same time, Yonah could feel beads of sweat forming at her hairline. Her chest swelled with joy, swallowing fresh air, floating with freedom. She almost felt happy.

Yonah saw the canyon and slowed the horse to a stop. She slipped off and took its lead, taking them down the path into the scar of the earth.

She hadn't been to visit the waterfall since the first time Naris had brought her. She felt a little bit like she was intruding on a sacred place without him with her. The feeling made her want to both leave immediately and take advantage of the place.

The small waterfall pounded into a pool at the bottom of the canyon. Surrounded by red rocks, small trees, and shrubs, it was an unusual oasis.

Yonah looped the gelding's lead over a tree branch and undressed. She waded into the pool. The temperature sent her shivering and clutching her arms around her body.

Of all the things she had learned to do after marrying Naris, swimming was not one of them. She knew from experience, though, that this pool was plenty shallow enough for her to safely wade.

Yonah sucked in a deep breath and let herself sink all the way into the rippling water. Weightlessness carried her, sending her dark hair floating wildly around her head. The sound of her heartbeat overtook all other noise, sending a calming sensation through her. She opened her eyes. Grey blue. Stillness. It was beautiful.

Her throat clenched. Yonah returned to the surface and gasped in air.

She looked up to see that the storm clouds had rolled in above her. The sky rumbled. But she wouldn't go back yet. Instead, Yonah continued to wade around the pool, weaving around the backside of the waterfall and out into the open again.

A low rumble came from above once again. The gelding shifted its weight and ground his hooves into the dirt.

"It hasn't even started raining yet," Yonah told the horse with some annoyance.

She felt a heavy raindrop plop onto her face. She looked up again. The clouds were darker than they were even a few minutes ago.

The raindrops grew more frequent, pricking the surface of the pool with needlepoints that rippled and were interrupted by other drops. Yonah's hair matted onto her head, and, in a matter of seconds, she was caught in a rainstorm.

Her clothes were already soaked when she waded out of the pool to get dressed. Despite their state, Yonah dressed, took the gelding's lead, and started for the path that would lead them up out of the canyon.

The dirt beneath their feet was fast turning to slippery mud. Each time Yonah took a step forward, she slid back a few inches. The gelding whinnied in protest.

"Keep coming, River," Yonah said, trying to sound calm despite her growing annoyance. "Come on, boy."

A boom roared through the sky that vibrated through Yonah's body and made her jump. The gelding cried out again.

"Whoa, River," Yonah said. She stroked the horse's long face. "It's okay. Just keep walking." She met the gelding's eye and willed him to calm. He snorted at her. Yonah started up the path again, holding tightly to the lead with one hand and clutching the canyon wall with the other.

By the time she reached the top of the canyon wall, Yonah was puffing from the exertion of pulling her feet out of the mud each time she stepped and holding herself in a squat position so she wouldn't slip right over and fall. She stood on the grassy plain, still holding the lead, her other hand on her hip. She shoved her matted hair out of her eyes. It was heavy from the rain.

The horizon held nothing in sight except for the murky greyness of the storm. Yonah only knew in what general direction Vaha lay.

Lightning flashed across the sky just as another boom reverberated through Yonah's bones. For a split second, she was blind by the light, then by the sudden darkness that followed.

The gelding whinnied, reared up on his hind legs, and bolted.

"River, no! Whoa!" Yonah sprinted after the horse, but she slipped on the wet grass and fell gracelessly to the ground. She cried out as her chin hit the earth. She screamed angrily, "River!" But the gelding was gone from sight, swallowed by the rain and the grey. "River!"

There was another crack of lightning and a rumble of thunder. Yonah realized she was completely alone in the storm without really knowing where home was. She tried not to let panic take over as she stood up and looked into nothingness.

CHAPTER ELEVEN

"Yonah!"

She turned her head to the sound of the voice, but she couldn't see anybody.

"Yonah!" he called again.

Relief swept through her. "Naris!" she called back. She scrambled to her feet.

He was a shadow at first, then a silhouette. Naris was riding one of the horses, pounding magnificently through the storm. When he saw her, his eyes lit up, and he said, "Yonah!" In a fluid motion, he slid off the horse before it had even stopped and swept Yonah into an embrace. "I'm so glad I found you."

Yonah buried her face into Naris' wet chest, happy to have a companion in the storm. She looked at him. "Naris, I'm sorry. One of the geldings, he ran away."

"Don't worry about it now. It's not safe for you to be out here. We have to go back." Naris took Yonah's hand and led her to his own steed. He held the left stirrup for her and waited as she climbed on. When he climbed on behind her and wrapped his arms around her to grab the reins, memories of them together like this took over Yonah's mind. They had ridden like this a few times when Naris was teaching her how to ride. They had laughed together. Yonah had liked the way it felt to have him helping her, cheering for her.

On the other occasion they had ridden like this, Naris had caught up with her after she had attempted to run away with her now-dead sister. He had been furious. And he had hurt her that night in a way Yonah hadn't thought him capable of.

Naris wheeled the horse around and set it off at a gallop. Within a few minutes, the shape of the palace and the stable came into view. They rode for the stable, dismounted the horse, and raced inside.

Despite the rain pounding on the roof, it was far quieter in the stable than it was outside in the whirling wind. The horses were skittish and scoffed uncomfortably. As Naris settled his horse into its stall, Yonah wrapped her arms around her body to fight against the chill that came with wearing wet clothes.

Having finished with the horse, Naris went to Yonah and hugged her again, placing one hand around her waist and cradling the back of her head with the other. "I was so worried about you."

"Worried I'd run away," Yonah said. It wasn't a question. She knew where Naris' priorities lay.

He pulled away but kept his hands on her. His expression was one of hurt. "No, Yonah. I was worried you would be hurt. Or worse."

Yonah couldn't help but feel shame at assuming Naris had a complete lack of sincere feelings for another human being.

"Even if we're arguing, I'll always love you, Yonah."

She could only nod in reply. An unintentional shiver suddenly ran through her body.

"We should get you out of those clothes."

"Let's get to the palace," Yonah said with a nod. She started for the door, but Naris held her back by holding her hand.

"I'm not going out there again," he said.

"Well, I don't have any dry clothes in here. Do you?"

Looking serious, Naris walked to a shelf at the back of the stable and removed a blanket from its spot. A mild fear made Yonah hesitate.

"What about Seidon?"

"I sent him inside when I came looking for you."

When he came looking for her. When he saved her from the storm.

"What about the horses?"

Naris chuckled. "They won't mind." He slowly walked closer to Yonah.

"What about our fight?"

He cupped her cheek in his hand. "You don't need to be afraid of being a mother. I know you'll do wonderfully." He kissed her other cheek, burning the skin where his lips touched.

Yonah watched Naris carefully. He kissed her forehead and her nose, then placed a gentle, whisper-like kiss on her scarred lip. The softness of that kiss made Yonah's heart flutter. It was reaching through her chest, trying to pull Naris closer.

He whispered, "I love you."

She looked into his eyes. There was that vulnerable, frightened look. He turned to her for assurance that he was a loveable man, that he was worthy of affection. It broke her heart and filled her with rage all at once.

"Do you love me?"

She nodded, pressing her lips closed.

"Will you say it?"

The words caught in her throat, but she coaxed them out, up into her mouth, past her teeth and tongue, through her lips. "I love you."

He smiled softly. Then he reached for her waist and started tugging her tunic over her head. She responded in kind, out of obligation, though the farther along they went, the more she found herself appreciating the warmth of Naris' skin beneath her hands and, eventually, against the rest of her shivering body.

When they were both undressed, Naris laid the blanket over a pile of hay. He took Yonah's hand and led her onto it as if he were leading her to a dance floor. They lay down together. The blanket was scratchy against Yonah's skin, and she instinctively drew closer to Naris. He wrapped his arms around her and pulled her into a deep kiss.

Words bubbled inside Yonah and erupted. "Thank you for coming to find me."

Naris looked slightly taken aback that she had interrupted the kiss, but the corners of his mouth turned upward. He folded a strand of hair behind Yonah's ear. "Of course. I'll always come for you."

To be cared for was a luxury Yonah hadn't experienced in a long time. Yes, her brother was still alive and checked in on her, but he was always so far away. Yes, Praha and Seidon wanted to know if Yonah was doing well, but their relationships had to remain secret. But here, now, Naris cradled her in his firm but gentle arms, looked at her tenderly with eyes full of want, promised to take care of her for always.

That promise, that hope made Yonah bring her fingers to Naris' face. Naris closed his eyes as Yonah's fingers ran along his cheek and chin. This calmness he wore on his face now was unlike the cool confidence he wore in public. This was real. Yonah knew Naris was himself around her. She knew that he was perfectly content right now. He was happy.

Yonah brought her lips to Naris! They breathed each other in. Their chests swelled against each other. Yonah hooked her leg over Naris' hip, and he brought his hand to her thigh. She was burning on the inside.

In moments like these, she didn't need to run away to escape. Her mind, her passion, and her hunger took care of that. Everything on the outside fell away and left space only for her body next to Naris. They became just two humans. Not a master who married his slave. Not a law-abiding citizen and a rebel. Just Naris and Yonah.

Just Naris climbed on top. Just Yonah tugged at her husband's hair with both hands. Just Naris brought his fingers to the area between her legs. Just Yonah moaned softly.

Naris pulled his lips away and looked down at Yonah. His eyes were alight with a warm fire. They invited Yonah in as a guest that was more than welcome to stay for as long as she liked. Yonah wanted to stay like this forever.

The fire in their eyes was spreading through their bodies, reaching towards each other until they connected into a fiery mass. Yonah clung tightly to Naris. He kissed her hungrily.

Then she was calling out in pleasure, her body writhing of its own volition. Naris removed his hand from between her legs and placed himself inside her. The new sensation made Yonah moan once more. Their eyes met, and their hungry fire cooled briefly before sparking again into desire and steady love.

How could she have let that happen?

Yonah let passion shove aside the warnings in her mind. She and Naris found a rhythm between their two bodies, slow at first, growing faster and deeper.

Naris' body tensed suddenly. His eyes closed, his brow furrowed, and his mouth dropped open. Although she couldn't feel it, Yonah knew that Naris could be impregnating her right now. This had happened before. She just needed to drink some of her potion as soon as possible.

Yonah started as she remembered that the reason she had been out in the storm was because she was frustrated that Naris had her room searched and had all traces of that potion removed from it.

She would go to town tomorrow, first thing in the morning. And she would find a new hiding spot for the potion. She could keep it here in the stable. Or somewhere in the library.

"What are you thinking about?" Naris asked her softly, panting slightly.

Lie. "I think the storm's letting up."

Naris kissed her gently. "We can stay here until it stops." He stood up, took another blanket from the shelf, and took it back to Yonah, lying down next to her and covering their bodies with it.

Yonah let herself automatically burrow into Naris' chest as he threaded his arm beneath her. She had been attracted to him from the night they met, but she had reminded herself all along that she had to remain detached, for her safety, for the safety of those around her, and then for the rebellion.

She knew she should continue to maintain an emotional distance from

Naris. He didn't truly love her, and she couldn't love him. The wedding beads they wore to mark their partnership through life were false. But she ached for a family just as much as Naris did, and Naris was the closest thing to family she could have for now.

Chapter Twelve

They awoke to the sound of the stable door opening and closing, then Seidon loudly clearing his throat.

Shame made Yonah bolt upright, clutching the scratchy blanket covering her and Naris' naked bodies to her chest. Her wide eyes met with Seidon's. His expression was serious. His eyes questioned her.

"Pardon me for disturbing you both, Master Naris, Master Yonah," the stable master said.

Naris shamelessly stood up from underneath the blanket and began dressing. Seidon turned his eyes away.

"I'll, uh, take the horses outside," he muttered.

"Oh, slave," Naris called to Seidon. Yonah cringed at the address. "We lost one of the geldings in the storm last night. It ran off."

With a brief nod, Seidon said, "I'll send out a search party, Master."

As Seidon took the horses from the stalls to the corral, Yonah glued her eyes to her knees, too embarrassed to look at Seidon. Once they were gone, she stood up and started dressing, keeping her eyes away from Naris.

"What's wrong?" Naris asked her.

"I'm embarrassed at Sei- At the stable master finding us like this."

"Yonah, you shouldn't be embarrassed." Naris placed his hand on the small of her back, but she continued to keep her eyes away from him. "We're the masters here. We can do whatever we want."

Yonah glared at him. He would never understand. "It's unprofessional."

This caused Naris to pause. "I suppose you're right." He smirked. "But it was fun, wasn't it?"

She didn't deign to reply but simply finished dressing. "I'm going to go to Kirash today."

"Aren't you tired from the trip?"

"No."

"I thought we could spend today together."

Yonah started for the stable door. "We can spend time together when I get back from town."

"Well, why don't I come with you?"

Yonah stopped in the open door and stared at Naris. "You never come to town with me."

He shrugged. "This will be something new for us to do together. You can show me your favourite spots to visit."

Yonah fumed. He wanted to ensure she didn't go anywhere that sold anti-pregnancy potion. It made her want to scream. Instead, she plastered a false smile onto her face. "Wonderful. I'll just go change into new clothes."

When she reached her room, Yonah rang the bell string by her bed that was connected to the slaves' quarters in the basement. She started changing her clothes as she waited for Praha's arrival. The slave woman entered a minute later.

"Where were you last night?" she asked.

"I was caught in the storm and spent the night in the stable," Yonah said, annoyance tingeing her voice. "I need you to do me a favour. Can you get to Kirash sometime today?"

"I suppose so."

"I need you to buy some of my potion for me." Yonah stepped into a pair of loose pants.

"Don't you get that at a special spot?"

"I'm sure you'll be able to find it somewhere else." She pulled on a plain shirt. "I would do it myself, but Naris insists on coming to town with me."

"The slaves say you two are angry with each other."

Yonah rummaged through her drawers in search of a shawl to wrap around her shoulders and head. "Yes. We were. We are." She shook her head as if to shake all thoughts of Naris from her mind. "Will you help me?"

"I'll do my best," Praha replied.

Yonah returned to her drawers, withdrew a drawstring bag, and handed it to Praha. "That should cover any expenses along the way. I have to go."

When she had first arrived at Vaha as Naris' slave, they had ridden to Kirash with Yonah sitting behind, clinging to Naris' waist. Today they would ride separately. Naris looked on at Yonah with pride as she mounted her horse.

"You've come a long way," he said. "You ride like a real master."

Yonah whipped her eyes to Naris, her ears pricking at the sentiment. "I am a real master," she replied.

Naris' smile dissipated. "I didn't mean anything by that."

Without bothering to listen to any further explanation, Yonah kicked her horse into a gallop and whisked down the path from Vaha's front steps, through the vineyard, and towards the road that led to Kirash.

There wasn't much for Yonah to show Naris that wouldn't incriminate her or put her operation within the rebellion at risk, so she simply walked down the main road that served as a market with him. They examined stalls exhibiting artisan jewelry, finely made clothing, decorations, flowers, spices, dried fruit, and more.

"This is all you do when you come to Kirash?" Naris asked in disbelief.

Yonah shrugged non-committedly.

"Why don't we go to the dress shop and buy you something new?"

"I don't need any more clothes," Yonah replied.

"You never know when you need something for a special event."

"I have plenty of clothes to take care of that."

Naris said in a gentle tone, "I'd like to buy you something." His eyes were earnest.

The look in Naris' eyes melted Yonah's hard-hearted annoyance and she sighed. "Fine." She led the way to a building with a sign hanging from it that read *Lenara's Dress Shop*. The dress shop was a warmly lit place with a sense of hushed business. All noise was cushioned by the rolls of fabric stacked along the wall. Mannequins dressed in luxurious clothes dotted the room. Yonah did enjoy looking at the clothes from time to time, though she didn't spend as much time here as Naris hoped she would.

A woman wearing her hair in a low ponytail emerged from behind a mannequin, smiled, and said, "Master Yonah, it's a pleasure to see you here."

"Lenara," Yonah said in greeting. "This is my husband, Master Naris."

The dressmaker bowed her head to Naris. "Master Naris, it's lovely to meet you."

"Does my wife come here so often that you know her by face?"

"Not at all," Lenara replied. "We make a point of knowing our guests by name. In fact, Master Yonah doesn't come here nearly as often as we'd like!" She chuckled at the joke. "What do you need assistance with today, Master Yonah? A fitting? Shopping off the shelf?"

Yonah wandered down an aisle, taking in the rich colours and patterns. "My husband would like to buy me a new dress," she said over her shoulder. "I can just take a look around."

"Let's have a brand new one fitted for you, my dear," Naris said.

"That's a long process," Yonah replied. "You might get bored."

Although Naris gave Yonah his usual coy grin, she could see a slight tension in his eyes. "I insist."

Wanting to remain in Naris' good graces, Yonah walked towards the fitting area and said to the dressmaker, "Let's fit me for a new dress."

After the dress fitting, Yonah and Naris started back down the main road towards home. On the way, Naris bought a handful of candied fruit, which the two of them amicably shared.

"I remember our first train ride together," Naris said, popping a piece into his mouth, "where we ordered fruit for the trip. The look of pure joy on your face was so endearing."

Yonah couldn't help but smile at the memory. She had certainly been childlike in her enjoyment of fresh berries, a luxury she hadn't experienced for years beforehand.

"I'm surprised you remember," she said.

"I remember a lot of things," Naris replied.

When they reached the edge of town, they rode away from Kirash back to Vaha, dismounting the horses at the front of the palace—Naris rarely went to the stable himself.

"That was a lovely morning," Naris said, his tone light. "I'm glad I got to share it with you."

Yonah only smiled in return.

"What else are you up to today?" Naris asked.

"I have a letter to write." Yonah started up the steps to the front door of the palace.

"And after that?"

"I suppose I'll check in on other correspondences I'm in the middle of."

"So, you'll be in your room all afternoon?"

Yonah paused, one foot through the massive front door. She stared at Naris. "What does it matter where I am for the afternoon?"

He, at least, showed Yonah enough dignity not to deny that he was keeping tabs on her whereabouts. He did not, however, say as much out loud.

"I'll be sure," Yonah said coldly, "to let you know if I decide to leave my cell." She continued to make her way inside. Naris followed.

"Oh, don't compare yourself to a prisoner, Yonah," he said. "It's lowbrow and crass."

"Yes, Master," she replied, her voice dripping with sarcasm. She immediately froze and watched Naris' reaction. He, too, was frozen in place. The reference to the power structure of their relationship in its beginning stages had jarred Yonah. She hadn't called Naris 'Master' in two years.

To Yonah's surprise, Naris' face softened into disbelief and hurt. His eyebrows and the corners of his mouth drooped. He lost an inch in height and cast his eyes downward.

"Is that what you think of me?" His voice was dull.

"Is it not how you think of yourself?"

His gaze snapped up to Yonah's. "No, it is not. And the fact that you have to ask that is extremely disappointing."

Yonah shook her head and tried to keep her face calm. She did not want to go deeper into this conversation. It would unravel their already poorly woven marriage. "I'm sorry I said it."

"But you meant it."

Yonah spoke with more force than usual. "I wish I could take it back."

The forcefulness of her voice made Naris take a step backwards, as if a strong gust of wind had suddenly whorled through the entrance hall.

Yonah composed herself and said more gently, "I'll see you at dinner?"

Naris' eyes were searching Yonah's, trying to read her. Again, she wondered if he had become as good at reading her as she was at reading him.

"Fine," he finally muttered, and strode up the stairs ahead of Yonah.

Yonah remained rooted to the spot so there would be more space between her and Naris. When she had waited enough to know that Naris would be well on his way to his office, she climbed up the stairs to her bedroom.

She sat at the table in the centre of the room where she lately kept stationery and a quill.

Dear Beneri…

All she could write was that she had successfully made contact with the minister, that Beneri could expect to receive letters on her behalf, and that Yonah was temporarily unable to get further instruction as to how the rebellion wanted to use the minister but would write as soon as she was able.

Yonah signed the letter and folded it into an envelope. She then got to work on her more legal correspondence for the winery.

The afternoon wore on, and Yonah eventually set her quill down, stacked her letters together in a neat pile, and stepped out onto her balcony.

There were still slaves working in the rows of the vineyard, their copper collars glinting in the waning sunlight. Yonah knew the slaves of this estate looked on her with disgust ever since she had arrived as a slave herself, especially now that she had seemingly taken advantage of her position of privilege to gain even more stature. Despite being so disliked by them, Yonah looked at the slaves as a stark reminder of what she was doing all this for. It was for them, for the maimed like Seidon, for the poor like Praha, for the orphans like herself.

She heard her bedroom door open and turned to see Praha walking in. She carried something, but Yonah didn't register what, as her attention was stolen by the large bloody welts on Praha's hands.

Chapter Thirteen

"Praha," Yonah said, alarmed. She strode back into her room from the balcony. "What happened?"

"I was brought to Master Naris when I arrived back at the palace," Praha explained. She was shaking. "He asked me what I had done in town. He asked to see what I bought."

Yonah realized that Praha carried a bottle in her hands, the bottle of anti-pregnancy potion she had sent for. It was empty but intact. Yonah's insides trembled with rage. She took the bottle and set it on the table with a dull thud.

"What did he do to you?"

Praha looked at her hands as if she hadn't realized they were bleeding. "He— He hit me with a strap."

Although it had been a long time, it wasn't the first time someone had been hurt by Naris on Yonah's account. Yonah forced herself to take in Praha's injury, bright red welts, peeling skin, caked blood. She forced herself to memorize the disgust she felt with herself for letting yet another friend of hers unwillingly take punishment on her behalf.

"I'm so sorry, Praha." Yonah's voice shook. She wasn't sure whether it was with sorrow or fury. "This is my fault."

Praha said nothing. Yonah met the slave woman's eyes. When she saw them, she immediately wanted to turn away. There was a darkness in them like a light snuffed out.

"Let's get you some help," Yonah muttered. She placed her hand on Praha's back and ushered her out of the room. They went down to the main floor, to a set of stairs that led down to the basement where all the slaves of Vaha worked and slept.

These stairs went straight into the kitchen, which was always a bustle of activity. Yonah wanted nothing more than to avoid going down these stairs. Nothing good ever came of her visiting the slaves' quarters.

When Yonah and Praha entered the kitchen from the stairwell, the room hushed for a moment as the slaves registered Yonah's appearance. Their confusion at her arrival was quickly eclipsed by their concern for Praha.

"Is Daza here?" Yonah asked.

Someone said, "I'll get him," and left the room. Someone else led Praha to the long kitchen table to take a seat. The others glared at Yonah. She grew hot under their stares.

The healer named Daza arrived, carrying a small case. He sat next to Praha on the bench, set his case on the table, and examined her hands.

"What happened?" he asked. His voice was gentle and soothing.

"A strap," Praha choked.

"Who did this?"

"Master Naris."

All the slaves present, including the healer, glanced over at Yonah.

"I'm not covering for her," Praha said. "It was Naris."

A man standing in the corner said, "But *why* didn't Naris hit you?" He kept his eyes on Yonah as he spoke, making it very clear that he knew why.

"Can you fix it or not?" Praha asked Daza.

The man nodded. "You'll be alright."

Praha looked up at Yonah. "You'd better go."

Yonah wasn't sure if she imagined it or not, but something about Praha's suggestion felt somewhat final. She glanced around the room at the unfriendly faces surrounding her, gave Praha a quick nod, and started up the stairs.

She paused at the top of the stairs. When Naris had punished the wine pourer and her friend Bana, she had just stood by. She hadn't fought back against Naris, hadn't told him that his actions were unacceptable. She had been a slave back then. She was a master now. She was his wife. She was supposed to be his equal.

She had married him so she could get to work protecting others.

With a fire in her chest, Yonah went straight to Naris' office. She didn't bother to knock on the closed door but instead grabbed the handle and barrelled through it. Her sudden entrance made Naris' head whip up in surprise.

"You're a monster," Yonah said, agitatedly pointing at her husband as she stood in front of his desk, doing her best to tower over him.

"Oh, I'm the monster?" Naris leaned back in his chair, apparently just as riled as Yonah. "You did see what your favourite brought for you?"

"If you have a problem with me, you tell me! There was no reason for you to hurt Pra—that slave woman!"

"Tell you like you've been telling me?" Naris stood and walked around the desk to stand just inches from Yonah. "No, Yonah, this is what gets you to listen. Now I have your attention."

"This isn't how a normal marriage works!" Yonah's arms flailed in the air as if she were trying to capture the proper message she was trying to convey with her bare hands. "This is the reason I'm afraid to have children with you! Because you're a lunatic!"

Naris plucked Yonah's wrists from the air and clutched them in his hands. "What did you call me?"

She met his heavy stare, afraid but unwilling to turn away. "I called you a lunatic. A sadistic lunatic."

The pressure on Yonah's wrist grew tighter as Naris clenched his hands. Just as panic started to set in at the tightness of his grip, he suddenly threw her arms away from him.

"I could just—" he sputtered. He lifted his outstretched hands to her skull, where they hovered an inch from her skin. "You make me— The things I would do to you, Yonah, if I lacked self-control."

"I wish you would hurt me," she said, hot tears welling up in her eyes.

Naris rolled his eyes. "So you can call a magistrate and have me sent to prison?"

"No." Yonah met Naris' eyes and, for the first time, wished that he would see her soul, her pain, her guilt. "Because I deserve it."

For all the mistakes and missteps Yonah had made, the consequences were so often left to other people to bear.

Concern erased any trace of anger from Naris' face.

"I'll stop trying to buy anti-pregnancy potion," Yonah said, "and you'll stop hurting the slaves."

Naris shook his head. "No. No, I have a right as a master to discipline my slaves as I see fit."

"And I have a right as a human being to decide what happens and what doesn't happen to my body."

They held each other with their eyes, the usual battle of wills raging.

Yonah pointed to herself. "No more potion." She pointed to Naris. "No more hurting the slaves. Do we have a deal?"

"You would have a monster father your children for a bunch of slaves?"

"Not for a bunch of slaves," Yonah replied. "For the sake of human beings."

Again, Naris' face crumpled as he let his hurt show. He turned and leaned on the edge of his desk. "Why do you care about the slaves more than me?"

Yonah closed her eyes and sighed softly. "Because the slaves need more care than you do right now."

"But you're my wife."

Unsure of what to say, Yonah leaned on the desk next to Naris. No longer being nose-to-nose suddenly made it easier to breathe.

"We have a deal," Naris said. The pair of them gave each other a sideways look. "I'll stop hurting the slaves. You stop buying potion. We have a family."

"Deal." She held her hand out to Naris to shake.

Naris hooked his fingers beneath Yonah's and stroked her knuckles with his thumb. "Instead of shaking, I'd like to kiss on it."

Yonah watched their hands for a moment, then turned her eyes to Naris' face. His expression was soft. There was that vulnerability. She could always count on that.

She leaned towards Naris. He met her halfway. Their lips pressed together in a soft kiss. She pulled away sooner than Naris. She could feel his lips puckering, reaching as she leaned back.

Chapter Fourteen

Normally, Praha would come to check in with Yonah during the evening, but she was absent, just as Yonah expected. She didn't come the following morning either.

Yonah needed to get word to Vitora that she had successfully contacted Minister Hara. Under normal circumstances, she would have simply gone to Kirash without worrying about telling Naris, but with the current tension in their relationship, she felt that would push Naris over the edge.

She tucked her stack of letters into a small shoulder bag, including the one for Beneri, and made her way to Naris' office, where he was already back for another day's work. Instead of storming in as she had done yesterday, Yonah knocked on the door and waited for Naris to call out for her to enter.

The skin around Naris' eyes was purple, and his eyes were heavy. He had apparently not slept the night before. "Good morning, Yonah," he said.

"Good morning." She stood in front of his desk, resting her hands on the chair that sat there. "In the interest of regaining your trust, I wanted to let you know that I'm going back to Kirash today."

"What business do you have there?" Naris asked grumpily.

"I have letters to post, and I'd like the walk. I can show you the letters if you like."

She was reaching into her bag when Naris shook his head and sighed. "I believe you."

A silence weighted the air between them.

"If it would make you feel better," Yonah said slowly, half-regretting the words already, "you could send someone with me."

"Yonah," Naris moaned. He cradled his forehead in his hand. "What am I supposed to say? I should let you go alone to prove that I trust you, but I'm afraid right now. And if I send someone with you, then I'm treating you like a master treats a slave." He looked up at Yonah, his eyes begging her to tell him what to do.

Yonah sat in the chair across from Naris. "I offered so I could ease your mind."

"What do you want me to say?"

So many things. Yonah wanted Naris to say that he was sorry. That he would never hurt her. That he, too, wanted to change the way things were.

"Pick someone to send with me," she said. "Ask them where we went. Ease your mind."

"Yonah, that feels wrong."

"Then don't."

Naris slowly nodded. "I'll see you when you get back."

Yonah stood and went for the door. She was just opening it when Naris called out.

"Yonah." His voice was pained. He was holding his head in his hands, his eyes pointed down. "I'll send someone to go with you."

Although Yonah was disappointed that she had come so close to a solo trip to Kirash, she wasn't surprised that Naris wasn't yet ready to let that happen. She silently walked around Naris' desk and laid a gentle kiss on his head. Naris looked up at her with searching eyes. Yonah held her hand to his cheek for a moment, then left.

A TEENAGE BOY wearing a slave collar met Yonah in front of the palace. They nodded silently to each other in acknowledgement, and Yonah led the way down the path to the edge of the estate. The boy walked a few feet behind her. They remained silent the entire walk.

When they reached town, Yonah made a point to look as if she was meandering down the main road for pleasure, taking care to pause at various stalls and enter different shops. She posted her letters when they reached the post office. She continued to meander down the street until they came upon the west end of Kirash, where The White Stallion lay.

"I'm going to have a drink," she said, speaking to the slave boy for the first time. "Would you like something?"

The boy looked bewildered at the offer. Yonah took some ora coins from her bag, placed them in the boy's hand, and went inside.

"Sit wherever you like," Yonah instructed. "I would like my own table."

The boy sat down on a stool at the bar while Yonah found a table on the other side of the room. Several of the wooden tables were occupied by men and women alike. For a mid-morning visit, The White Stallion was quite busy.

A woman with beautiful long hair, a slender waist, and wearing a slave collar stepped up to Yonah's table.

"I haven't heard from your brother since your last visit," said Meerha.

"I have a chaperone," Yonah said, disregarding the comment about Obi. "The boy at the bar."

Meerha turned to look at the boy, then turned back to Yonah. "What do you need?"

"I need you to pass on a message to Vitora. Tell her I made contact with a minister."

Meerha's eyebrows rose. "Oh, really?"

"And I'm not sure about the next time I can see her myself."

"What happened?"

Yonah glanced at the boy at the bar to see if he was watching.

"My husband and I got into an argument."

"Hm." The barmaid seemed unsatisfied by Yonah's vague answer. "You staying for a drink?"

"I have to."

Meerha left Yonah to retrieve a drink for her. Yonah looked at her chaperone again, but he was merrily chatting with a man behind the bar.

When Meerha returned with a drink for Yonah, the barmaid said, "Is there a way we can send a message to you in case of an emergency?"

Yonah wasn't sure if Praha wanted anything more to do with the rebellion after what Naris had done to her. "Take any messages directly to the stable master."

Meerha nodded. She placed her hand over Yonah's and looked steadily into her eyes. "Take care, Yonah."

"I'll try."

After sitting for an appropriate amount of time with her drink—though she barely touched it—Yonah and the slave boy started back towards Vaha. As they stepped into the shade of the entrance hall, Yonah said to him, "Go find Master Naris. Answer everything he asks. He'll be in his office."

The boy swiftly started up the stairs, and Yonah went up at a fatigued pace. All she could do now was wait. For a letter, a message, instructions, she didn't know.

YONAH AND NARIS ate together that evening in their usual spot on the patio where they were married. It was a quiet affair, to begin with. They exchanged polite greetings, carefully sipped their wine, and wore curated expressions on their faces.

Naris finally said, "I don't think I properly told you how grateful I was to have you with me in Kelab."

"Oh?"

"I was glad for your company among so many strangers," he explained. "You make me feel less alone."

Yonah gave him her standard wifely smile. "I was happy to be with you in the city, to help you in whatever way I could."

The response didn't seem to please Naris, as he turned downcast. "The slave boy told me you made him come to my office after you returned from Kirash."

"Yes," Yonah replied with a cool voice.

The conversation faded from there, replaced with the sound of silverware on plates, of glasses thudding to the table.

Naris asked, "Whose party was your favourite?"

Yonah was a little startled by the earnest question, but she took a moment to ponder her answer. "I think Master Lania's was my favourite."

"I was sure you would say Master Beneri's," Naris said with a soft smile.

"Just because he's a friend doesn't mean I think exactly like him. Master Lania's party was grand, but it was also just fun. It was a little more sincere than the others. The masters in Kelab like to compete with each other, but I think Master Lania just wanted to put on a good event."

Naris rested his elbows on the table and leaned forwards. "So, you don't go for anything over-the-top?"

"You know that I don't."

"Is Vaha too over-the-top?"

Yonah looked around the grey brick patio, stared out over the lush green grounds, and thought of the decorated interior. "Vaha is nearly perfect."

"High praise! Where do you find fault?"

"It tells a beautiful story of you and your family. I sometimes feel like a stranger in it."

Naris furrowed his brows in thought. "I don't like that. You're a master of this house. You should feel at home."

Yonah shrugged.

"I have an idea." Naris stood up and held his hand out to Yonah. "I think it might help, just a little bit."

Yonah's eyes drifted from Naris' outstretched hand up to his face. Part of her wanted to keep her distance from Naris as much as possible, so she could freely do her business with the rebellion, so she could keep her body her own. Her curiosity at what Naris' next gesture might be held her close.

"Please," Naris said.

Yonah couldn't recall a time when Naris had said that word to her.

She took his hand and stood up. A soft smile lit up Naris' face. He led her inside and up the stairs. Yonah knew better than to ask him where they were going. She would find out when they arrived.

They went up the staircases that wound around the exterior walls of the palace, then down the long hallway on the third floor, past the paintings and tapestries and small sculptures.

Naris removed a lamp from the wall and opened a small and inconspicuous door at the end of the hall, which led to another staircase Yonah hadn't known about before. The staircase was narrow, dark, and tunnel-like. They went through one more door at the top of the stairs and stepped into a dark room.

"One moment," Naris muttered. He edged along the nearest wall, his hand searching. Within moments, another lamp had been lit, illuminating a portion of the room.

The room appeared to be a storage space. Forms shrouded in white sheets cluttered the centre of the room. Yonah had to guess the sheets covered furniture and unused decor.

As Naris continued around the perimeter of the room, lighting lamps as he went, Yonah removed a sheet from the nearest form.

Her guess was correct. She had uncovered a purple chaise with gold trim.

"Uncover them all," Naris said.

"Why, what are we doing here?"

Having finished lighting the room, Naris stepped next to Yonah. "We're here to find your favourite piece and put it somewhere in the house. So you can start to feel more at home."

Yonah met Naris' eyes. His consideration for her never failed to surprise her. Even this temperamental and bullying man continued to try to be thoughtful and kind to her in his flawed way.

Naris nudged his head towards the shrouded furniture. "You'd better take a look."

The pair uncovered everything in the room, Yonah pausing to look closer at an item that drew her special attention, Naris stopping to tell a story as his memories and family history were uncovered.

"Everything has meaning here," Yonah noted. This excursion wasn't helping her to feel like she fit in with the palace.

"Maybe." Naris sat in an oddly wide chair. "I imagine the things that hold meaning for me were meaningless to other members of my family. And that things that hold one meaning for me hold meaning in a different way for another."

"Is there something in here that doesn't hold meaning for you?"

"Plenty." Naris' head swiveled as he looked around the tightly packed furniture and decor.

"Like what?"

"Well, why don't you pick something you like first, and I'll tell you?"

"Because I want to pick something that's just mine." Yonah couldn't help but smile at her and Naris' playful stubbornness over these small matters.

"What's your favourite thing in this room?" Naris asked. The coy smirk on his face reminded Yonah of the first time she met him.

Yonah glanced around the room and sighed, overwhelmed at the sheer number of items at her disposal.

"There was a tapestry," she muttered, lifting her leg and stepping over a chaise. She climbed through the rejected furniture until she found the tapestry in question. It was rolled and lain on the floor, buried beneath a row of dining chairs. From the corner that Yonah was able to peer at, she saw luscious blues and sandy red. "I'd like to look at this."

Naris stood and made his way to Yonah. He looked at the only visible portion of the rolled tapestry, his brows furrowing. "I'm not sure I know what this is. Let's get it out of here."

They started lifting the chairs out of the way, threading through the other furniture, and setting them down. The entire roll was twelve feet long.

With a laugh, Naris said, "Well, you'll certainly make your mark on this house if you choose this!"

"I didn't realize it was so big," Yonah said.

"I'm just teasing you, dear." Naris kissed the top of Yonah's head, and her nerves quelled to quietness. "We do need to clear more space to unroll this."

"How did anybody ever get it up here?" Yonah thought of the narrow stairwell just outside this room.

"With great difficulty, I imagine." Naris continued to push furniture away from the tapestry towards the perimeter of the room. Between the two of them working, a space was cleared within a few minutes.

"I'm excited to see what's in here," Naris said. He stood at one end of the tapestry, and Yonah stood at the other. They bent over and began the task of unrolling the fabric. As more of the image revealed itself, Yonah realized she was looking at it upside down. Even so, she thought she recognized the image.

"Wonderful!" Naris exclaimed.

Yonah rounded the tapestry and stood next to Naris.

The tapestry depicted the very waterfall Yonah had visited the other day. The blues cascaded from a grey and yellow sky, surrounded by the red rock of the canyon.

"That's very well done," Naris said. He looked at Yonah. "What do you think?"

It was beautiful. It showed true skill. But it was anything but meaningless. Naris had initially brought Yonah to this secret spot to woo her. She loved the place, but it reminded her of her strange relationship with her husband. Perhaps that wasn't necessarily a bad thing.

"I love it," she replied.

"Where should we hang it?"

"Where can we hang it?"

Naris cradled Yonah's elbows in his hands, standing close to her. "Anywhere you like."

Yonah watched Naris. His eyes were soft and hungry, his lips parted slightly, heat emanating from his body.

"Is this whole excursion just a way to seduce me?" Yonah asked, putting on a playful tone.

There was a flash of hurt in Naris' eyes that came and went so fast Yonah wasn't sure if she imagined it or not. "You underestimate just how much I love you."

"Maybe I do," she conceded.

Naris placed his hand on Yonah's cheek and kissed her with a strange mixture of gentleness and force, with a longing that pulled Yonah's chest closer to him. Without meaning to, Yonah clutched Naris' shirt into her fists and leaned into him, searching for more of this feeling. Heat propelled her, motivating her movement and driving her into action. Her hands roamed his body just as Naris' hands explored hers.

Naris pulled away from the kiss and looked around the room. He took Yonah's hand and led her to a chaise they had uncovered.

The pause in activity had sobered Yonah a little. "We should go back to our room." Maybe by the time they got there, Naris wouldn't be in the mood anymore, then he wouldn't have another chance to impregnate her.

"You are the master of this house," Naris replied. He spun Yonah around, so she stood against the chaise, then kissed her while pressing her down until her knees buckled and she was sitting. "You can do whatever you like," he kissed her neck, just below her ear, "wherever you like." He kissed the other side of her neck. Yonah's skin prickled with pleasure. Her eyes involuntarily closed at the sensation.

Naris' lips found hers again and Yonah emphatically kissed him back, leaning and turning until she was lying on the chaise with Naris straddled on top of her.

Chapter Fifteen

They migrated back to Naris' room afterwards, leaving the mess they had made in the storage room to be dealt with another day. After a game of chess, they climbed into bed, where they kissed goodnight, and blew out the candles.

Naris was asleep in a matter of minutes. Yonah had work to do.

Guilt tugged at her insides as she silently walked to her room in the darkness of night, having memorized the path. That guilt escalated when she opened the door and found Praha waiting for her.

"What are you doing here?" Yonah asked. She noticed the bandages on Praha's hands.

"There are escapees arriving tonight," Praha replied without emotion.

"I didn't expect you to help after what Naris did." Yonah wished she could disappear as she added, "After what I let happen."

Praha shook her head and held her palms out to Yonah. "This is why I need to help."

She didn't absolve Yonah of the role she had to play in Praha's punishment.

Yonah gave Praha a stiff nod and started to dress in her black pants and shirt. Together, the two women snuck down to the front path. Yonah remained in front of the palace while Praha walked to the edge of the estate where the road forked, one heading east, the other west towards Kirash.

It was from the Kirash road that a wagon rolled towards Vaha and stopped where Praha stood. Yonah knew that one of Vitora's representatives—perhaps even her husband—was driving the wagon, and that the cart held a handful of escaped slaves.

Yonah glanced up at the palace. All its windows were dark. She noisily slid her foot along the gravel, signalling Praha to bring the escapees.

A group of figures hopped out of the wagon and dispersed into the vineyard at Praha's instruction. Yonah waited patiently for them to emerge from different rows at the front of the palace.

"How many are you?" she asked in a quiet voice.

"Six."

She counted six figures. Two were children. "Follow me."

They started around the side of the palace, towards the back. She led them back into the cover of the vineyard and headed for the stable.

Although the stable was dark, Yonah knew Seidon was watching for them. She glanced again at the dark palace as they started up the hill. At the stable, Yonah knocked twice, then twice again. The same knocking pattern came from the other side of the door before it opened. Yonah ushered the escapees inside, where Seidon led them to an empty stall.

"Take care, Yonah," he said to her once the escapees were settled in.

Yonah nodded. "I will."

Seidon closed the stable door, and Yonah made the lonely walk back to the palace. When she slid back into bed, Naris barely shifted.

"YONAH," A VOICE whispered.

She was dreaming of her family. It had been a long time since she had dreamt of them. It was blissful. Yonah didn't want to wake up.

"Yonah," the voice said again, louder.

She moaned, and the vibration in her throat brought Yonah back to the real world. She was in Naris' bed. She was a master. She had helped escapees onto the estate last night. Naris could never know.

"Yonah, where did you go last night?"

"What?" she mumbled, still not quite conscious.

"Did you go looking for a stash of potion?"

Yonah slowly opened her eyes. She didn't realize Naris had noticed her disappearance last night. Had she been more awake, she might have felt annoyed at Naris harassing her with the same worry. Mostly, she was glad he didn't suspect her of anything worse than trying to weasel her way out of their agreement.

"No, Naris," she said, her voice growly. "I told you I would stop. I just wanted some water."

"Why didn't you call for a slave?"

"Because it was the middle of the night."

"That doesn't matter."

Yonah closed her eyes, too tired to argue any further. "Can I go back to sleep?"

"Only if you promise to dream of me."

"I'll do my best."

Before she fell back asleep, Yonah felt Naris kiss her cheek and the bed wiggle as he climbed down to the floor.

It didn't feel as though she slept very long after that, but Yonah felt a little more rested when she awoke. Deciding she would start her day with a walk and perhaps even check in on the escapees and Seidon, Yonah dressed in a long skirt and a cropped shirt and started for the back door.

She was just about to open the back door when she paused, seeing something strange from the corner of her eye.

Yonah turned and saw the tapestry of the waterfall hanging from the wall. In the few hours Naris had been awake, he had already had Yonah's decorative pick put up in one of the most trafficked rooms of the palace. Yonah stared dumbly at the tapestry for a moment, a mixture of emotions stirring within. She loved the tapestry. It was beautiful. She had shared a wonderful moment there with Naris. Naris, who was kind and thoughtful towards her, yet also dangerous, self-centered, and frankly ignorant when it came to the plight of the lower classes of Harasa.

Rousing herself from her pondering, Yonah exited the palace and walked through the vineyard to the stable. Seidon was in the corral with the horses. The cat, Saza, was weaving in and around his ankles.

When the aging man saw Yonah coming, he nodded to her and rested his elbows on the fence that kept the horses contained.

"The escapees are fine," he said once Yonah was close. "Praha sent me out with some food for them this morning. Her hands looked sore."

Yonah nodded without meeting Seidon's eyes. "Naris caught her doing an unsavory errand on my behalf. I won't ask her to do that again."

"You and the master have a strange relationship."

Yonah tried not to blush at the memory of Seidon catching her and Naris sleeping naked in the stable just two mornings ago. "I told him to stop hurting the slaves."

"Will he listen to you?"

"We have an understanding," Yonah said with a nod.

"Does he suspect anything?"

Yonah paused to think. The only trespass he showed concern over was her use of the anti-pregnancy potion. Once his worries were quelled on that front, and as long as she acted normally, there would be no reason for Naris to suspect that his estate was being used as a safe house in a network used for sending slaves to the countries of Modeef and, now that slavery had been eradicated there, Jalid.

But he knew that Yonah had left their bed last night without her realizing it. Yonah couldn't know how many times Naris had noticed her nighttime walks without her knowing.

"I don't think so, but I can't be sure."

"We need to take care."

"We always have."

"And we've been very lucky," Seidon said with a little force. "Our luck will run out if we don't stay vigilant."

"Don't say things like that," Yonah said. "You don't want them to come true."

"If my words had that kind of power, Master Yonah, I would have been freed and sent back home a long time ago."

Seidon turned and limped towards the stable.

"Where is home?" Yonah called out.

Seidon looked back at her. "Along the southern border. A place called Savala."

As Seidon returned to his work, Yonah picked up Saza and watched the horses for a while. She noticed the lost gelding named River galloping with the others. A smile lifted the corners of her mouth as she watched him, glad he had been found after the storm.

Duty called to her, and Yonah returned to the palace.

THE SLAVES WERE successfully sent away on the next part of their journey that night. Just as it went every time, Seidon took the slaves via horseback through the plains to a meeting spot that even Yonah didn't know the location of. All she could do was wait for the stable master's return with the horses, hopeful that Seidon wasn't caught in the meantime.

As Yonah stepped inside the palace on her return from the stables, moonlight poured into the entrance hall and illuminated Naris standing on the stairs.

Yonah jumped when she saw him.

"What were you doing out there?" he asked. "It's the middle of the night."

Yonah composed herself and said calmly, "I couldn't sleep, so I went for a walk."

Naris narrowed his eyes at her, trying to determine whether she was lying or not.

"It's not as if I would find any anti-pregnancy potion out in the vineyard,"

Yonah said, trying to distract Naris from thinking about any other suspect reasons for her to be out of bed in the middle of the night.

"Have you always had such restless nights?" Naris asked. He walked down the rest of the stairs to the door and peered outside. Yonah followed his gaze, but there was nothing to be seen in the darkness of night.

"I don't sleep very well," she replied.

"Perhaps we should get a healer to look at you." Naris looked at Yonah, his face stern. "I don't like you going off into the night all by yourself. You never know who could be out there."

Yonah smiled. "Nobody's out there, Naris. They're too afraid of you."

She could tell that Naris wasn't sure whether that was a compliment or an insult.

"Let's get back to bed," he said. "In the future, I'd much prefer you kept your midnight wanderings to the palace."

Yes, Master.

FOR THE NEXT two days, Yonah waited impatiently for word from Beneri or Hara from the city, but none came. She was finally able to visit Kirash without a chaperone to check in with Vitora.

"All I need you to do is wait to hear from your contacts in Kelab," Vitora told her.

Yonah pressed for more responsibility, but Vitora was adamant. "I don't want to send any escapees your way for the next while. Not after that scare."

"We're not expecting visitors right now," Yonah argued.

"Just wait," Vitora said, "to hear from your contacts, alright? And then report to me."

Yonah could tell the discussion had come to a close and asked, "Have you heard anything more about the rebels coming from Jalid?"

"Everybody around here has a heard rumour from one place or another, but nobody has actually met any of them. I hope your friend in the city can let us know if they've bypassed the north and gone straight to Kelab."

When she returned to Vaha, Yonah asked Naris if they had ever received an order from Minister Hara's estate.

He looked brightly up at her from his office desk. "Yesterday. That's all thanks to you, my dear."

Ignoring the compliment, Yonah said, "May I see the order form?"

Naris' brows furrowed in confusion, but he said, "Alright," and removed a paper from his desk and passed it to Yonah. She examined the form, but there was nothing about it that was out of the ordinary.

"Minister Hara also sent us a note," Naris said. Yonah looked up from the order form. Naris was reading a small rectangular card. "'It was wonderful to meet both of you. If you ever find yourself in the city again, be sure to stop by and say hello.' Signed, Minister Hara." He flipped the card onto his desk and smiled. "Congrats to us."

It wasn't the concrete update Yonah was looking for, but it was certainly a good first step.

Chapter Sixteen

Yonah woke up that night choking. When she opened her eyes, a figure stood over her, its hand pressed to her mouth. Yonah tried to gasp, but she couldn't breathe. Her eyes bulged in terror as the figure leaned closer to her. It whispered, "Yonah, it's me—Praha."

Yonah's muscles relaxed when she realized who it was. Praha cautiously took her hand away from Yonah's face. Yonah sharply turned her head to see if Naris had awoken, but his eyes were closed, and his breathing was slow. She stepped out into the hallway with Praha and whispered, "What is it?"

"Something happened down the line," Praha replied, referring to the intricate system of safe houses, roads, and rebels who were involved in helping slaves escape. "Some escapees are waiting in the basement."

It felt as if a giant hand was clutching Yonah's heart, squeezing. She started towards the basement at a brisk pace. "Why are they there?" She couldn't help but let anger colour her voice.

"Their handler knocked on the slaves' quarters door looking for help. Somebody answered, and now everyone is awake down there. I came to get you."

"Someone will be coming to get Naris," Yonah said, fear's grip squeezing harder on her chest.

Praha shook her head. "I let them know I was going to find a master."

"They'll be expecting Naris," Yonah muttered, still walking at speed. Her mind raced to find a reasonable excuse for him to have stayed in bed and left her to deal with a stranger at their door. "Maybe I can say he's feeling ill right now and needs to rest."

"Nobody will question you," Praha said. "You're their master."

The statement jerked Yonah to a stop, so suddenly that Praha didn't realize Yonah wasn't with her until she had continued several more steps. "Yonah," she said, firmly.

Yonah shook off the uncomfortable feeling oozing over her at the reminder of her position and followed Praha into the basement.

It seemed as though all the slaves of Vaha were awake and crammed into the kitchen. A low but excited murmur lay like a blanket over the room as the slaves spoke with each other.

"Out of the way," Praha called as she and Yonah came to the bottom of the stairs. "Master Yonah is here."

The slaves parted, glancing uncertainly at Yonah as she walked through the crowd. At the long table where the slaves usually ate sat seven escapees still wearing their slave collars. There was an elderly woman who looked to be Seidon's age, two men, one of whom had a sleeping baby strapped to his back, a young woman about Yonah's age, and two teenage boys who looked to be twins. A collarless man Yonah assumed to be their handler also sat at the table, looking tensely around the room.

Yonah's eyes flitted about the household slaves that surrounded her. She caught sight of her old friend Bana in the corner and immediately felt self-disgust wash over her. He was the first friend of hers to be punished on her account.

"What's this?" she asked, putting on her most formidable voice.

"This man says he's transporting these slaves," replied a man belonging to the Vaha household. "And they lost their horses and need a place to stay for the rest of the night."

Yonah turned her eyes to the handler. "Transporting slaves in the middle of the night?"

The man returned Yonah's firm gaze and spoke slowly. "Like I said, our horses ran away, so our progress has been slow. We were supposed to reach Kirash several hours ago."

"Hm," Yonah said shortly. "All of you, go back to bed. I'll deal with this."

A handful of the slaves shifted, but many stayed to watch.

"Go to your rooms, now! I assure you; you do not want to know what I am going to do with these slaves." She purposely veiled the statement in a threat, but, truly, it was a warning for their own good. The less the slaves of Vaha knew, the better.

As the household started for their rooms, grumbling along the way, Yonah grabbed Praha's wrist, silently calling for her to stay. She saw Seidon hovering in a back corner and subtly jerked her head towards the stairs. He waited a while and went out to the stable. Once the kitchen was empty, but for Yonah, Praha, and the escapees and their handler, Yonah spoke quietly.

"Relax, I'm not turning you in."

The group let out a collective sigh of relief. The man wearing the baby gave an audible gasp and dropped his face into his hands.

"But why are you here?" Yonah asked.

"I was supposed to take them to a countryside inn north of here, but the place was filled with Guards," said the handler. "They were ransacking it."

"They knew it was a safe house?"

The handler shrugged. "They suspected something. I knew Vaha was a safe house, so I thought I'd try here."

"If that ever happens again, you go straight to the stable," Yonah instructed. "The household doesn't know anything about the line. We'll take you out there now."

"Thank you," the man wearing the baby said. "Thank you so much!"

"Just stay quiet," Yonah said, worried the man was working himself into hysterics. "My husband doesn't know about this either."

She moved to the edge of the kitchen, where she knew there was a door to the secret passageways that criss-crossed the palace. She was just reaching for the hidden latch to open it when she saw it was already open a crack.

The familiar sense of squeezing in her chest returned. Yonah turned around and caught Praha's eyes. She mouthed the word "Run," to the woman.

Praha's eyes widened as she realized what was happening, and she started to shove the escapees towards the stairs. "Move. Faster. Now!"

The secret door behind Yonah slammed open, and Naris stepped into the kitchen. He wrapped his hand around Yonah's arm and hissed at her, "You sneak!" He yelled to the escapees, "Stop!"

They were already racing up the stairs, Praha behind them.

Naris went to the wall of pull strings and wrenched one over and over again. It was for the guard house where his hired guards slept. "Guards!" he yelled, fury heightening his volume. He raced to the stairs, grabbed the back of Praha's shirt, and pulled her back, causing her to fall past him back into the basement with a terrible pounding sound.

"Stop that!" Yonah yelled. She ran to Praha and knelt over her. "Praha, are you alright?"

"I'm fine, I'm fine," the woman grumbled, pain edging her voice.

"You stay here!" Naris said, pointing down at Praha from his perch on the stairs.

Yonah whispered to her, "Can you run? Through the passage?"

The woman met Yonah's eyes, and Yonah felt an unspoken farewell. Yonah helped Praha to a standing position as Naris yelled, "Stay down!"

Yonah shoved Praha to the passage and stepped to block Naris' way as he jumped down the stairs. Her whole body quivered with fear and adrenaline as her husband came to her.

"Get out of my way, Yonah," he said, his voice dangerously low.

"No," she said.

"Get out of my way, or I will make you."

"Then make me." Her voice shook with anger. She would not let him hurt Praha again.

Naris grabbed her arms and pushed her aside. As he ran past, Yonah clasped her hands around his wrist. He turned and struck the palm of his hand across her cheek. Yonah shrieked in surprise as a stinging pain tickled her face, and her eyesight shook.

She quickly recovered and chased after Naris, who had disappeared into the passage. He was running for the exit to the side of the palace, where the door was left haphazardly open. Naris paused, circling around in search of Praha. He turned back to Yonah, his eyes crazed with anger, and took her arm.

Yonah let him lead her. As long as he was focused on her and not Praha, then she would stay. Naris led them around the side of the palace to the back patio. Yonah saw Praha running to the stable. She knew Praha would be able to warn Seidon. They could steal some horses and run away.

Naris' hired guards were scrambling in the back, some already chasing after Praha, others headed for the vineyard in search of the escapees. The young woman had been caught and had her hands bound behind her back. Her face was streaked with tears.

"Did you see them all?" Naris asked one of the guards, who appeared to be in charge. "There were seven of them and one of my own. The stable master is in on it, too."

"We're searching for them now."

Naris let out a frustrated yell and turned to face Yonah. "You!" He took her inside and up, up the stairs of the palace. As they took an exterior stair, Yonah saw a pair of horses galloping north away from the stable. She couldn't tell who was riding them.

As Naris took her down a hallway at the top of the palace, Yonah realized where he was taking her. They went through the small door at the end of the hall, up the claustrophobic stairwell, and through the door into the storage attic. Naris released Yonah's arm from his grip and slammed the door shut. She heard him let out another anguished yell before he stomped down the stairs, leaving her alone in the darkness.

SHE WOKE UP with the sun, although she felt anything but rested. Sunlight stole through the cracks of the shuttered windows. Yonah had slept on the same chaise she and Naris had shared in a bout of passion only a few nights ago. How quickly things could change.

She checked the door and found it, unsurprisingly, locked. She opened one of the shutters and looked outside. Up at the top of the palace, there was no way down. Perhaps if she were a few years younger and in the physical shape she had been as a teenager, she might have attempted escape.

Yonah knew that, according to the law, Naris had to turn her in. She was a rebel, the worst kind of criminal in the eyes of President Althu and his corrupt government.

Rebels were enslaved for life.

Sometime that morning, the attic door opened, and Naris slowly stepped into the room. Yonah stood up from her seat in a large, cushioned armchair.

Naris didn't meet her eyes for several moments. Instead, he shifted his weight back and forth, his fingers balled into fists. When he finally turned his gaze towards her, she saw a deep pain and a sorrowful hope.

He was struggling to find words. It took Naris a few moments to speak, and when he finally did, he spoke slowly, as if the words were trying to crawl back into his throat.

"Is… Is everything between us a lie?"

Even though she could still feel where Naris had struck her the night before, even though she knew he would be sending whichever slaves he had caught back to their masters, Yonah felt pity for her husband.

"It's complicated," she finally said.

"It's complicated?" Naris took a couple forceful steps closer to Yonah. "Did you or did you not lie to me for our entire marriage? Did you or did you not lie about loving me?"

It baffled Yonah that the man standing in front of her could be a monster and just a man at the same time. All Naris wanted from the night they met was to be loved.

"I've always been lying."

Naris exhaled a sharp breath and started to pace back and forth, shaking his head.

"And I've grown to love you," Yonah added.

"No," Naris said, his shaking head growing more fervent. "No, if you loved me, you wouldn't have done this."

"Naris, we could spend days arguing over all the things we wouldn't have done if we truly loved each other." Yonah felt the corners of her mouth pulling downwards at the terrible truth of that statement.

Naris stopped his pacing. "What did I do to you?"

Bewilderment nearly knocked Yonah off her feet. "Are you honestly asking me that right now?"

"I'm honestly asking you that because, from what I can tell, I've given you everything! I took you away from Master Puru's, I pulled you out of slavery, I made you a Master, I dressed you and fed you--"

"You didn't do that for me. You did it for yourself!"

"I did it because I loved you!" Naris raised a finger and shoved it in Yonah's direction.

It was Yonah's turn to shake her head. Naris didn't know what love was. And yet, she had let herself fall for whatever facsimile of it he presented.

Naris' voice was soft as he said, "I loved you, Yonah."

She could tell him that she had loved him, too, or at least part of him.

Part of her loved him, and part of her despised him. It was too complicated to put into a simple three-word sentence.

"Aren't you sorry?" Naris asked.

He was like a child sometimes, trying to figure out the world around him.

Yonah sighed. "I'm sorry I hurt you along the way. I really am. But I'm not sorry for what I did. This is bigger than you and me, Naris. It's more important."

"You always put the slaves ahead of me."

"And you always put yourself ahead of the slaves."

Naris sharply turned his eyes to Yonah, a spark lighting them. "What's going to happen to me?" Yonah asked.

Naris' eyes softened. "I've sent word to the local magistrate that you've committed an act of rebellion and that we'll be on our way to Kelab starting today, so you can face trial."

Yonah hadn't expected a trial. Perhaps that was a perk of being a master at the time of her crime. She nodded to let Naris know she had heard him.

"And the others? Did any of them get away?"

Naris frowned at Yonah. "Why would I tell you that?" He left the attic.

Chapter Seventeen

Despite technically being a prisoner on her way to trial, Yonah travelled in style, just as she had on her and Naris' previous tour to Kelab. The intense silence that weighed heavy between them was not so different from their return home from Kelab, either.

While they travelled with Naris' personal guards, members of the national Guard, dressed in black uniforms and red sashes, met them at the train station in Kelab. Yonah saw them immediately upon stepping down from the train. Although she knew she would have to go with them, an instinctual part of her itched to run.

She let two of the Guards take her arms and escort her to a carriage. She was glad, for Naris' sake, that her ride to the prison wouldn't be so public. Once seated in the carriage, Yonah looked through the open door across the station to where Naris stood. He watched her departure, but his face was oddly void of emotion. The carriage door was shut, and, moments later, Yonah was taken away.

The prison lay beneath the courthouse, a clean white building with a rounded facade. Yonah was taken to the back of the building, where there lay a small wooden door. A set of stairs led down from the door into the dark stone basement. Sandwiched between two Guards, Yonah was led down the stairs and along the hallway lined with cells. Of the twenty or so cells, only half were filled. The inmates appeared to have been there for a short time, their faces still coloured from the sun and their clothes not yet grungy with overwear.

One of the Guards opened an empty cell with a key and held the barred door open for Yonah.

"Do you know when my trial will be?" she asked, remaining in the hallway.

"Get in there," the Guard grumbled, taking Yonah's arm and roughly pushing her into the cell. He shut the door with a clang, locked it with the key, and left without bothering to look at her.

Yonah watched the Guards go until they had disappeared up the stairs, and she heard the door slam shut. She looked around her cell. It was a small square space with barred walls. She had no immediate neighbours, but she could see a prisoner on either side of her two cells down through the bars. There was a tiny, barred window at the top of the cell letting in a little daylight. A bucket sat in the corner, and a bed pallet stacked with a couple thin blankets was pressed against the stone wall. It was a far cry from her luxurious bedroom at Vaha.

Yonah gingerly sat on the bed pallet, sitting tall and clasping her hands together, and waited.

SHE WAITED THREE days in her holding cell. A few of the other prisoners were escorted out to their trials, returned briefly, and taken away. Another prisoner was brought into an empty cell on the second day. Sometimes a visitor was escorted inside and had a hushed conversation with a prisoner.

Yonah had no visitors. No Naris. No Beneri.

During her first afternoon, she tried talking to one of the other prisoners, but, between the distance between their cells and the lack of interest they showed in talking to her, Yonah quickly gave up on that endeavour.

Instead, she worried about Praha, Seidon, and the escapees. She wished she could know if they were safe or not. The young woman escapee would receive the standard punishment of an additional two years to her labour sentence. Yonah received the same sentence when she tried to escape from Naris with her sister. If she hadn't married him, Yonah would be free of Naris now. But she had chosen to use her influence with him for rebel activity, and it had gotten her locked up in a cell, likely to be sentenced to slavery for life.

Something in Yonah had known that she wouldn't be able to keep her secrets from Naris forever, but that was the risk she had to take. Her risk was making a difference. *Had been* making a difference. Her time was up.

On the morning of the fourth day in her holding cell, two Guards entered the prison and stopped in front of her. Yonah's heart started to pound as they unlocked the cell and opened the door.

"It's time for your trial," one of them said.

Yonah took a long deep breath and stepped into the hallway. One of the Guards put her wrists through a set of manacles, and she was escorted up the stairs and out the door. They re-entered the building through a different set of doors and walked through a labyrinth of narrow hallways until they stood in front of a closed black door with an ornate golden handle.

They waited for only a few minutes, but it felt like hours to Yonah. Her insides were squirming uneasily. One Guard shifted his weight from one foot to the other. The other looked up at the ceiling and sighed every few minutes.

From the other side of the door, Yonah could hear a woman speaking as if to a large room. The door suddenly opened, and the two Guards waiting with Yonah started to attention and took her through.

The first thing Yonah noticed was the rows of people looking at her. Some were strangers wearing expressions ranging from mild interest to disgust, and some were masters she recognized from her previous visit to Kelab. Beneri was sitting in the middle of the crowd, and when his eyes met with Yonah's, he turned away.

Sitting in the front row, back uncomfortably straight, was Naris. He did not look in Yonah's direction. Would not look in her direction. He kept his face forward. Yonah tried to will him to look at her, but he resisted whatever energy her look sent his way.

There was a short square pedestal between the onlookers and a raised dais at the front of the room. Yonah was led to the pedestal and made to face the dais. A massive and ornate chair sat on the dais, and a woman dressed in blue robes sat in the chair.

"Can you confirm that you are Yonah Muran?" the woman asked in a commanding voice.

Momentarily dumbfounded, Yonah nodded. She quickly found her voice and said, "I am."

"And do you admit to participating in rebel activity against President

Althu and the great nation of Harasa?"

Memories of living on the streets of Kelab came to Yonah suddenly. With the little money she and her siblings managed to earn each day, they went to the market to find food for their humble evening meal. Her sister Sayzia would always barter for a better price. Yonah was always too intimidated to try it, but Sayzia said, "Why should we settle?"

Yonah squared her shoulders and said, "What do you define as rebel activity?"

There was a low murmur from the spectators behind her.

The magistrate narrowed her eyes. "Were you a participant in a scheme to assist slaves in escaping their terms of labour?"

She had a sudden urge to look behind her so she could see Naris. "I attempted to assist a handful of slaves off my estate."

"Assisting slaves in escape is considered rebel activity."

"I said I was having them removed from my estate," Yonah said loudly, her limbs shaking. "I did not realize that was illegal."

"Master Yonah," the magistrate said with a sigh, "You are being deliberately difficult. You did not notify anyone of the presence of escapees on your estate until you were forcibly caught by your husband. Masters are to report escapees to a magistrate. You intended to set them free."

Yonah remained silent and stared unabashedly at the magistrate.

"Do you deny these accusations? Or do I need to bring your husband up to testify against you?"

The room was silent. Yonah felt dozens of pairs of eyes on her. She turned around and looked at Naris. His eyes were on his knees. There was no point in dragging Naris any deeper into this scandal than he already was, except for spite.

"Master Yonah," the magistrate said. "Do you deny it?"

Yonah turned back to the front of the room. "I don't deny it."

"Then you shall be enslaved for life as a rebel. You will be sold on the next market day. Guards, take her back to her cell."

As the magistrate stood and swept out of the room, the two Guards took hold of Yonah's arms and pulled her off the pedestal.

"Naris," Yonah said as she was taken away. "Naris!" But he did not look up.

Yonah was taken back through the maze of the courthouse, back outside, through the prison door, down the stairs, and to her cell. She stood dumbly in the middle of the small square space as the Guards started back outside.

She knew it was coming, but hearing the words out loud brought a sense of hopeless finality through Yonah's bones. She would be a slave for the rest of her life. There was no chance for freedom, no chance for happiness, no chance for making a difference.

Her hand drifted up to her bare neck. Soon, she would be fitted with a new copper collar.

"Bad news, then?"

She looked to the cell across from hers. A woman wearing plain brown clothes was leaning against the bars of her cell.

Yonah nodded. "But not unexpected."

"Doesn't make it any less bad," the woman replied.

That made Yonah nod, too. Her luck had changed so quickly. She had gone from living a life of luxury and comfort to a lifetime of forced labour, disdain from the masters, and hopelessness.

She sat on her bed pallet, folded her arms over the top of her knees, and wearily lay her forehead on her arms.

Many minutes later, the sound of the exterior door opening echoed through the prison. Yonah didn't bother to look up. It was likely a Guard bringing in a new prisoner. She listened to footsteps coming down the stairs and along the hall, ever closer to her cell. The footsteps stopped, and a voice she instantly recognized said, "I can find my own way out."

Yonah's head snapped up. Naris was standing in front of her cell. He watched the Guard leave the prison, then, for the first time that day, looked at Yonah.

Her breath hushed to a stop, and every inch of her body froze. She had missed familiar interaction, but she hadn't realized just how much she had missed Naris over the past three days. Part of her wanted to go to him and apologize for dragging him into her mess, and another part wanted to scream at him to leave her alone.

Naris sighed and wrapped a hand around one of the bars of her cell. "I'm sorry I didn't come to see you before the trial."

Yonah didn't respond.

"I was just so angry with you," Naris continued. "And I knew if I looked at you in there today, I would do something reckless. Something to embarrass us. More so than you've already done."

Yonah had to resist rolling her eyes. "Well, I won't embarrass you anymore, Naris. I'll be far away, a slave to a master again."

"Actually," Naris said, "that is why I'm down here. I just spoke with the magistrate. Since we were married—"

Now that Yonah had permanently lost her status as a free woman, she had also lost her right to marriage.

"—I asked to have priority over purchasing you."

Yonah's limbs started to feel heavy like they were slowly filling with sand.

Naris said, "She agreed with the caveat that, if you were once again found doing anything untoward, I would be investigated as well. You're coming home with me. Only now, I can ensure you remain obedient."

The look in Naris' eye made Yonah draw away from him, even though they were already several feet apart.

"I didn't think you'd want me," she said, trying to sound unperturbed.

"I told you before, Yonah. I'll always come for you."

Chapter Eighteen

The following morning, Yonah was removed from her cell, placed into a carriage, and taken to a blacksmith. She was to be fitted with a new slave collar.

She had been sixteen when she and her siblings first received their slave collars. Thinking back on that day still brought a grave sense of sorrow to Yonah. It was the day she had failed her family.

The process was just the same as before. A rounded strip of copper was heated on the ends enough that it was pliable. Two blacksmiths maneuvered the copper around Yonah's neck with long heavy pliers, twisted the ends together, and removed any excess. Yonah remained perfectly still so as not to bump the tools preventing the heated copper from burning her skin. A bucket of water was poured onto the copper, sending steam hissing around Yonah's ears. She closed her eyes at the heat and held her breath.

The collar was released and fell against Yonah's chest. She brought her hand up to her neck, wrapping her fingers around the still-warm metal ring.

"Stop crying, slave, and let's go," one of the Guards escorting her said.

Yonah glared at the Guard. "I am not crying."

The Guard roughly grabbed her arm and led her back outside to the carriage.

Yonah wasn't sure if she was being taken back to the prison or not. The carriage had no windows for her to see the city by. All she could do was wait until the next part of her fate was revealed to her.

There came a loud boom from outside the carriage that made Yonah clutch the bench beneath her. The carriage horses whinnied in fear, and the carriage turned roughly and started to tip sideways.

"Whoa, whoa, whoa!" Yonah yelled, trying to keep her body upright and failing. She slid towards the side of the carriage as the whole thing toppled over.

In the stillness of the up-ended carriage, Yonah could hear shouting from outside.

The carriage door above her head wrenched open, and a large figure wearing burnt red clothes, including a matching scarf to cover his face, looked inside.

"Are you Yonah?" he asked.

"Why, who are you?"

He yelled, "Are you Yonah!"

"Yes, yes!" Yonah cried, startled by the sudden anger aimed towards her.

"Then you're coming with me."

"Who are you?"

A body struck the man, and he disappeared from the top of the carriage. Yonah could hear him scuffling with whoever had tackled him – likely a Guard. She stood up on her tiptoes to peer outside the carriage.

Red smoke was billowing from a nearby rooftop, fogging over the fighting between Guards and six people dressed entirely in the same burnt red Yonah had seen on the man who was now wrestling on the ground with a Guard. A crowd of spectators was gathering around the melee, and more Guards were coming down the road.

Yonah hooked her elbows over the edge of the carriage door and, using the interior walls of the carriage as a boost, hoisted herself out and stood on the carriage.

The horses were still whinnying angrily, still attached to the carriage by their twisted harnesses, writhing on their sides. Yonah clambered over to the front of the carriage, took hold of the harnesses, and started to unclip the horses. As the horses began to stand, Yonah took their reins and pointed them towards the man and the Guard he was wrestling. The panicked horses followed the lead and ran.

"Look out!" Yonah yelled. The two wrestling men looked and split apart, leaving the path of the two horses just in time to avoid being trampled.

There was another boom, and another puff of red smoke came from a second rooftop. Yonah ducked at the noise, but the man in red, unphased, strode over to her, took her wrist, and led her in a run.

He shouted something in a language Yonah had never heard before, and the other people in red started running, too.

The man dragged Yonah down an alley. She looked over her shoulder to see if they were being followed.

"Stop it!" the man shouted. "You're slowing us down. Just run."

He pulled her into a kitchen, which they passed through to a back door while indignant shouts were sent their way. They crossed a road into a second alley where the man pulled Yonah into what looked to be someone's home, although it was covered in a thick layer of dust, and released Yonah's wrist.

"Who are you?" Yonah asked.

The man ignored her. He pressed his hands into a piece of wood countertop and pushed upwards. A panel opened to reveal a massive hole.

"Get in," he said.

Yonah took a single step forward to get a better look at the hole. There was a wooden ladder waiting on one edge.

"Where does that go?" Yonah asked. "Where are you taking me?"

"I know it seems like we're safe right now, but there'll be Guards all over this city looking for us for the next few days, so you need to get in there now."

Yonah's options were sparse. She could let herself be recaptured by the Guard and sent back to Vaha with Naris. Or she could leave this stranger and try to continue her escape on her own. But she didn't have a working knowledge of Kelab like she did before she was captured by the Guard. She wasn't sure she would be able to make it across the city to Beneri's home to find sanctuary.

Or she could follow this man.

"Alright," Yonah said. She stepped forward and hoisted herself over the counter edge and started down the ladder into the dark hole.

Once she was down a few feet, the man followed her, closing the countertop behind him, and sending them into complete darkness.

Yonah felt her way down the ladder, clinging onto the sounds of her and the man's feet on the wood. She eventually found the hard ground beneath her reaching toe instead of another wrung, and she gratefully let go of the ladder.

The man landed next to Yonah and rummaged in his clothing. There came a scraping sound, and a match lit, casting his eyes and otherwise covered face in an eerie glow. He used the match to search the wall by the ladder and lit one of three lanterns hanging from hooks. He retrieved the lantern and silently started down the tunnel at a comfortable walking pace.

"Will you tell me who you are now?" Yonah asked. "And how you know who I am?"

The man was silent for so long that Yonah thought he wasn't going to answer her. He finally said, "You'll find out when we reach the others."

Yonah tried to ignore the rising sense of unease bubbling within herself. This was the path she had chosen; she would just have to find out where it took her. She wondered where Naris was right now. He would be furious at her disappearance.

They had been walking in silence for about ten minutes when the man stopped at another ladder with more hooks and lanterns. He blew out his lantern and, presumably, hung it with the others.

"We're going up," he said. "Follow me."

Yonah felt his body leave the space next to her, then climbed up after him. She blinked against the light that streamed in when the man opened the exit. After climbing out, the man turned and took Yonah's arm to help her out of the tunnel. He held his finger to his mouth to signal her to stay quiet.

They were in what looked like a storage room for a shop. Shelves packed with boxes surrounded them.

A door opened somewhere in the room, and the man shoved Yonah into a crouching position next to him by pushing down on the top of her head. They waited with breath held as someone walked through the room, moved some boxes around, then left.

"Are we not supposed to be here?" Yonah whispered.

The man shook his head. He wiggled two fingers towards himself. Follow me.

Yonah followed the man away from the door they had heard to a dark corner where there lay another door. They stepped outside into an alley.

"That particular location," the man said, "doesn't know about that tunnel." He removed the scarf from his head, revealing his face to Yonah. His sharp features and curly hair reminded her of Naris, but his eyes, rather than Naris' brown and gold, were a pale blue.

"How did that happen?"

The man shrugged. "A change in ownership, likely."

As the man started towards the street, Yonah followed, trying to piece together who he was and how those tunnels came to be.

When they emerged on the street, it took Yonah a moment to realize that they had travelled a fair distance in their short walk underground.

"Where are we going?" she asked.

"We're almost there."

"That wasn't my question."

The man took them through the doors of a four-storey building and up all three sets of stairs to the top where a single door stood. He knocked an odd rhythm on the door.

A voice came from the other side of the door. "Who is it?"

"A friend of a friend."

The door opened and Yonah followed the man into a spacious apartment, where several people dressed in the same burnt red clothes and a few others gathered. They all turned their heads to the man and Yonah.

"There you go, Sayzia," the man said. "The others have probably told you already, but that rescue was a disaster. She better be worth it."

At the sound of her sister's name, Yonah's skin prickled. Her sister had died nearly two years ago when she had tried to escape with her. This was someone else with the same name.

A young woman using a walking stick to assist her, with serious eyes, stepped forward.

A sound of surprised exclamation burst from Yonah's mouth. It was a ghost. A beautiful, wonderful ghost of her sister.

Sayzia smiled. "Hi, Yonah."

Chapter Nineteen

For a moment, Yonah wondered if she might be dreaming, or she might be undergoing a trauma response, or she had even died when the carriage tipped over and was meeting her sister in the afterlife.

"Are you real?" she finally asked.

Sayzia stepped closer to Yonah and took her hand. "I'm real."

Yonah's mouth dropped open, and her eyes and nose started to burn with tears. "But you were dead."

"Someone saved me. The rebellion saved me."

Yonah glanced around the room at the people watching her and her sister's reunion.

"The rebellion?" Yonah asked.

"When you tried to take me with you," Sayzia replied, "when you tried to escape, I woke up in the heart of the rebellion in Jalid. And because my master had abandoned me and thought I was dead, I was free."

"Is it true that slavery's gone in Jalid?"

Sayzia nodded. "It's true. And some of us have come back to Harasa to see if we can't do that here, as well."

"But how did you find me? Why did you help me escape?"

"Now, that," said the man who had escorted Yonah, "is a great question."

Sayzia shot the man a glare. "We decided as a group that we would perform this rescue, Thari. Now, let it be."

"What does she have that can help the rebellion?" he replied snarkily.

"She was married to a prominent slave master," Sayzia said. "She was a slave and a master herself. She has some knowledge that can be of use to us."

"She's also a fugitive."

"We're all fugitives here!" Sayzia snapped. She turned to Yonah. "Do you have anything that could help us?"

Yonah took an involuntary step backwards, trying to put more room between her and the expectant stares of the rebels. "Wait. I don't even know what you're trying to do. How did you end slavery in Jalid?"

The man Sayzia had called Thari shook his head and folded his arms over his chest.

"Yonah," Sayzia said quietly. "You need to give us *something* before we can tell you more. I had to do a lot of convincing to get these people to help you escape."

Yonah looked carefully into her little sister's eyes. They were not as readable as Naris', but she could see that she needed to listen to Sayzia.

"The estate I lived on was a safe house for escapees, so I know a few people involved with the rebellion around there. I have a friend among the masters here in Kelab who is for the rebellion. And I recently made contact with a minister who is sympathetic to the cause."

"A minister?" someone asked.

"Which minister?"

"Yes," Thari said. "Which one?"

"Have I proved myself useful enough to stay?" Yonah asked. "Or will you send me back to the Guard?"

The rebels shared a few glances amongst themselves. Sayzia and Thari appeared to be having a staring contest until Thari sighed and said, "Fine. Now, who's your minister?"

Yonah looked at Sayzia. Her sister nodded to her. "Minister Hara."

"That's the new one," a woman said. "She can't have much sway in the government."

"Her father was very influential," a man added. "Maybe some of that rubbed off."

"Not likely," someone else said.

"Yonah could make contact and ask her."

"No, not yet," Thari cut in. "We have to let the city cool down a little. Just for a few days."

Sayzia spoke. "Thari's right. The Guards will be looking for Yonah for the next while."

"And my husband," Yonah said.

The room hushed. Sayzia furrowed her brow. "He's not your husband anymore. He's a master, and you're a rebel."

Yonah felt the watchful eyes of the rebels on her. "I know," she said to assuage them. "Habit."

"Who's your other contact?" Thari asked. "Here in the city."

"Master Beneri."

"I haven't heard of him," Thari said. He looked around the room, but everyone shook their heads. "Good thing you have a minister to fall back on."

Yonah glared at the man.

"Sayzia, Thea, let's talk." Thari started across the large room to a door. One of the women who had spoken earlier followed. Sayzia quickly wrapped her arms around Yonah. She let go too soon and followed Thari and Thea through the door.

Yonah looked nervously around the room at the remaining rebels.

"You hungry?" a woman just a few years older than her asked.

Yonah nodded and the woman took her to the kitchen on the other side of the room. The others dispersed, breaking off into smaller groups to debrief or relax. Some even unrolled blankets on the floor and lay down to sleep.

"I'm Dani," the woman said. She opened a cupboard sparsely packed with food. Some flatbread, a bag of beans, and a jar of jam inhabited the shelves. The woman named Dani removed the flatbread and jam from the shelf.

"And you're Yonah. Sayzia's big sister."

Yonah looked at the door through which her sister had gone. She was still coming to terms with the fact that Sayzia was alive.

"How did she... How did she survive? She was dying. We left her in the cold." Yonah's eyes burned as she thought of that terrible night. "I left her."

Yonah could feel Dani watching her. "I don't know the details of who helped Sayzia that night, but she was nursed back to health by some of our friends. And you all leaving her is what made it so easy for her to join the abolitionists."

"Is that what you call yourselves?" Yonah asked. "The abolitionists?"

Dani frowned slightly. "What do you call them down here? Oh, yes.

Rebels." She was smearing jam onto the bread with a knife. "Who came up with that?"

"Probably our government."

Dani pointed the knife towards Yonah. "That was on purpose."

"What do you mean?"

"Which sounds more dangerous, and which sounds more reasonable between 'rebel' and 'abolitionist?'"

Yonah said thoughtfully, "I suppose 'abolitionist' sounds more politically inclined. And 'rebel' has a criminal connotation to it."

Dani raised her eyebrows pointedly at Yonah, then slid a plate over to her. Yonah looked at the food that had been prepared for her. Jam on flatbread, just like her mother used to make for breakfast on school days.

"So, what's your story?" Dani asked.

Yonah looked up at the woman. "Sayzia hasn't told you?"

"She said you had a master that was in love with you. With a little investigation, we found out that you were married to him. How did you manage that?"

Thinking of her complicated relationship with Naris sent a dull ache through Yonah's chest. "I don't really want to talk about that."

She could feel Dani's eyes hovering over her. "You're safe from him now," the woman said.

Yonah nodded to Dani, but she wasn't sure what being 'safe' from Naris meant. It felt hollow like someone had carved a piece of her chest out. She decided to change the subject as she ate.

"So, are you all abolitionists from Jalid?"

Dani nodded. "But many of us are Harasan-born. Most of the

abolitionists stayed in Jalid to help rebuild the country. Everything's a mess there, right now, with the new rules and people looking for work and the economy being suddenly very different."

"Why can't it just go back to the way it was?"

"Stuff like that takes time. The rest of us came south to see if we could help the rebel factions in Harasa unite and become strong enough to finally end slavery here."

"There are different factions?"

"There's no organization down here," Dani explained. "You've all just been doing your own things in different regions. There are some weak connections through the escape lines, but rebel activity in Harasa is mostly small, isolated groups. While that works for short-term help, it won't really make a difference to create big change."

Yonah tried not to feel too downcast at the news that the rebellion was not very far along in Harasa, and that her work as a safe house was small scale.

"But you're uniting the factions?"

Dani replied with a shrug, "We're trying to track everyone down, but it takes time, especially when you can't make a mistake."

"We should talk to the woman I report to," Yonah said.

"Why? Who do you report to?"

"A woman in Kirash. She's in charge of our area. I know she plans our portion of the escape line, among other things for the rebellion."

"Tell that to Thari and he'll be more than glad that he helped you escape."

As if saying the name had summoned him, the door to the other room opened, and Thari, Thea, and Sayzia stepped out into the main room.

"How do you communicate with your minister?" Thari asked as if their conversation hadn't been over for several minutes.

"I write to my friend among the masters, Beneri. He passes it on."

"I don't like that," Thari muttered, turning to Sayzia. "Too many people involved."

"I trust Beneri," Yonah said.

"We don't know him."

"Look, I can put a letter through the post like normal. He doesn't have to know where I am or who I'm with."

Sayzia said, "No, Yonah, you're a wanted criminal now. You can't just put a letter through the post. You can't do anything right now."

Yonah already missed the freedom and flexibility she had as a master. "Then we'll pretend to post it as someone else. Or drop it off directly at his house."

"I'd rather do a direct drop-off than involve forgery and postage," Thari grumbled. "All of that leaves too much room for trouble."

Sayzia nodded. "Then let's do that."

"But she doesn't tell this Beneri person anything."

"Alright!" Sayzia replied, annoyance tingeing her voice.

Thari glanced at Yonah. "And I guess we'll have to get that collar off her."

"Why don't you get to work on that, and I'll help Yonah draft the letter," Sayzia said, her suggestion coming out at a firm command.

Thari and Sayzia exchanged fierce looks before Thari turned and left the apartment. The woman named Thea patted Sayzia's shoulder as she passed by on her way to sit on a sofa.

Just Sayzia, Yonah, and Dani were left in the kitchen. The sisters took a long look at each other, finally given room to take pleasure in each other's presence.

Sayzia's eyes flicked down to Yonah's empty plate. "I see Dani's looking after you. Thanks, Dani."

"It's no trouble," Dani replied with a shrug. "I guess I can leave you two to catch up."

Sayzia took Yonah's hand. "Let's go to another room." She took Yonah down a hallway and through a door into a room lined with pallet beds, closing the door behind them.

"I don't understand," Yonah said. "How are you and I standing in the same room together after all this time? After everything that's happened?"

"When slavery was abolished in Jalid, a group of us wanted to come back to Harasa to do the same thing here. I asked around to find out if you were still with Master Naris. It wasn't that hard for me to find you when I heard you were not only married to him but had a trial coming up for helping escapees!"

"And then you convinced Thari to rescue me?"

Sayzia nodded, her eyes bright. "Yonah." Her demeanor changed, growing more cautious. "Did you ever find Obi?"

The question was a startling reminder of just how long it had been since all three siblings had been together.

Yonah nodded. "I saw him only weeks after returning home from Jalid. He's fine. He's a slave for a captain from the isle. We're still in contact with each other."

Her sister sighed wistfully. "I'm glad he's alright. Soon, he'll be free."

"We can get to work on that letter."

"No, Yonah, let's sit for a while." Sayzia pressed her back against a wall and slid down to a seated position, using her walking stick for support. "I think you haven't relaxed once for the past couple of days. Why don't you tell me about your escape? Thari makes it sound like everything went wrong, but he can be a little dramatic sometimes."

"He doesn't seem too pleased about me being here." Yonah sat down next to her sister.

"He just doesn't like putting too much at risk," said Sayzia, shaking her head. "And he doesn't like newcomers. Everyone's a potential threat to our agenda. But he'll warm up to you eventually."

So Yonah told her sister about her carriage ride, how it tipped right over, how Thari (though she didn't know, then, it was him) yelled at her and was tackled by a Guard, how she had let the horses loose, how she and Thari had run away. Sayzia laughed at Yonah's retelling of Thari's role in the story. She explained to Yonah how he reminded her of an elderly woman who had lived in their neighbourhood when they lived in the big house, always worrying and fussing far more than necessary. Yonah laughed at that, too.

"Who made the smoke?" Yonah asked. "And how did they make it red?"

"That was Ravi. He's a bit of a chemist. He can make explosions, but we can also make smoke signals for each other."

"Did you use that in Jalid?"

Sayzia shook her head. A cough erupted from her throat, a leftover symptom from an illness that had swept through Harasa several years earlier, and she had to pause before speaking. "We just started doing that in Harasa. Things are a lot more intense down here."

"That's what I hear," Yonah replied with a nod.

Sayzia stayed with Yonah for the rest of the afternoon. At suppertime, well over a dozen people gathered in the common room of the apartment, where the delicious scent of spices wafted through the air. There was a modest buffet waiting for them in the kitchen, which everyone sat to eat wherever there was room—on a chair, a countertop, or the floor.

Yonah mostly listened to the chatter around her as she ate. Everyone seemed to know each other intimately. It felt like a large family dinner instead of a rebel gathering. Perhaps this was what Vitora had meant when she said the rebel group in the north was something akin to family. Yonah had never been privy to that level of intimacy with anyone besides her own family and Naris.

She wondered if Naris was out looking for her right now or if he had stopped for the night. He was likely back at the hotel they usually stayed whenever they visited Kelab. He would be undoubtedly furious that she had escaped, but it was possible that he was also sad to see Yonah go in his twisted way.

Sayzia sat next to Yonah while they ate, and Thari sat next to Sayzia. Thari and Sayzia's legs touched, and they leaned towards each other. They shared quiet remarks that only they could hear and special looks that Yonah couldn't translate.

Not everybody stayed at the apartment for the night. Several left after the sun had set, but Sayzia stayed and led Yonah to one of the rooms down the hall and set up a new pallet for her to sleep. As she lay down and closed her eyes, Yonah was taken back to her time as an outdoor slave at Puru's estate, surrounded by the calming sound of steady breathing and snoring.

Chapter Twenty

The following day, Thari and Sayzia helped Yonah write her letters to Beneri and Minister Hara:

Master Beneri,

I hope you are well. Please have this sealed envelope sent to Minister Hara.

Your friend

Minister Hara,

May this letter find you with ease and without suspicion. I have friends who wish to ask for your aid in pursuing our goal of abolishing slavery in Harasa.

I am safe. That is all I can disclose at this time.

Two friends and I will be at Government Garden on the 52nd day of summer. We will wait there for one hour.

Your dance partner

Later that afternoon, a rebel arrived at the apartment bearing cutters that looked just the same as the ones used at Yonah's wedding to remove her slave collar.

"Where did you get those?" she asked the rebel.

"I borrowed them from my employer," the rebel replied.

Yonah held still as the woman brought the cutters to her collar. With a familiar chunking sound, the collar gave way and clattered to the floor. Yonah's hand instinctively went up to her once more bare neck.

"That's better, isn't it?" Sayzia said.

"I was almost used to it again," Yonah replied. "Isn't that terrible?"

Two days later, Yonah, Sayzia, and Thari were perched in a tree not native to Harasa in a massive garden near Government House. It was well known that the garden contained just about as many political dealings as Government House itself, as it was a popular place for the ministers and the city's members of the upper classes to wander and meet. The walls of the garden crisscrossed in a maze-like pattern, providing privacy in the obscure corners.

It was here that Yonah and her companions hoped to meet Minister Hara. They were hidden from view in case the minister brought unwanted guests.

This corner of the garden wasn't well travelled. In the thirty minutes Yonah had been sitting in the tree, she had seen one sole person pass by.

"This had better be worth it," Thari muttered.

"Or what?" Sayzia asked, calling his empty threat.

Thari frowned grumpily at Sayzia. "Or I'll be very annoyed that we sat in this forsaken tree for over an hour."

"We can't have that, Yonah," Sayzia said. "Wouldn't want Thari to be *annoyed*."

Yonah tried not to smile too big at her sister's teasing Thari.

"Someone's coming," Thari said.

The three of them hushed and watched the person walking closer to their perch. It was the minister, looking particularly imposing in her silver clothes that the politicians wore to Government House.

"Is she alone?" Sayzia whispered.

Minister Hara paused in the centre of the walled path and looked around. The three rebels glanced at each other and, with a nod from Thari, descended from the tree.

The minister's eyes widened in surprise at their sudden arrival. She looked up at the tree. "What an odd place to wait for a meeting," she said with a soft smile. She nodded to Yonah. "I'm glad to see you're alright."

"Minister Hara," Yonah said, "this is my sister Sayzia and our friend Thari."

"Can I credit you with helping Yonah escape?" Hara asked.

"Well," Sayzia replied, "not me. But Thari certainly helped."

Brushing past Sayzia's comment, Thari said, "Yonah says you're partial to the cause. Since you're here talking to us, I guess that must be true."

"It is."

"We're trying to contact everyone in Harasa who wants to get rid of the slavery laws. Is there any way you could send your contacts in our direction?"

"Why? What is your plan?"

"A political assembly," Thari replied. "Same as we did in Jalid."

Hara shook her head. "That won't work here. Jalid wasn't nearly as militarized as Harasa is."

Sayzia asked, "So? We're not going to attack Government House."

The minister stared hard at Sayzia. "Althu maintains control of this country through fear. A simple political proposal will not entice the general public to risk their lives."

"We're not asking for the general public," Thari said. "We're asking for your contacts who are already involved in rebel activity."

Hara turned to Yonah. "What do you think?"

"They just want a united force," Yonah replied. "All of us together will be much stronger than we are now."

The minister nodded in understanding. "I'll let my people know. They can decide for themselves what they want to do. Where should I tell them to find you?"

"They can come to the market in Middlerow," Thari answered. "Tell them to wear a scarf in our colour." He motioned to the burnt red clothing that he and Sayzia wore.

Hara said to Yonah, "They haven't let you become a full member?"

Yonah shrugged and joked, "Thari's picky."

"I'd better head back," Hara said. "I have work to do."

"We'll let you go first," Sayzia replied.

As the minister headed back down the path, the three rebels huddled around each other.

"I think that was a success," Yonah said.

Thari shrugged. "We'll see what comes from it."

There was a shout from around the corner that caused Yonah to look up. Hara was backing away from something. As she rounded the corner, so too did a group of Guards, all pointing pistols at her.

"Minister Hara, Yonah Muran, and you two," yelled one of the Guards, "are under arrest for suspected rebel activity against President Althu and the country of Harasa."

Thari whispered, "We're going up the tree and getting out of here."

"What about the minister?" Yonah hissed.

"We can't help her right now. Now, run."

Thari led the three of them in a sprint back to the tree. He nimbly climbed up, assisted Sayzia up and onto the nearby wall, then grabbed Yonah's hand as she climbed.

Gunshots pierced the air, and Yonah felt air rippling near her as bullets whizzed by. She remembered the searing pain of her bullet graze wound from when she was a child.

The moment she stepped onto the top of the wall, she ran, keeping her focus on the line of stonework that stretched beneath her feet. She looked up and saw Sayzia a few feet ahead of her. She followed.

When Sayzia suddenly stopped, Yonah almost crashed into her. She felt Thari grab her arms to stabilize himself after the sudden stop.

"I wanted to make sure you were still with us," Sayzia said to Thari, panting. She broke into a coughing fit.

"We have to keep going," he said.

Through her coughs, Sayzia nodded. She started along the wall again, but at a much slower pace.

"Sayzia, push it!" Thari yelled from behind Yonah.

Yonah's sister nodded, but they didn't speed up.

They were at the edge of the garden. It was a ten-foot drop down to the street. Without fear, Sayzia dropped down, rolling off her feet onto her side. She cried out in pain.

A group of the Guard mounted on horses came riding down the street towards Sayzia. She must have noticed them at the same time as Yonah because she yelled, "Thari, you and Yonah go a different way!"

Thari glanced towards the Guards, pounding closer. "What will you do?" His features, normally firm, were stretched into concern.

"Don't worry about me."

Yonah recognized the look on her sister's face. It was one of resignation, of acceptance of the hard truth. "Sayzia, no! You hide!"

"No, Yonah!" Sayzia's voice was full and fierce. "You run!" Her eyes turned to Thari. "Both of you! Go!"

Yonah squeezed her eyes shut, which were wet with hot tears, as if that would erase all that was happening. When she opened them again, she nodded once to her sister and grabbed Thari's arm. The man was staring hopelessly down at Sayzia.

"Thari!" Yonah snapped at him. He looked at her. "We have to go."

He sent one last look down to Sayzia, then led the way along the wall in a different direction. Yonah didn't look over her shoulder to see the Guard gathering around her sister, but she could imagine the horses circling Sayzia, making her look even smaller against their tall frames.

Yonah shook the thought from her head. She couldn't help her sister at this moment. Right now, she had to get away.

The rebels hadn't yet taught Yonah all their secret pathways through the city, so Yonah had to blindly follow Thari as he wound through alleys, in and out of buildings, up and down levels. He finally stopped in a quiet alley, crouching low with his back against a wall, his face cradled in his hands.

Yonah, panting, placed her hands on her hips and paced back and forth.

Her sister wouldn't go to trial–she didn't have the luxuries of masters like Yonah and Naris. She would go to market as a slave as soon as possible, sentenced to life as a rebel. No one would buy her in her condition, forever touched by the sickness that ravaged Harasa several years back. She would go to the government labour camp, wherever that was. If she went that far, Yonah wasn't sure they would be able to get her back from there.

"We have to help her before they take her away," Yonah said, her voice shaking.

Thari looked up from his hands, his eyes stormy. "You said we could trust your contacts." His voice was like a low rumbling thunder.

Yonah took an involuntary step backwards. "I thought we could. Beneri has been helping since–" She faltered. Beneri. He was the only person that could have possibly tipped off the Guard. She couldn't believe that he would betray her.

"Thanks to you," Thari said, standing up, "Sayzia is being fitted with a slave collar as we speak!"

Yonah's shame choked her, preventing her from attempting to defend herself. Thari was right. It was her fault that Sayzia was in trouble.

"And while we're at it," Thari continued, "our only potential contact with the government will be going to trial, too."

A tear bled from the side of Yonah's eye and dribbled down her cheek.

"What, you're crying now?" The disdain in Thari's voice billowed the dying flame in Yonah's chest.

She wiped the tear away. "I cry when I'm upset."

"Crying doesn't fix anything."

"Neither does yelling at me. I know I'm the reason Sayzia's in trouble.

Believe me, that is *killing* me." She glared at the man. "Now, let's stop sulking and whining about it and find the others so we can put together a plan."

"No, you're not coming with me," Thari said, shaking his head.

Yonah's chest clenched. "What do you mean?"

"You're a liability."

"I want to help my sister! I want to help the rebellion."

"Then do it on your own time." Thari started walking towards the street.

Yonah followed him. "What happened to uniting the rebellion?" Thari kept walking. "I know where your headquarters are. Who knows who I'll tell it to?" Panic sent her insides trembling as her one remaining ally continued to walk away from her. "Please! She's my sister!"

He stopped, his back still towards Yonah. He bowed his head but remained silent. Yonah didn't dare speak for fear of undoing any progress she had made in convincing him to bring her.

Without turning, Thari said, "Let's go." He stepped onto the street, and Yonah followed. They walked in silence back to headquarters, each burning with anger and frustration. As she walked, Yonah was already making plans to confront her so-called friend.

Chapter Twenty-One

Master Beneri's house was quiet, a stark contrast from the evening of his party just a few weeks earlier. That felt like a lifetime ago.

Yonah crept around the tall house to the back, the darkness of night hiding her from any watchful eyes, and searched for an open window on the main floor. That was not difficult to find, as letting in the night breeze was quite common. She climbed through the window, landing as softly as she could.

From a glance around the room, Yonah could tell she was in a drawing room. Beneri's home had several of these rooms. Yonah crept into the front room of the house and started up the stairs. She knew where Beneri's bedroom was. She knew where he was sleeping. And his slaves were likely far away.

Ever so slowly, Yonah withdrew a small blade from her belt. It belonged to someone at the rebel apartment. She eased the door open. Beneri was curled up in the bed, looking child-like in sleep.

Before walking over to Beneri, Yonah went to the open window and looked outside. There was a small balcony the width of the window. From the balcony to the ground, it was over ten feet. There was, however, a lattice running along one side of the balcony that Yonah knew she could use to escape.

Staying on the side of the bed nearest the window, Yonah placed her blade at Beneri's throat. Her hands shook with nerves as she used her other hand to cover his mouth and nose. Within a moment, the man's eyes opened in a rising panic that went even higher when they saw a figure standing over them.

"Don't move," Yonah hissed, pressing the blade so it just touched Beneri's skin. The slight pressure helped still her shaking. "Don't call for help. What did you tell the Guard about my letter?"

Yonah slowly removed her hand from Beneri's face, keeping the knife at his throat.

"Are you going to kill me?" Beneri said with a dark frown.

No, she didn't want to kill him. They were friends. Used to be friends. He had betrayed her. "Answer the question."

"Yonah, I didn't want to do it, but the Guards came here and started ransacking the place. They saw one of my slaves leave the minister's palace and wanted to know what business I had with her. They were going to arrest me."

"Arrest you for what, Beneri?" Yonah hissed. "You didn't do anything wrong!"

"They said they were going to arrest me, Yonah! And I have zero interest in seeing what the local jail is like, let alone slavery!" Beneri tried to press his head deeper into his pillow to inch away from Yonah's blade.

"Nobody wants to be a slave!" Yonah snapped. The flame in her chest was burning. "That's why we've been doing this! And you just threw me and our entire plan to the Guard!" She pressed her lips together and leaned even closer to Beneri. "What did you tell them? Did you read the letter?"

"No, I didn't, and I told them as much." Beneri's breathing was starting to calm. "The Guards didn't believe that at first."

"So, you didn't tell them about our meeting? And they didn't know about it?"

Beneri shook his head. "I told them that you and the Minister were planning something, something I didn't know anything about."

"And they just let you go," Yonah said with a sneer.

"They told me not to leave the city." Beneri's voice trembled. "That they would be back."

"Now you're their informant." This relationship had run its course. "You will never see me again. You will never speak of me again. You are now an enemy to the cause."

"Yonah, I'm sorry."

She shook her head. "That doesn't matter." She removed the knife from Beneri's throat and went to the window. "Goodbye, Beneri." She climbed over the edge of the balcony to perch on the lattice and lowered herself to the ground. Once she had hopped down from the lattice, Yonah looked up and saw Beneri standing on the balcony watching her.

Without a word or even a nod, Yonah turned and started running back to the rebel apartment, taking a circuitous route to throw off anyone that may be following her.

WHEN YONAH WOKE the next day, she found she was alone in the bedroom and the sun was high in the sky. She went out into the main room of the apartment. Thari was the only person there, standing in front of a small window and gazing out upon the city. He turned at the sound of Yonah's footsteps.

"Where did you go last night?" Although his voice was firm, his features were soft with gloom.

Yonah thought she had successfully snuck out and back without anybody knowing of her absence. She had taken great pains to put the knife back exactly as she found it.

"Nowhere," she replied.

Thari shook his head. "And you want us to trust you. I know you were gone last night. Where did you go?"

She felt like she was being interrogated by Naris again. "I went to confirm whether Beneri had betrayed us or not."

"You made a house call? Without consulting anyone?" Yonah saw Thari's cheeks tighten as he clenched his jaw. "You put all of us at risk with that little visit. Were you followed?"

"No. I made sure." Thari was treating her like a child.

He was shaking his head again, his nose wrinkling in disgust. "You've brought nothing but trouble. I don't know why Sayzia begged us to help you."

Yonah couldn't pretend that the words didn't sting, but she kept her face impassive. "You can ask her when we get her back."

Thari's eyes fell, and his shoulders dropped. He nodded slightly.

"We'll intercept her at the next market day, right?" Yonah said.

"If she's there, yes."

"Why wouldn't she be there?"

Thari lifted his eyes to Yonah's. Their seriousness reminded Yonah of her sister.

SAYZIA WASN'T AT the slave market. Hidden beneath a brown scarf, Yonah stood in a crowd of onlookers. Newly captured slaves stood in rows in the centre of the square, their hands and feet bound in chains, copper rings around their necks. Six years ago, Yonah had stood in this square with her brother and sister, waiting to be bought.

She couldn't see Sayzia's face in the rows. Yonah watched as masters took their turns picking out new slaves, watched as their numbers dwindled, watched as children were separated, watched as they cried, watched as the few that were left were rounded up by the Guard and taken away, presumably to the government labour camp.

The crowd began to disperse, and Yonah moved with them, her heart weighing heavily with the knowledge that Sayzia was already gone.

"We're too late," Thari muttered as he walked alongside Yonah. "They probably sent her away a few days ago."

He didn't say where, but both he and Yonah were thinking it. If she hadn't been at the slave market for a master to purchase, Sayzia would have been sent to the government labour camp. The rumours that surrounded it sent Yonah's insides trembling. It was a place for slaves to be worked to death.

"She could still be at the courthouse prison," Yonah said.

Thari shook his head.

A drawing on a notice board caught Yonah's attention.

It was Naris. Whoever had drawn him had done a fair job of capturing his features. Yonah stopped to read the bulletin.

Naris Muran on trial for suspected rebel activity on the fifty-sixth day of this season. Open to the public.

The bulletin left Yonah staring dumbly at it for a moment. She had assumed Naris was out looking for her or, at the very least, had gone back to Vaha. It had never crossed her mind that the magistrate who had overlooked her trial would have had Naris arrested after she escaped.

"Hey," said Thari, bumping Yonah. "Let's go." Yonah followed Thari, although she was still deep in thought.

The trial was tomorrow. Naris had been sitting in jail, the same jail Yonah had inhabited, for about a week. And she had no idea. Yonah wondered who, if anyone, had been keeping Naris company while he awaited his trial. Perhaps now he knew the loneliness Yonah had felt as she waited for hers.

If that were true, Yonah knew that Naris was also very bored while being a little afraid of what was to come. Except he was innocent. He could look forward to going home after his trial.

Unless the state didn't need any proof to decide he was guilty. Then he would be a slave indefinitely.

Yonah knew she had to see the trial.

Chapter Twenty-Two

"Absolutely not," said Thari.

After returning to the apartment with Thari, Yonah had informed him of Naris' trial and her intention of going.

Yonah blinked. "I wasn't asking for your permission."

As Thari sighed loudly, Yonah had to resist the urge to roll her eyes. He said, "As long as you're with us, Yonah, you don't get to just do whatever you want. Everything you do has an effect on us. On our attempts to gain traction here in Harasa."

Yonah glanced around the room at the other rebels. Most were occupied with their own conversations and activities, but a few were watching Yonah and Thari's argument.

"It's a public trial," Yonah said. "I'll blend in with the crowd. I'll keep my face hidden with a scarf."

"If the high attendance at your trial is any indication," Thari said, "I'm sure your ex-husband's trial will be just as busy, especially with Guards, who, in case you forgot, are on the lookout for you."

"Like I said. I'll blend in with the crowd. Thari. I just need to know what happens to him."

Thari shook his head. "Why?"

"He was her captor." The woman named Dani had stepped into their conversation. "She wants to make sure that he stays under lock and key so she can put her mind at rest." The woman turned to Yonah. "Right?"

It wasn't as simple as that, but Yonah nodded and said, "Something like that."

"Then she can wait for the bulletin announcing the results of the trial," Thari replied. "It's too risky."

"Well, I'm going," Yonah said, jutting her chin towards Thari.

He leaned towards her. "Then don't bother coming back here."

"Thari, be reasonable," Dani chimed in.

"Who will help you find Sayzia?" Yonah added.

"I don't need your help to get Sayzia back," Thari said smugly. He held his hands open and gestured to the room. "I have everybody else."

Dani cleared her throat and shook her head.

Thari glared at her. "What."

Dani said quietly, "Thea doesn't think it's a good idea to use our resources to get Sayzia back."

Thari grew so still with his glare upon Dani that Yonah wondered if he had turned to stone. The man finally blinked and said quietly, "Thea doesn't want to get Sayzia back?"

Dani kept her lips pursed together, clearly uncomfortable under Thari's gaze.

"Thea!" shouted Thari. He swept past Dani and Yonah and went towards the kitchen, where Thea was conversing with some other rebels. Thea looked towards Thari, visibly steeling herself for whatever he had to say.

"We're going to plan a rescue mission for Sayzia, yes?" Thari demanded. He stopped just in front of Thea, towering over the shorter woman. His closeness and his height didn't seem to intimidate Thea one bit. She simply kept her eyes firmly on him as she spoke.

"No, Thari, we're not."

"Why not?"

"Because." Thea placed her tented fingers on Thari's chest and nudged him a step away from her. "Our resources are better put to use focusing on uniting the abolitionists in Harasa and getting a move on with our protest."

"We went and rescued her sister!" Thari yelled, waving an arm in Yonah's direction.

"Against your better judgment, and you were right. Rescue missions are not our strength."

By now, everyone was watching the battle of wills between Thari and Thea. Some people had even come to the hallway from the other rooms to peer into the kitchen.

Thari's voice was pleading this time. "But Sayzia is one of our own. We've been with her for so long."

"And that's what makes this choice so much more painful," Thea replied with an acknowledging nod. "But the sooner we can abolish Harasa's slavery act, the sooner Sayzia gets out, too."

Thari's face broke into something between helplessness and disgust. "The three of us decided we would take charge *together*. Don't I get a say in this?"

"Thari. Even Sayzia would tell you to smarten up and focus on the bigger picture."

For a moment, there was silence between the two of them. Yonah had been in several of these moments with Naris, where two wills have said all they can say, have born their dreams to the other, have proved themselves unpassable, and there's nothing left to do but stand there in defiance of the other.

"Well," Thari finally said, "I want to hear those words from her lips."

"That's a bad idea," Thea said.

"I suppose you'll try to stop me from using any supplies or asking for help from our friends?"

Thea shook her head. "I won't stop you or anyone else here from doing anything." She spoke louder so everyone would know she was addressing them. "But if there's trouble at this mission, I don't want any suspicion sent in our direction. You do not wear our colours. You do not lead the Guard back here." She turned back to Thari. "And you replace whatever you take."

Thari addressed the room. "Who will join me in getting one of your fearless leaders back?"

Everyone who was watching looked as if they wanted very badly to leave. Thari was scanning a room of apologetic eyes and averted glances.

"Not one of you?" he asked.

Yonah stepped forward. "I will."

Thari cast her a brief but stormy glare before turning back to the others. "Who will help free Sayzia? Who helped bring you all here?"

One man walked silently towards Thari and took his hand in his own. Even though he spoke quietly, everyone could hear what he said. "I'm sorry.

To both you and Sayzia. She will be safe when we finish what we came here to do."

Thari ripped his hand away. "You're all cowards. I'm ashamed of you." He started for the apartment door.

Thea called out, "Thari, where are you going?"

He didn't reply, only slammed the door shut behind him. Yonah watched as the rebels slowly shifted back into their own activities. She turned to Dani.

"Why will no one help? Don't you care for Sayzia?"

"Of course, we do," Dani replied. "But we just can't afford to perform a rescue mission every time someone is arrested."

The weight of Yonah's escape lay heavily on her. Sayzia had convinced the rebels that they needed Yonah, that she would help them change the country. Sayzia was the reason she was free.

She left. She didn't hear Dani calling after her. All she could think of was her sister and finding the man that would help get her free.

As Yonah ran down the stairs to ground level, her mind raced over where Thari might have gone. She didn't know enough about him to know his favourite spots, to know what places held meaning for him. Maybe he went straight to the courthouse to see if Sayzia wasn't there after all.

Yonah stepped out onto the street and nearly tripped over a man sitting on the stoop. She looked to see who it was and realized Thari was seated there, his head bowed.

"I thought you would have gone farther," she said.

He lifted his head, his tired eyes finding Yonah. Then he sighed and let his head drop again. Yonah shifted her weight from side to side, searching for the right thing to say. She suddenly sat on the stoop next to Thari, who gave her another one of his dirty looks.

His glare set Yonah's chest aflame. "What is your problem?"

"With you? You're the reason we're in this mess."

"Yes, Thari, yes, I'm aware that everything's my fault. And I'm trying to fix it! I want to help you get my sister back."

He sighed. "I know you do. I just wish at least some of the others did, too."

"Well, they do," Yonah said. "It's just not a priority for the rebellion."

Thari rubbed his face. "The rebellion, the protests, the sneaking. It doesn't matter without her."

Suddenly, everything became just a little bit clearer to Yonah. She understood why Thari was so desperate to rescue Sayzia. She had witnessed this hopelessness before. She knew what could make a man who was so calm and logical in other areas of his life be otherwise a mess of emotions and whim in this one.

"You love her." It wasn't a question. She knew.

Thari cast her a sideways glance as if looking her head on was too much to bear. He finally nodded.

"Does she love you?"

His face softened in a way Yonah had never seen before, and he nodded.

"I didn't know." Yonah thought she would have noticed if her sister was entwined in a romance. Thari didn't respond.

"Well," Yonah said, "then, we're the two people best suited to getting Sayzia back." She met Thari's eyes. "We'll never give up on her." Not like she had before. Never again.

"You might be right," Thari conceded.

"Of course, I'm right. Now, will you let me go to Naris' trial in peace?"

"I still think it's a terrible idea." He sighed and rubbed his face with one hand. "But since you're the only one who'll help me, I guess we could make it work."

Chapter Twenty-Three

Just as Yonah suspected, Naris' trial was a well-attended event, and she was able to slip into the courtroom with the crowd without attracting any unwanted attention. She wore a scarf loosely over her head to shield much of her face.

"Here," Thari said, pointing to a row. As they shuffled down the length of the bench, Yonah's eyes scanned the front of the courtroom and found the door behind which she knew Naris was waiting right now.

Once they had sat down, Thari muttered to Yonah, "If anything goes wrong, you remember our meeting spot?"

"Nothing is going to go wrong," Yonah muttered back.

"You're here. Of course, something is going to go wrong."

Someone a couple rows behind them was talking loudly. "They're still looking for his wife."

"Ex-wife," someone else cut in.

"My brother told me they're supposed to be watchful of her today, that she might come to the trial."

"Why ever would she do that?"

"That's what I asked my brother. He said she might have an emotional attachment to him."

"But that was all an act."

"Somebody thinks it might not have been."

Yonah could feel Thari's eyes on her, but she pointedly kept them towards the front of the courtroom.

"Well, it would be very foolish of her to come here," the second person said.

The intensity of Thari's look grew stronger. Antagonized by the feeling, Yonah turned her eyes and glared at him, daring him to say something out loud.

Soon after, the trial began with a man in sweeping blue robes walking down an aisle to the front of the courtroom and stepping onto the dais. He stood in front of a massive chair, his eyes fiercely bright on the onlookers. The courtroom started to quiet and rise to their feet with only his look as their cue.

Once the courtroom had settled, the magistrate balled his hands into fists and placed the knuckles together. He spoke. "We bear allegiance to our country, to its government, to its president. We believe in the significance of a united nation. We will not condone anything undoing of our government's goals, for we are Harasa first and foremost."

Yonah noticed that everyone else in the courtroom held their arms in the same manner the magistrate did. She slowly floated her fists upwards and touched them together, hoping she didn't appear anti-state.

The magistrate released his hands. "We are here to bear witness to the trial of Master Naris Muran, who is suspected of assisting the rebel Yonah, previously known as Master Yonah Muran, with escape. Bring in the suspect. You may be seated."

As they sat down, Yonah whispered to Thari, "How long has that pledge been a thing?"

"Ever since we arrived from Jalid. Haven't you seen it before?"

Yonah shook her head. She and Naris had never been to any official state events together, just parties with the other masters.

She looked to the front of the courtroom again and saw Naris entering from the side door, accompanied by someone wearing a paler blue than the magistrate.

"Oh, he has a lawyer," Thari said quietly.

"A lawyer? I didn't get a–" Yonah cut herself off. "His wife didn't get a lawyer."

Thari gave Yonah a look that said something along the lines of, 'Of course, the slave-turned-wife with no connections among the upper class besides the husband she betrayed and embarrassed didn't get a lawyer.'

Naris was placed on the short podium in front of the magistrate. His lawyer stood on the floor next to him. The magistrate, now sitting in his chair, gazed haughtily down at Naris.

"Can you confirm you are Master Naris Muran?"

Naris' voice was firm and resolute as he spoke. "Yes."

"You are being tried for aiding a convicted rebel with escape from the state, Master Naris. How do you plead?"

"Not guilty."

"I see you have brought representation with you today. State your name."

"Lawyer Zaren Burani."

"State your case, Lawyer Zaren."

"My client," the lawyer began, "comes from a family that has been highly regarded for generations. His family's estate was one of the first to embrace the Harasan Slavery Act because they saw it for what it is–an opportunity to rehabilitate both the people involved and the country itself."

The lawyer was such a fine speaker that Yonah couldn't tell whether he believed what he was saying or if he just knew it was the way to ensure Naris' plea of innocence. Either way, the words sent a hot rage through her body and limbs.

"We have witnesses, including honourable members of the Guard," the lawyer continued, "who can state with conviction that they saw Master Naris at the train station at the time of the rebel Yonah's escape."

"And are any of these witnesses present?" asked the magistrate.

"Yes, a member of the Guard is here, Magistrate."

"Bring them forward."

A member of the Guard, dressed in his black clothes and red sash, stood up from the front bench and stepped forward. He corroborated the lawyer's statements and was asked to sit down.

"I conclude that Master Naris was, in fact, not at the scene of the crime," the magistrate said, "but that does not necessarily prove his innocence. Who's to say he didn't hire those involved to carry out the task of assisting in his wife's escape?"

"Magistrate," the lawyer said. "Firstly, the rebel Yonah is no longer Master Naris' wife. He retracts all legal and emotional bonds with her. Secondly, I insist that proof of Master Naris' involvement in this crime be brought forward to enable his conviction."

"I cannot let an enemy of the state go free, Lawyer Zaren."

"But you can let an innocent man remain in prison?"

"I can keep him in prison for questioning until the details of this crime finally come to light."

"Master Naris has already told you everything he knows."

"I have one new piece of information," Naris said suddenly, his voice cutting through the argument.

There was a shift in energy in the entire courtroom as everyone refocused their attention on Naris.

The magistrate furrowed his brow. "Master Naris, how can you possibly have new information when you've been in prison the last seven days? Perhaps you mean you have 'withheld' information, which is also a crime."

"It is not withheld information," Naris replied. Yonah could hear the surly impatience in his voice. "I learned of it after my questioning."

Naris' lawyer rushed over to him and whispered hurriedly at him. Naris replied in the same hushed volume but with a still calmness. Whatever Naris said made his lawyer pause for a moment, then nod. The lawyer stepped away from Naris and spoke to the magistrate.

"Did you know you have a relative of the rebel Yonah in custody?"

The courtroom murmured. Yonah's skin prickled.

"Is that relevant?" the magistrate asked.

"It is if you want to know the last known whereabouts of the rebel Yonah," Naris said.

Thari shook his head. "How does he know?" He looked at Yonah, his eyes pleading. "How does he know?"

But Yonah couldn't bear to answer him, to tell him that Naris had met Sayzia before, that he already knew they were sisters, that Yonah would do anything for Sayzia, including attempting escape, and that it was likely her sister would do the same for her. It was possible that Naris and Sayzia were both being held in this prison beneath their very feet. It was possible that they were placed in cells close enough for Naris to recognize Sayzia, even to talk to her.

"Can we count on the revealing of this information to prove Master Naris' innocence of the crime for which he is being tried?" the lawyer asked.

"Now you are withholding information," was the magistrate's answer.

"And you are denying the inarguable fact that Master Naris did not help the rebel Yonah escape. But he knows someone who did."

The magistrate sat with his elbows resting on the arms of his great chair and his fingers tented together. "This new witness will be questioned. While he is currently considered innocent of directly helping the rebel Yonah with escape, Master Naris will remain in Kelab, under guard, at a location of his choice. Now, Master Naris." The magistrate leaned forward. "Who is this witness?"

Naris glanced over to his lawyer, who, with a dejected sigh, nodded.

"She's my wife's sister. Sayzia."

More murmurs rumbled through the courtroom as a tiny smile crossed the magistrate's face. Thari leaned forward in his seat, earnestly awaiting what the magistrate would make of this news. Yonah's theories were confirmed. Naris and Sayzia had spoken.

And, while everyone else was referring to her as Yonah the rebel, Naris called her his wife.

"Master Naris," the magistrate said, "where in the city do you wish to stay until we have finished questioning Sayzia, the sister of the rebel Yonah?"

Naris named the hotel he and Yonah had stayed at during their last visit to the city.

"Very well. You shall remain there under guard until the court has stated otherwise. You and your belongings will be escorted there now."

The magistrate swept out of the courtroom through a door at the front while the Guards moved towards Naris. They started down the aisle with Naris walking between them. Yonah's eyes couldn't help but remain on Naris' face. Relief smoothed out his features, but Yonah could see impatience lurking there, too.

As Naris' eyes scanned the room, his eyes flicked briefly over her, then returned. Time seemed to stand still as their eyes locked. Several emotions battled within Yonah. Even her breathing stopped, and she was completely frozen.

Though the look felt like forever, Yonah and Naris were caught in each other's gazes for only a brief second before Yonah felt a harsh tug at her arm that made her turn her head.

"Keep your head down!" Thari hissed at her, keeping his own face turned downward.

Yonah turned her face to her feet. She used to wear jeweled and strappy sandals. Now she wore cloth shoes with leather soles. Once she was sure Naris was past their row, Yonah looked over her shoulder to catch one more glimpse of him. The spectators of the courtroom began to stand and leave, and Yonah and Thari followed suit.

As soon as they were outside, they started down the street and slipped into the convoluted alleys of the city, walking in silence.

Eventually, Thari deemed they were safe from being recognized, stopped walking, and said, "How does Naris know about Sayzia?"

Yonah stopped a few feet ahead of him. His eyes were blazing in her direction. She was quickly growing used to being on the receiving end of his death glares. "They met. A couple years ago. I tried to take her and escape."

"That's when you left her for dead."

Yonah staggered backwards as if the words themselves had sprouted hands and pushed her. "Is that what she told you?"

"She said she fell asleep in a stable and woke up in a rebel house," Thari said, his voice hard. "I put the pieces together."

"That's why you dislike me so much." Thari didn't respond, but his silence confirmed Yonah's conclusion. "For your information, our masters caught up with us that night. They took me by force. Her master said to leave her." She remembered the cold wintery air of the north, the brightness of flame cutting through the darkness of night, Naris' fury, his hands on her. "I was punished for what I did."

Thari scoffed. "Please, he married you after that."

Yonah shook her head. "You don't know what goes on behind the closed doors of a marriage. No one does." Her eyes drifted away from Thari as she thought about the past two years. "Even I don't know what happened."

Her marriage to Naris was a jumble of deceit and honesty, manipulation and earnestness, hatred and, somehow, love.

"I don't understand," Thari said. "It's not like you liked him or anything."

Yonah buried her confusion deeper into her chest and looked up at Thari. "Right. It was just a marriage of convenience."

The look on Thari's face told Yonah that he didn't quite believe what she was saying, but he didn't pursue the subject any further.

"We should warn the others," he said. "We don't know how much Naris knows about our hideouts."

Yonah nodded in agreement, and the pair started back to the apartment, not speaking the entire way.

While Thari explained to Thea what had transpired at the trial, she listened intently, her face furrowed in thought.

"What do you think we should do, Thari?" she asked.

"I think we need to get Sayzia out of there before they torture some answers out of her!"

"And the hideouts? Do we leave and start over?"

Before Thari could give his opinion on that matter, there came a massive thudding sound at the apartment door that sounded as though a very strong, very large person had thrown their entire body against it.

All the occupants of the apartment swiveled their heads to stare at the door. The booming noise came once more, and the door started to give way.

Chapter Twenty-Four

As though it had been rehearsed, everyone but Yonah sprang into action, collecting supplies and heading for the window.

"They're outside!" someone shouted.

"You all know where to go when it's safe!" Thea yelled with authority. "Good luck!"

Everyone started out the windows, like mice swarming out of their flooding burrow. Yonah could now see why this apartment had been chosen as a rebel hideout. It was tall enough for people to escape onto the rooftop of the next building, it was lined with several balconies that allowed for fast travel along the building itself, and it was in the middle of a maze of alleys and streets.

Yonah felt a large and warm hand wrap around her wrist. She looked to the owner and saw Thari's fiery eyes on her. "Let's go!"

Yonah followed him onto the balcony. Memories of living on the street with Sayzia and Obi flickered through her mind. She shoved the memories aside.

"We'll climb down and make a break for it," Thari said.

"No," Yonah replied. She could see one Guard standing in the street below them. There was a good chance there were even more. She pointed to the rooftop across from them. "We jump. That's our best chance."

"Can you make that?"

Yonah glared at Thari, climbed onto the balcony railing, crouched perched on top, glanced down four stories to the chaos below, and pushed hard with her legs. She was flying through the air, arcing, then falling. The next rooftop came barrelling towards her. As soon as her feet hit the rooftop, her knees buckled, and Yonah collapsed. But she was safe.

Her entire body was throbbing with blood and adrenaline coursing through it. She stood and smugly looked at Thari, who was already atop the balcony railing. Behind him, the apartment door flung open, and red-sashed Guards spilled inside. Thari pounced and landed next to Yonah, letting himself fall upon landing.

"Let's go," Yonah said, leading the way. It had been years since she had run across rooftops, but the strategy of it all came back to her quickly. Keep moving. Stay high, away from the Guards. Easier to jump down to a new rooftop than straight across. If you can go inside and get higher, do it. Outrun.

She didn't hear Thari calling her name the first few times. Then his hand was on her shoulder.

"Yonah!"

She turned around, startled at the touch. Thari's hands were on his hips as he panted. "I think we did it," he said. "We can stop."

Yonah nodded and glanced around to get her bearings. Though it was different from years ago when she regularly ran around on these rooftops, Yonah could recognize the city she had once called home.

Perhaps it was home again, after all. Yonah didn't know where she lived anymore. She was displaced, floating between spaces.

"You're good at this," Thari said. "The rooftop running."

"I did it for years. With Sayzia and Obi. Are we supposed to meet the others somewhere?"

"Yeah, there's an emergency safe house, but I want to give it a day or two."

"And where do you propose we stay in the meantime?"

Thari folded his arms over his chest. "I don't know."

Yonah looked out over the city, its brown and cream buildings making the day seem hotter than it was. They had nowhere to stay. They were living on the streets. Or on the rooftops…

"We could stay up here," Yonah said quietly.

"What?"

"Do you know about the children who live up here?"

"Pardon me?"

"Did no one tell you? Not even Sayzia?"

Thari shrugged. "I'm gonna need you to start making more sense."

"When our mother was murdered," Yonah said, "and we became orphans, we lived up here. Above the city. There were dozens of us."

"What do you mean you lived up here?"

Yonah held an arm out wide, gesturing at the landscape. "The orphans of Kelab live on its rooftops where the Guards can't reach them, where they can sleep in peace, where they can stay invisible. We can stay here, too, for now." Despite having just sprinted for several minutes, Yonah felt a new burst of energy. "We could ask them for help."

"Orphaned children who live on rooftops?"

"Why are you looking at me like I'm crazy?"

"Because I think you're a little crazy."

Yonah sent her most deathly glare towards Thari. "And I think you're unnecessarily stubborn and judgmental."

Thari said dryly, "Well, now you've hurt my feelings."

"Then you think of a better idea!" Yonah snapped.

"I'm not from here," Thari said. "Don't you know anybody who could help us?"

"I haven't spoken to anybody from my old life since before we were captured." There was their neighbour who sometimes looked after them before their mother was murdered. There were her parents' friends. There was the baker who always gave the children a loaf of bread each morning while they were living on the streets.

Yonah wondered if he would be willing to provide them with a place to sleep.

"Follow me," she said and started searching for a way down to the streets.

"Where are we going?"

"To see if an old friend of my family will talk to me."

Chapter Twenty-Five

The baker still lived in the same building, selling his goods from a window and sending delicious scents wafting out onto the street. The only thing that seemed different was the new coat of paint.

Yonah had instructed Thari to go to the baker to initiate a conversation about the three children he had once helped. They needed to find out if he was still sympathetic to them, especially the oldest one, who was now a fugitive.

As Thari spoke with the baker, a man whose hair was now completely grey, Yonah hovered at a display just next door, doing her best to pick their conversation out from the noise of the market.

"Why are you asking all these questions about the past?" the baker asked, keeping his voice pleasant.

"What if I could tell you where the oldest sibling is?" Thari replied.

"Then you would be a great help to the state." The baker's voice was dry.

"I don't want to help the state find her. Do you?"

Yonah snuck a look from behind her scarf at the baker. His eyes looked quizzingly at Thari, puzzling out what to say.

"I wanted nothing more than for those children to be safe. If Yonah could stay out of the hands of the Guard, I would be very happy for her."

Yonah took that statement as her cue and stepped beside Thari. She looked boldly into the baker's face, waiting for him to recognize her.

He only needed a few seconds. His eyes widened as he realized who was standing before him, then he caught himself and looked down at his hands as they worked out of view.

"Is it really you?" he asked, looking back at Yonah. "Yonah Praliv?"

Yonah hadn't heard her original surname for a long, long time.

"The stories I've heard about you since your arrest..." The baker shook his head. "What about Sayzia? And Obi? You have no idea how glad I am to see you, how glad I am that your parents' sacrifices were not in vain."

Yonah's throat suddenly felt tight. She stammered, struggling to formulate words for a few moments before finally saying, "Obi's fine. In servitude, but fine. Sayzia's in trouble."

The baker furrowed his brow. "What kind of trouble?"

"She's being held for questioning."

The baker's eyes flitted between Yonah and Thari. "Are both of you working with the rebels? And Sayzia, too?"

Yonah gave a miniscule nod. "Will you report us?"

The baker's shoulders drooped, and he sighed. A distant sadness filled his eyes. "I could never. I spent all that time doing the little I could to help you kids when you were younger."

It hurt Yonah to think of asking a favour of this unnecessarily kind man. She was the one that owed him. "Then I have one more favour to ask of you. Of course, you can say no."

"What is it?"

"We're looking for a place to sleep for the night. Our headquarters was raided."

The baker stiffened, and his eyes darted around the street behind Yonah and Thari. "Did they see you there, Yonah?"

She shook her head. "I don't think any of them really registered that I was there."

"Come inside." The baker disappeared from the window and opened a wooden door just next to it. He ushered Yonah and Thari inside.

As Yonah stepped through the doorway past the baker, she whispered, "Thank you, Elder Bayim."

"Oh, I think we're past formalities, Yonah," he replied and closed the door behind them.

The warm scent of baking was even stronger inside the shop and sent a soft and cozy sensation through Yonah's body. For the first time in a long time, she relaxed into happy memories: the family walking to this very shop together, helping her mother bake by stirring batter, licking icing off her fingers.

"I'll put you upstairs. In my daughter's room."

They went through the cluttered kitchen and living quarters and up the stairs. There was a narrow hallway lined with four doors. Bayim opened one of the doors and ushered Yonah and Thari inside. "Stay quiet. It's best if my wife doesn't know about this. What she doesn't know can't hurt her. I'll bring you some food later on."

"Thank you," Yonah said.

Bayim nodded, and he closed the door.

The room was very small and cramped, even though the only piece of furniture inside was a small bed.

"He's a nice man," Thari said, breaking the uncomfortable silence.

"Yes, he is." Yonah climbed onto the bed and sat with her back resting against the wall. "It's going to be a long day if we're stuck in this room until morning."

"Better this room than a cell."

"You're right," Yonah conceded. "Which reminds me, how are we going to get Sayzia out? And what about Minister Hara?"

Thari frowned. "What about Minister Hara?"

"Don't you think we should try to get her out, too?"

"The whole point of contacting her was to use her position to gain more traction. She has nothing, now."

"So, we just leave her in jail? Leave her to be enslaved?"

"We can't help every rebel who gets arrested."

"But that's what Thea said to you about Sayzia."

Thari opened his mouth to respond, but froze, caught up in his hypocrisy. "Sayzia's a different story."

"The only difference," Yonah said, "is that each of us has a personal relationship with Sayzia."

"I thought you wanted to help Sayzia?"

"I do. And I also want to help Hara."

"Well, then, why don't we just break everybody out of prison?"

Yonah shrugged. "Why don't we?"

Thari shook his head. "You are just full of crazy ideas today. Can we just focus on one thing at a time, maybe? Besides, you already know that helping just you escape was a mess, never mind helping an entire prison full of people."

"It would boost morale among the rebels. And it would certainly force the state to pay attention to the cause."

"The wrong kind of attention, Yonah," Thari said. "Back in Jalid, everything was done properly. Legally. Politics abolished slavery, not guerilla warfare."

Yonah shook her head but didn't respond.

Thari continued. "Tomorrow morning, we're going to meet at the emergency safe house to regroup, and we'll make our plan for helping Sayzia."

"I guess you're in charge," Yonah muttered.

"Yes. Sayzia, Thea, and I were put in charge of the Harasa group. Because we proved ourselves in Jalid."

"Fine." Yonah was fed up with trying to converse with Thari.

"Yes. It's fine. It's good. I know what I'm doing."

"I'm sure you do."

Thari glared at her. "I do."

"That's fine!"

He paced to the covered window and back to the door. "Sayzia never mentioned that you were so difficult."

"Maybe you're the difficult one."

"Says the woman who's caused nothing but trouble since we rescued her. You're welcome, by the way."

Yonah tiredly turned her attention to her hands, which rested across her bent knees. For all the arguing she and Naris had done, at least Naris seemed more reasonable than Thari.

Naris was now likely back in his favoured hotel while they questioned Sayzia. Yonah wondered if Sayzia would reveal anything about the rebel group, enough to set Naris free, enough to get them to stop interrogating her. She wondered how much they would hurt her little sister.

Even if Thari refused to consider trying to help other prisoners escape, at least he was ready to help Sayzia. Yonah would do anything to save her sister.

It must have only been an hour or so later when Yonah heard a woman's voice speaking loudly from the floor below. Bayim answered the voice, then footsteps on the stairs, coming closer.

Yonah sent a panicked look in Thari's direction and scanned the room for a place to hide, but there was nothing.

The door opened, and the baker's wife burst into the room. The corners of her eyes crinkled as her mouth pulled into a smile.

"Yonah. It's good to see your face."

Yonah's eyebrows shot up in surprise at the same time her heart melted into a sorrowful warmth. "Thank you, Mathim."

Mathim opened her arms, walked towards Yonah, and embraced her. At the feel of the woman's firm hold around her body, a swirl of emotions welled up inside of Yonah, and she felt her body tightening, trying to keep them all in. They grew and swelled and whirled. Yonah felt her own mother in this embrace. She felt all the times she had been comforted by a caring adult. She felt taken care of.

Her body released, and tears streamed silently down her cheeks. She didn't care that Thari was watching this odd reunion. She just leaned into Mathim's body and let herself be held.

When Yonah finally pulled away, she saw that Mathim had been silently crying, too. The aging woman used her thumbs to wipe Yonah's cheeks.

"I'm sorry we didn't help you," she said.

"You helped us," Yonah argued. "You fed us."

Mathim shook her head. "We could have done better. We should have done better. We failed your parents."

"That wasn't your job. It was mine."

"You were just a child, Yonah. You're still just a child."

"I'm of age now."

"Just a number. Although I'm sure your circumstances have aged you quickly."

Yonah glanced at the baker. "I thought Bayim wanted to keep us secret from you. So you wouldn't get in trouble."

Mathim sent a scolding look in her husband's direction. "My husband is too chivalrous sometimes. He can't keep secrets from me. Besides," she took Yonah's hands in hers, "I'm more than happy to help you. Come downstairs. We'll get supper ready."

Yonah and Thari followed the couple downstairs into the kitchen. The bakery window was shut up and locked, leaving the living quarters shadowy, lit with only lanterns.

They all helped to cook supper—a vegetable stew with flatbread—and Yonah asked about the family. Bayim and Mathim's children were all married and living in their own homes. Two of their daughters were expecting.

"That's wonderful!" Yonah said. "And are they comfortable? I don't really know anything about how people make money anymore. Without the schools, jobs have surely changed."

The baker sighed. "We, of course, had been hoping to send our children to the university when they were older, but that was not meant to be. Mora sometimes helps me in the shop. Lara takes care of her friends' and neighbours' children. Abin is apprenticing with a tailor."

"I thought you had four children," said Yonah.

The baker and his wife exchanged a sorrowful look.

"Dayi became a member of the Guard a few seasons back," said Mathim. "We haven't spoken to him since."

Yonah opened her mouth to speak but couldn't find the words. She remembered playing with Dayi when they were still in school. They had exchanged pleasantries whenever he happened to be in the bakery when she and her siblings came to pick up baking before and after they were orphaned. He knew what kind of terror the Guards inflicted on families, how corrupt they were, and that the work they did was wrong.

"Why did he do that?" Yonah asked quietly.

"He said he was desperate for work," Bayim said in a low voice. "We tried to talk him out of it, but he wouldn't listen." He rubbed a single tear from his eye. "Who knows? Maybe he'll come back to us."

"Not in that uniform, he won't," Mathim said harshly. She was vigorously stirring the stew. She stopped suddenly and took a breath. "What about you, Thari?" She looked up from her work. "What's your story?"

Thari, who had been quietly setting the wooden table, looked at the three sets of eyes suddenly watching him. "I'm from Jalid. My parents were lawyers. Even though they disapproved of the slave trade, they didn't really do anything about it. So, I found a group that would let me help make a difference."

"I thought you were from Harasa," Yonah said.

Thari shrugged.

"Then why did you come here?" she asked.

Their eyes met, but Yonah couldn't make out what was there. Thari muttered, "To help," before turning his face back to the table.

She suddenly realized. "To be with Sayzia?"

Thari rolled his eyes and cast Yonah a glare.

Mathim said, "'To be with Sayzia?'" There was a coy tone in her voice.

"To abolish slavery here," Thari replied so firmly that the conversation ended there.

Mathim and Bayim shared a knowing look that made Yonah smile.

As they sat down at the table, bowls filled with steaming stew, Yonah asked, "Is there much support for rebels or the rebellion in the middle class?"

"Only in a figurative way," replied Bayim.

"What do you mean?" Thari asked.

"The people you see going to protests are just a fraction of the population. The rest..." he cast his gaze down to his food, "us included, don't make our dislike of the slavery act so public. We're just quiet bystanders."

"Didn't you ever go to a protest with my father?" Yonah asked.

"We decided the risk was too great," Mathim said quietly, placing her hand on her husband's arm. "We wanted to be sure that we would remain alive to raise our children."

Looking between Bayim and Mathim, at their small but cozy home, at the life they had built for themselves and for their children, Yonah saw what her life might have been: two loving parents, working to support them, perhaps even happily married and expecting a child.

Hadn't Naris been trying to offer her that life? Something like that life?

"I'm sorry, Yonah," Mathim rushed to add. "I don't mean to belittle your parents' choices. They were trying to make a difference. We didn't have the courage to do that."

Yonah nodded, her mind still thinking of what might have been. "Your children still have you."

"Now that they're grown," Thari said, "you could join the abolitionists."

Husband and wife looked at each other, speaking in the silent language of a long-time partnership.

"We hadn't really considered—"

"It's a possibility."

"But with the babies on the way—"

"It's something to think about."

Yonah couldn't blame them for letting fear lead their way. They had watched Yonah's family fall apart, piece by piece, and wanted to avoid letting the same happen to theirs.

But as Yonah was lying down trying to fall asleep, she considered that perhaps Bayim and Mathim's family was already beginning to fall apart in a different way. They had seemingly disowned their son, who had joined the Guard. Maybe that was enough to convince them to do more to make a difference.

Shame washed over Yonah as she realized that they were doing something. They were providing refuge to a known fugitive and an abolitionist who was a stranger to them. They weren't activists like Yonah's father, but they made a difference in their own way. They had done their best to make a difference in Yonah and her siblings' lives when they fed them breakfast as orphans.

If Yonah's father hadn't been at that protest, he would likely have been alive today. But Yonah's mother had been needlessly murdered by a power-hungry Guard.

There was no telling what could happen, not with the way things were.

Chapter Twenty-Six

Yonah and Thari departed the bakery the following morning with packs filled with bread, some meat and cheese, and even a few cinnamon rolls that reminded Yonah so much of her childhood.

"Be safe," Bayim told Yonah. "I hope you're able to find Sayzia."

"Thank you for your help," she said, hoping that Bayim and Mathim realized just how much she meant it, even if they did feel guilty for not doing more.

She and Thari started down the street and watched as Kelab began to wake.

"Look," Yonah said, pointing to a pair of children walking ahead of them. "The orphans. They're all looking for work for today, so they can feed themselves and stay away from the Guard."

"And you say they sleep on the rooftops."

"It's where we slept when we were younger."

A hand gripped Yonah's arm and dragged her into an alley. She cried out in surprise, then hushed when she realized it was Dani tugging her.

"Dani!" Yonah gasped. Her heart was beating at an unreasonably fast pace. "You're alright!"

Thari, who had followed Yonah into the alley, said, "Dani, Ravi, what's going on?"

Yonah noticed a man standing behind Dani. He spoke. "The Guard are in there. They've got Thea and many more."

"How do they know about the safe house?"

The man named Ravi shrugged. "They've been ambushing people all morning. We just barely got away. We've been trying to warn others."

"How many have you helped?" Thari asked.

"Just you two."

Dani added, "I saw them taking Thea away."

Thari slapped the palm of his hand against a building, his face clouding over in rage. "So, we're done? There's no one left?"

No one replied. There was nothing good to say.

Thari moodily peeked out of the alley to look at the safe house. Yonah still didn't know what building it was. "Well, we have to wait," Thari said. "We have to see if there are any others still coming."

"I think they're all gone, Thari," Dani said.

"Well, we're waiting," he snapped. "Until nightfall."

It was a long, slow, silent day. The sun rose higher into the sky, but the shade of the brown buildings kept the alley at a bearable temperature. Yonah passed around the bread that Bayim had given them. Thari glared miserably onto the street just outside the alley all day, watchful eyes searching for a member of their party.

Nightfall arrived, and no one else had come by to go to the safe house.

"Either the Guards got them all," said Ravi, "or they've heard the news and they're not coming."

Yonah, Dani, and Ravi stood behind Thari's crouched form. He continued to stare into the darkening street. After a long period of silence, he stood up.

"Everything we worked for," he mumbled. "It's all gone."

"We can rebuild," Dani said.

"With what? With who?"

"The abolitionist movement in Jalid came from nothing, too, Thari," said Ravi.

Thari sighed and leaned against a wall.

Silence enveloped the quartet once again. Yonah looked from one dejected face to another.

"Why don't we help them all escape?" she said.

"Do you want me to go crazy right now?" Thari answered, his eyes wide. "Enough with your stupid ideas."

Yonah's chest burned. "Well, your stupid idea is to give up!"

"You want just the two of us, maybe four if these two also feel like getting captured," Thari motioned to Dani and Ravi, who were helplessly watching the argument, "to break into Kelab's prison, which is constantly monitored because it lies beneath the courthouse, and perform a massive jailbreak?"

"We were going to do it for Sayzia. What's the difference?" Yonah's voice rose in volume as her frustration grew.

"We would have over a dozen fugitives to hide from the Guard. It's difficult enough keeping you out of their sight. And we're running out of places to hide." Thari glared at the safe house from the alley. "How did they find it!"

When no one answered him, he turned and glared at the others.

Ravi's eyebrows coolly rose up his forehead. "Oh, are you wanting an answer? I didn't realize you were done yelling."

"Either they followed someone who went straight there from the apartment," said Dani. She hesitated before adding, "or someone told them where it is."

Thari shook his head. "No. You are not accusing her of anything."

"We don't know what they're doing to her, Thari," Ravi said. "No one would blame her."

"She wouldn't do that to us."

"That's the thing; nobody was supposed to be there. Sayzia didn't know the apartment had been infiltrated."

"You think Sayzia gave away this place?" Yonah asked, her stomach dropping. Her eyes turned to Thari, who looked like he was going to be sick.

"What are they doing to her?" he muttered. He looked at Yonah and darkness clouded his eyes. "They want you. They know she's your sister. They're hurting her to get to you." He pressed his shaking fists to his face. "Why did we help you escape? Everything was fine until we got you out." He glared at Yonah with a fresh wave of anger. "It's your fault that everything's fallen apart! We should send you back to them!"

Ravi stepped between Thari and Yonah and took Thari's shoulders. "Okay, Thari, go take a walk. You need to relax."

"I need to get rid of her!"

"You're going to draw attention to us. Get out of here." Ravi pushed Thari onto the street. "You can come back later. We'll be here."

With one final glare in Yonah's direction, Thari stormed down the street, shaking his head.

Yonah leaned against a wall and slid down into a seated position, her arms folded over her knees. Her mind reeled over the possibilities of what they—whoever questioned prisoners—might be doing to Sayzia to find out where Yonah was, to find out where the rest of the rebels were.

Dani crouched next to Yonah. "You alright?"

"He's right."

Dani pursed her lips. "Maybe, but just a little. Everything's more complicated than that. Sayzia's the one who pushed for the rescue mission. So, you could say this is all her fault." As Yonah turned to frown at Dani, the woman added, "I'm just saying, trying to find where to put the blame doesn't necessarily do any good. Now." She stood up and dusted off her pants. "Where are we going to sleep for the night?"

Chapter Twenty-Seven

Yonah didn't want to impose on Bayim and Mathim for a second night, but between herself, Dani, and Ravi, it was the best solution they could come up with for their situation. Dani and Ravi hadn't slept until the early hours of the morning when they catnapped in a park, taking turns keeping watch for the Guard.

Now, the four of them stood on the street just outside the bakery. The window was shuttered as it was after dark.

"Wait here," Yonah said to the others. She crossed the near-empty street to the bakery door and knocked tentatively. She clutched her head scarf closer to her face, anxious about being recognized.

The door opened to reveal a young man about Yonah's age. Her brows furrowed. "Can I help you?" he asked.

"Oh," Yonah stammered. She took a step backwards. "I didn't realize there was company here. I'll come back another time."

"Wait, let me tell my parents you're here," the man said. "What's your name?"

"No, that's not necessary. I'll come back." She didn't want to put Bayim and Mathim's children at risk of arrest with the knowledge of her location.

"Abin?" came Mathim's voice. "Who is it?"

"I'm not sure," Abin replied. "She won't tell me."

Yonah cringed as Mathim stepped next to her son and saw her face. "Oh!" the woman exclaimed.

"I didn't know your son was here," Yonah said, her voice apologetic. "I'll just go."

"Is everything alright?" Mathim asked.

"Wait, who are you?" Abin asked. "Ma, how do you know her? Do I know you?"

She had to leave. Too many people were finding out she was still wandering the streets of Kelab, a wanted fugitive. "It's fine," she said.

"I thought you would have met your friends by now."

"What friends?" asked Abin. He narrowed his eyes at Yonah. Even though she had covered the lower half of her face with her scarf, faint recognition slowly pooled in Abin's eyes. "You're one of the orphan kids. From the house a few streets over. What was your name again?"

Yonah shot Mathim a panicked look.

Mathim said, "This is Esra. She recently came of age and came to us for help yesterday. Come in, child. Is your friend with you?"

"And a couple others," Yonah mumbled. "But if you don't have room, I understand. Please don't feel obligated. I don't want to cause you any trouble."

Mathim raised an eyebrow at Yonah. "Does anybody else know they're here?"

Will the Guard come looking for them here?

Yonah shook her head.

"Then you had all better come inside. Abin, get them something to drink."

Abin glanced at his mother, then Yonah, before heading into the kitchen. Yonah turned to the dark street and waved the others over.

"What was that about?" asked Thari in a hushed tone.

"Her son is here. My name is Esra."

The others nodded and followed Yonah inside.

"So, Esra," Abin began, pouring cold tea into four cups, "were you looking for work today? And a place to live, I guess."

"That's right," Yonah replied.

"What about your friends?"

"We all worked at the same estate. They're all a little older than me, so I knew they were in Kelab. There was a fire in their building today."

"I didn't hear about a fire," Abin said.

"It was over by Sandhill," said Thari.

"That's a long walk from here."

"Which is why we're happy to give you a place to rest your head for the night," Mathim interrupted. "Sit down, all of you."

"Where's Bayim?" asked Yonah.

"I'm here." He was coming down the stairs but paused at the full kitchen. "There are more of you than before."

"There was a fire, and Esra and her friends need a place to stay for the night," said Mathim. "That shouldn't be a problem, right?"

Yonah caught the silent conversation between husband and wife again.

Bayim quickly said, "Not a problem at all. Someone might need to sleep on the floor if Abin decides to stay for the night."

"No, I can go home and sleep in my own bed. You all have enough problems right now without having to worry about getting a good night's sleep."

"You're a good boy," Mathim said to her son, a soft smile in her eyes.

"I'll leave now."

"You don't have to rush."

"It's fine, Ma. Walk me out?"

Mathim and Abin both stepped outside the house. Yonah could hear them whispering to each other through the slightly ajar door. Eventually, Mathim came back inside and closed the door behind her.

"So. What happened?"

"Mathim, I'm so sorry," Yonah said, ignoring the question. "If I had known your son was here, I wouldn't have come. I know you're worried about your family's safety."

"It's fine."

"He's suspicious of us."

"Why are you back here?" the aging woman asked calmly.

Yonah sighed. "The Guard beat us to the safe house. We waited all day to see if there were any others. Tomorrow we'll look for somewhere else to sleep."

"Yonah, I'm not upset that you came back," Mathim said. "I just want to be sure you're not luring the Guard here."

"Nobody knows we're here," Ravi said.

"What is your plan for tomorrow, then?" asked the baker.

Yonah looked at the others. Thari pointedly kept his eyes lowered though his jaw was clenched. "We're in disagreement over that," she said.

"Well, you might want to leave the city, Yonah," Mathim said. "Abin just told us that Master Naris has been released from custody."

Yonah's eyes shot up towards the woman. "When? Today?"

"I believe so."

Yonah looked at Thari, who was watching her. Naris would be looking for her now that he was free to go home. He might, first, go back to Vaha to check on the state of the business. They had been away for a few weeks, although Naris' business advisor was probably handling it perfectly fine.

Whether he stopped at Vaha or not, Naris would certainly come looking for Yonah.

"WE HAVE TO go north," Yonah said. She, Thari, Dani, and Ravi sat in a circle on the floor of the men's bedroom, a candle burning between them. Bayim and Mathim had gone to bed, and all was quiet in the house.

"North?" repeated Dani. "To where?"

"To meet up with my contact in the rebellion."

Ravi frowned, the movement in his brow casting a shadow over his eyes. "You're from the Kirash area, right? That will take us days to get there. Our friends will be sold into slavery by then."

Yonah nodded solemnly. "I know." She could feel Thari's eyes on her, trying to penetrate her skin. All evening, she had been trying to figure out a way for them to break into the Kelab prison, to free not only her sister but all the rebels that had traveled here all the way from Jalid. But the only people she knew with the power to do anything were either in jail themselves, had already betrayed her, or could never trust her again because of her own act of betrayal.

"I thought the whole point of your crazy ideas," Thari said, "was to help everyone escape *before* they were sold into slavery."

"Yes, but, as you've pointed out, we don't have the resources to do that. If we go north, we can meet up with some people who probably have the resources. Or we can at least start working on your original plan to unite the rebels."

"Abolitionists," Dani said.

Yonah shrugged in response.

"I really, really wish we could help Sayzia and the others," she said. She looked directly at Thari. "I know I've failed my sister too many times. And I'm doing it again." Yonah was grateful that the candle between them cast very little light, so they couldn't see her watery eyes. "I wish I could do better."

Dani placed her hand over Yonah's. The touch felt strange to Yonah, unfamiliar and uncomfortable, though she was appreciative of the gesture.

Nobody spoke for a moment. This was the first suggestion of moving away from a rescue mission, of leaving their lost friends behind to their fates as slaves.

"They deserve better," Ravi finally said. "But so do many people."

Thari shook his head. "No, Yonah, what were you saying about the orphan children? And what about the masters you met? Can nobody else help us?"

"There's nobody. I wish there was."

Thari stared into the candle flame, his face softening into defeat.

"Then we'll head north tomorrow morning," Dani said. "How will we get there? We risk Yonah being recognized on the train."

"I'm not sure we have enough ora to hire a carriage," Ravi replied.

Thari silently retreated to the bed and lay down with his back to the others.

Dani whispered, "We'll figure it out in the morning. Come on, Yonah."

As she followed Dani out of the room, Yonah took one last look at Thari curled up on the bed, totally still, keeping his turmoil to himself.

THE FOLLOWING MORNING, the four of them went straight to the train station, stopping across the street. It was as busy as ever, with carriages stopping in front of the building and loading and unloading passengers, masters trailed by slaves encumbered with luggage.

There were also about a dozen Guards spaced throughout the station, simply keeping watch.

"That will make things difficult," said Dani.

"Yes," grumbled Thari. "Yes, it will."

Yonah watched as a pair of women stepped out of a carriage dressed in brightly coloured clothing. One of them wore a bare face, while the other was clearly wearing makeup that painted her eyelids in beautiful browns and oranges and her lips in a dark red.

"I have an idea," Yonah said to the others.

Nearly an hour later, with Dani's help, Yonah had purchased some makeup at a nearby store and covered her scar with a tinted cream and a neutral lip colour.

Thari shrugged. "So, your scar's gone."

"It's my most defining feature," Yonah replied, trying to hide a scowl. "Most of these guards won't know my face without it."

"I'm not sure that's a risk I want to take."

"I'll walk in with her," Ravi said to Thari. "You and Dani go in separately. Then you won't risk getting caught if they recognize Yonah."

"Oh, and you will?" Thari asked.

"I will."

With a scowl on his face, Thari shook his head. "We'll all go together. It'll be easier for her to get lost in a group of four."

Thari bought their tickets at a booth, and the four of them started for the train together. Yonah wore a headscarf low on her forehead, hoping to cover her eyes, but pointedly let the lower half of her face remain out in the open. She thought the Guard would be making a point to look for women covering their mouths.

They had no problem boarding the train and found seats in the public car. Without first-class tickets, they couldn't have a booth to themselves.

Yonah tried to still her pounding heart. She sat in the window seat, so she continued to make a point of keeping her scarf low over her eyes. Thari was in the seat next to hers, with Ravi and Dani in front of them.

The car was quickly filling up. A Guard was meandering down the aisle, looking from one rider to another. Yonah kept her face forward.

A conductor also moved down the aisle and checked that everyone had a ticket. Thari showed the man both his and Yonah's tickets. The conductor stared at the tickets for what seemed an exceedingly long time, then passed them back to Thari and continued. Yonah relaxed her shoulders and unclenched her jaw.

In a few minutes, the train started to chug away from the station. Yonah couldn't help but watch as the station went by, slowly at first, then faster. Soon, the station disappeared entirely, and she was looking upon the city streets, then the desert that lay outside of the city. They were officially out of Kelab.

Chapter Twenty-Eight

The train took them to the town of Araha, where they hired a carriage to take them to Kirash. Ravi pointed out that they had virtually no money left after hiring the carriage, but Yonah knew that once they reached Kirash and met with Vitora, they would be able to figure everything out.

The road to Kirash took them past Vaha, and Yonah watched the estate go by. Something tugged at her heart as the white palace became clearer the closer they came. Something tried to pull her towards it. Yonah wished she could pretend she didn't feel it.

Within a matter of minutes, they were rolling into Kirash. Yonah's arrival into the town felt a little like coming home. It was nighttime, however, and not quite as busy as usual.

"Where are we going?" Thari asked her.

"Let's just get off here," she replied.

For a moment, Thari fumbled over how to draw the driver's attention from within the carriage. Yonah thumped on the front of the small booth twice, and the carriage slowed to a stop.

"Will you be recognized here?" asked Ravi.

"Yes." She pulled her scarf over her head and folded a piece over the lower half of her face. "We'll get off the main road."

"We could get the boys scarves, too," Dani suggested, as she adjusted her own scarf to match Yonah's.

"With what money?" Thari said.

"My contact might be willing to help us there," Yonah replied.

The four of them stepped out of the carriage, Thari gave the driver the rest of their fare, and Yonah led the way down the street. She took them to the next road that peeled off the main thoroughfare and wound through the maze-like streets of the residential parts of Kirash. In an effort to ensure nobody followed them, Yonah took a circuitous route. Eventually, they emerged from a narrow road into a square lined with trees on one side and a well in the middle. The stalls that lined the other sides of the square were gone.

"Do you even know where you're going?" Thari hissed at her.

"We're here," she said calmly. She took the group around the edge of the square to the candle sellers' door. Yonah knocked quietly and waited until the door opened.

Vitora's eyebrows shot upwards when she opened the door, then narrowed as she looked at Yonah.

"Is that who I think it is?" she asked.

"The sand burns my feet at night," Yonah answered, "but candles keep me warm during the day."

Vitora's eyes flickered in shock very briefly before returning to their cool demeanor. "You've brought friends."

"They're trustworthy."

"How can I be sure?"

"They helped me. They're the reason I'm here."

Vitora glanced at Yonah's three companions. With a somewhat grumpy voice, she said, "Come inside."

Yonah's muscles relaxed, and her breath came easier once she was hidden inside the dark house. She removed the scarf from her head and shook her hair loose.

"Loni!" Vitora called as she walked down the narrow hallway to the back of the house where the kitchen lay. "The fugitive herself has returned."

Loni's voice came from upstairs. "Which fugitive would that be?"

Vitora didn't answer. She started pulling chairs out from the small kitchen table, then asked, "A drink?"

"Please," Yonah answered. Vitora began to pour cups of cold tea, and Yonah and the others sat at the table. Footsteps announced Loni's descent from upstairs.

"Never would have guessed it'd be you," he said, still standing on the stairs. There was a gentle smile on his face. "How are you, Yonah? How did you escape? You've been the talk of the town for a couple weeks now. First, the slave master's favourite, then his upper-class wife, then a rebel, then a fugitive!"

"That's a bit of a story," Yonah replied.

"I don't suppose you have anywhere else to be, though," Vitora said, setting cups on the table. "You're in hiding. We're the first place you came, aren't we?"

Yonah nodded solemnly.

"Well, tell us everything," Vitora pressed. "Especially how you got caught in the first place, so it doesn't happen to anybody else."

Yonah told her story of the night the group of unexpected escapees arrived at Vaha, and Naris caught them all.

"Do you know where they came from?" Vitora asked.

"I didn't get a chance to ask."

Thari said, "I didn't know you were helping slaves escape to Jalid."

"Surprised?" Yonah asked.

Thari shrugged but didn't say anything.

Yonah continued her story, describing her arrival at Kelab, her stay in the jail, her trial, and the attempted transfer, at which point she introduced Thari, Dani, and Ravi to both the story and to Vitora and Loni.

"You came from Jalid?" Vitora's eyes lit up. "How large is your network? Have you made any headway in Kelab?"

"No, Vitora," Yonah said. She continued to explain how Hara was captured, how their safe house was found and all the other rebels arrested, and how Naris was rumored to have been released.

"There's been no news of him around here," Loni said. "He must still be in Kelab."

"Looking for her, maybe," Thari added, nodding towards Yonah.

"The rebellion in Kelab," Vitora said. "There's nothing left?"

"Nothing left of our people, anyway," Thari replied.

Vitora tapped her fingers on the kitchen countertop. "You have nothing to show for your adventure, Yonah. That's a disappointment."

Yonah's chest burned with shame. Vitora was right. When hearing her story all at once, it became obvious that all she had made of her time in Kelab and with the rebels from Jalid was to make more of a mess.

"Well, she brought us along, didn't she?" said Dani, indignation colouring her voice. "We can tell you how we found success abolishing slavery in Jalid, so you can apply those techniques here."

"That should have been happening in Kelab," Vitora replied.

"We can spread the cause to Kelab from the northern part of the country," Ravi said. "We might even be able to gather more support if we come from afar rather than keeping abolitionist support only in the centre of Harasa."

Vitora didn't speak for a moment. Her gaze was heavy on Ravi's. Yonah kept her eyes lowered, unable to bear Vitora's disappointment.

"Well, I suppose we have to do it that way now," Vitora finally said, with a sigh. "And you'll all be wanting a place to sleep, too?"

"You can tell us where we can start looking," Ravi replied. Yonah appreciated his calm demeanour and the way he could defuse a situation.

"You'll stay here for now," Vitora said. "Until I can be sure you won't betray us. Loni will get you some blankets. You three can sleep upstairs."

"Where will Yonah sleep?" asked Thari.

"She's a wanted woman," Vitora said. "I have a special spot for her."

Yonah shifted her eyes to the rug lying beneath their feet and returned her look to Vitora. The woman lifted her eyebrows in acknowledgment. Of course, she wanted to keep that location a secret from these newcomers.

"It's alright," Yonah said. "You three go on upstairs."

Loni led the others upstairs to start putting together a place for them to sleep, leaving Yonah alone in the kitchen with Vitora.

"I don't think you should go outside for a while," Vitora said. "You're too recognizable around here. Even with that clever makeup."

"This clever makeup got me on the train in the middle of Kelab."

"But you're a local celebrity in Kirash."

Vitora was right. Yonah had often frequented the town as a slave, but once she had married Naris, everybody had wanted to catch a glimpse of the slave-bride. As the first month of their marriage morphed into two years, Yonah became a well-known citizen of the area, with accounts at several of the local upscale shops, and a habit of wandering the marketplace.

"So, what can I do?" she asked. "To help with the cause?"

"Right now, Yonah, I'm not sure you can be of any help." Yonah gawked at the words coming from Vitora's mouth. "You've brought me new recruits, and I thank you for that. But your worth lay in your connections to upper society and now that's gone and you can no longer be invisible because of your notoriety. Until we can send you away, you'll just have to stay in hiding."

It was a prison sentence. She had moved from imprisonment in Kelab to imprisonment in Vitora's house.

"Help me with the furniture," Vitora instructed Yonah.

The two of them moved the kitchen table and chairs off the rug lying beneath them. Vitora flipped the rug over to reveal a trap door.

Yonah had been inside this secret room a couple times before. She never would have expected herself to sleep in it. She opened the trapdoor, revealing nothing but darkness.

"Everything you'll need to make a bed will be down there." Vitora removed a lantern from a shelf, lit it, and handed it to Yonah. "Make yourself comfortable. Tomorrow morning I'll wake you early so we can put the kitchen together again without the others seeing."

Yonah resolutely began her descent into the cellar, one hand on the ladder and the other holding the lantern.

"Goodnight, Yonah," Vitora said. "I'm sorry it has to be this way."

The trapdoor closed over Yonah's head, and Yonah lowered herself to the cellar floor.

She knew she certainly wouldn't want for any items down here. The room was packed with shelves, trunks, and boxes filled with innumerable items. This was Vitora's stash that she used to trade with people who didn't have any money. Yonah had used this system to barter for items to give to her informant—Meerha.

Maybe she could convince Vitora to ask Meerha to come by to pass on any news from her brother Obi.

Yonah pushed two flat trunks together to build a bed and placed some flat cushions on top for a mattress. She even found a bedpan to keep close by, just in case.

The jail in Kelab had windows, she remembered.

You're not in prison. You're free.

But Yonah wasn't sure that she was.

Chapter Twenty-Nine

Vitora woke Yonah early, though Yonah only knew the time of day once she climbed out of the hidden cellar and looked out the back window. Within a few minutes, the other three came downstairs to eat breakfast.

Yonah looked around the table at the odd grouping of adults.

"You will spend today looking for jobs," Vitora said. "I can't have you living here and eating our food without contributing. And it will ensure the Guard has no reason to arrest you." She named several shops and owners who might be looking for help.

Once everyone had finished eating and cleaning up breakfast, Thari, Dani, and Ravi started for the front door. When Yonah didn't follow, Thari paused. "Isn't Yonah coming with us?" he asked.

"She'll work for me here," Vitora replied. Yonah knew that she would not be spending any time manning the candle stall. Vitora would keep her inside, away from anybody who might recognize her face.

With a furrowed brow, Thari caught Yonah's eye and jerked his head towards the door. Yonah glanced at Vitora, who nodded once, and followed him as far as the doorway.

"What will you do today?" Thari asked Yonah.

"I don't know yet. Vitora doesn't want me to be recognized. Especially if I'm living in her home."

"We'll find you a different place to live, then," he replied. There was a look of concern on his face that seemed out of place to Yonah, who was used to him glaring at her. "Where did she have you sleeping last night? Why weren't you with us?"

"It's a safe place from searching eyes," Yonah answered. "I'll see you later."

With a soft frown, Thari turned and jogged to catch up with the others. Loni shuffled past Yonah and started unpacking the stall. "Vitora wants you inside," he said to Yonah.

Yonah retreated into the house, closing the door behind her, and found Vitora in the kitchen. She set Yonah to do various chores around the house: cleaning the kitchen, organizing the cellar, and preparing food for storage. All the while, Vitora sat at the kitchen table, pouring over a handful of letters.

"Is that for the rebellion?" Yonah asked.

"Yes."

"Can I help?"

"No."

Yonah tossed the knife she was using to chop vegetables aside. "I didn't come to you to become a housemaid."

"What do you expect me to do, Yonah?" Vitora kept her eyes on the letter in front of her.

"Let me help! Or else let me go somewhere that will let me help."

"You're not a prisoner, Yonah," Vitora said, lifting her eyes up to Yonah. "You're free to go whenever you like."

Yonah blinked. "I thought–"

"You just can't come back here if you do."

"But I want to help with the rebellion, and you're the only person I know."

Vitora didn't answer. She returned to reading her letters. "If you are patient, I might be able to find some work for you to do from within this house."

The slight chance at doing something more meaningful with her time sent a glimmer of hope through Yonah. "And in the meantime, I'm just supposed to cook and clean? Can't I go see Meerha and ask her about my brother?"

Vitora gave Yonah a wide-eyed stare. "Go to the most popular gathering place in Kirash? It's a wonder you've survived this long."

"Can she come here, then?"

"Meerha can't come here. She's a slave."

Yonah sighed. "Then can I send Thari to go talk to her?"

Vitora pondered over the suggestion for a moment. "I think that should be fine. You're sure you trust him to know your business?"

The man was in love with her sister. He might as well learn about their brother.

Thari put up a bit of a fight that evening when asked to go talk to Meerha on Yonah's behalf. "Why doesn't Yonah just go?" But he gave in and went with instructions on how to get to The White Stallion and what Meerha looked like. He returned only with news that Obi was worried about Yonah and was ready to help her if she ever made it back north again. Meerha would let Obi know that she was safely out of Kelab.

"And is Master Naris back in town yet?" Vitora asked Thari.

He shook his head. "Meerha said she hadn't heard anything."

"He must think you're still in Kelab," Vitora muttered.

With Naris still away, Yonah wanted to try to get to Vaha to see if Seidon and Praha were alright. She didn't voice her wishes out loud, knowing that Vitora would quickly forbid it.

All three of the others had managed to find work that day. For the next few days, they settled into a routine of going to their respective jobs after breakfast, returning home for supper, and having a quiet evening discussing either the rebellion or other more light-hearted topics until bedtime. Meanwhile, Yonah's routine consisted of hiding out in the house all day doing various chores, wistfully wishing she could even help sell candles just outside the front door.

One evening, the group gathered in the kitchen late into the night, sharing stories and laughing. It felt good to laugh, but Yonah could feel her joy was being held back by the need to do something now.

She and Thari happened to meet each other's eyes. Thari subtly nodded towards the door. Yonah nodded, and they removed themselves from the kitchen and went outside to sit on the stoop.

"I'm appreciative of Vitora and Loni letting us stay here," Thari began, "but what is going on? I feel like I never see you. And all you can tell me about your day is that you've been doing housework?"

"I'm a risk for the rebellion right now," Yonah answered. "So, I have to stay hidden."

"And locked away somewhere even I don't know?"

"It's in case of a raid or something."

"Won't you tell me where?"

"Vitora doesn't trust you."

"Don't you trust me?"

A closed-lipped smile spread across Yonah's face. "I trust you," she said with a nod.

"Then where does she have you sleeping?"

Yonah glanced into the kitchen through the open door to see if Vitora was watching. The woman was engaged in the conversation inside.

"In the cellar," Yonah whispered.

Thari furrowed his brow. "There is no cellar."

Yonah shrugged. Thari's eyes lit up. "It's hidden?" he asked.

"Don't say anything about it," Yonah said.

Thari nodded and looked across the dark square. It was empty of sellers' stalls. "I still don't like that she won't let you leave the house."

"She says as long as I want to sleep here, I can't risk being recognized out there."

"Then I'll start looking for a different place to live. Somewhere I can rent since I have a job now." The tone of his voice told Yonah that he was surprised to be living such a domestic life. She chuckled. "And you can live there and not be cooped up like a prisoner."

Yonah hesitated to say the words, but they eventually came out. "I'm not sure how long I'm going to stay here, anyway."

"What do you mean? Here, in the house?"

Yonah gave Thari a sideways look. "In Kirash. If I can't help with the rebellion, then there's something else I need to do."

This time, Thari glanced inside to see if anyone was watching them, then shifted, so he was facing Yonah. "If you're going to help Sayzia, I'm coming, too."

"You're going to stay here. The rebellion needs you."

"They don't even have us doing anything yet!"

"Vitora's just trying to figure out if she can trust you. Soon, she'll figure out she can, then she'll give you some real work to do."

"Not if you leave," Thari said. "I'm coming with you."

"Well," Yonah replied, "I haven't really decided yet what I'll do."

Thari wrapped his hand around Yonah's arm and gently squeezed. His eyes held onto Yonah's. "Don't leave without me. Please."

YONAH TOLD THARI to meet her at The White Stallion the following afternoon. If he could scrounge up a pair of horses, though that was unlikely, even better.

Around noon, the others had gone to their respective jobs, and Yonah was stuck at the house with Vitora. Yonah was preparing lunch, and Vitora was upstairs. She took some food outside to Loni, who was minding the stall. She had used makeup to cover her scar again and wore a scarf over her head. Without a backwards glance, Yonah strode through the square, towards an alley that would take her towards the east end of town.

"Hey!" she heard Loni yell. He was jogging after her. She pressed on, hoping he would leave her alone. Then his hand was on her shoulder, pulling her until she turned around to face him.

"What are you doing?" he asked. He wasn't angry, just surprised.

"I'm leaving."

"There'll be something for you to do soon. You just have to be patient."

Yonah shook her head. "I can't."

Loni's look pleaded with Yonah. "Don't do this. You're being rash."

"I'm needed elsewhere. Goodbye, Loni. Thank you for your kindness. And for Vitora's, too."

The man shook his head but didn't do any more to try to make Yonah stay. Yonah, about to turn, saw Vitora standing in the doorway of the house, leaning casually against the doorframe. The woman didn't look upset or betrayed in any way. She was just watching events unfold so that she would know what her next step should be. Maybe this was her plan all along, to make Yonah want to leave.

Yonah turned and continued through the square, keeping her gaze straight ahead, avoiding looking at anybody. As soon as she stepped into an alley, out of sight of Vitora and Loni, she felt a weight lift off her shoulders. She was free again.

She found the eastern edge of Kirash without trouble and started down the road towards Vaha.

The farther down the road she went, the more she felt like her old self: the version of herself that was walking to and from town right under Naris' nose. But Naris wasn't waiting for her at Vaha. That was for the better. He would certainly turn her in to the Guard if he found her or take it upon himself to enslave her how he saw fit.

She could not walk down the main path onto the estate. It was the middle of the day. The slaves were out working in the vineyard and would recognize her immediately.

About a kilometer from the estate, Yonah veered off the road and into the grassy plain. She walked around the circumference of the grounds of Vaha, checking periodically that no one was watching her from the rows of vines until she reached Naris' childhood treehouse. She took refuge from the sun there for a few minutes, watching the movement of the workers in the vineyard. She waited for the opportune moment, then dashed towards the stable, throwing herself into the corral with the horses, and hid on the backside of the building.

Yonah sat with her back to the stable, panting for breath. Her eyes were drawn to the horses grazing in the corral. One turned its long face towards her—the gelding named River.

A figure rounded the building, and Yonah pulled her scarf over her face.

Seidon was standing over Yonah. His eyes went wide with shock as he realized who had snuck into the corral.

"Yonah!" he gasped. "What are you doing here?"

Yonah stood up and threw her arms around the man. His body was tense at first, and then he softened, returning the hug.

When Yonah pulled away, she saw pale yellow and green splotches on Seidon's face, as well as a faint line along his brow that used to be a scab. Her heart ached at the sight.

"He must have hurt you pretty badly for the bruises to not be gone yet," she said softly, sadly. "I'm sorry."

Seidon shrugged. "I'm already enslaved for the rest of my life. I'm already lame. There wasn't much else he could do to me and still have me able to work. Though my ribs still hurt."

"Oh!" Yonah took a step back from the man, realizing her embrace may have caused him some real pain. "Did I hurt you?"

He chuckled. "Yes. But it's fine. I'm glad you're alright. I didn't think I'd see you again."

"If everything went according to Naris' plan, I would have been back here in no time, back in a collar. How is Praha?"

"She's quiet. Keeps to herself these days."

Yonah's skin began to tremble. "What did he do to her?"

"I don't know. She would only let Daza see her after it was done." Daza was the resident healer among the slaves at Vaha. He had healed Yonah after Naris cut her lip. "Yonah, Naris isn't here, but if anybody recognizes you, I don't know that they won't report you to him. I understand he was doling out punishments for the slightest things after we were caught."

"Don't worry. I'm just passing through. I just wanted to see how you and Praha were doing. If you get a chance to talk to her, will you let her know I'm thinking of her? And hope she's able to heal like she helped me heal?" Praha's tough love had shaken Yonah out of her stupor after she and Naris had returned from the mountains before their marriage.

Seidon nodded. Yonah looked out over the plain. She could feel herself being drawn towards the waterfall.

"Could I borrow a horse?" she asked. "Just to go that way," she pointed away from the estate. "Not even an hour."

Seidon squinted in the direction Yonah pointed. "You'll be sure to bring it back this time?"

Yonah smiled. "Barring another natural disaster, yes."

"You be quick," Seidon said as he started for the stable. "I want to see you gone from here safely this time."

"You've always been a great help to me," Yonah said. "And a dear friend."

Seidon turned to look back at Yonah. He nodded. "Yes. I care for you. I want to see you safe."

Seidon helped prep a horse for Yonah—not the gelding, River—and, within a few minutes, Yonah was galloping across the plain towards the waterfall. She just needed one last look before she moved on with her life.

She wasn't sure what she was expecting to feel when she arrived. Nothing felt different about the place. It was a mixture of good times and bad, of love and frustration. It was a cool pool of water that would otherwise be at peace if it weren't for the pounding of the waterfall.

Maybe Yonah could be a clear, unrippled pool of water if she could just forget about Naris.

She saw his golden-brown eyes giving her that desperate and searching look. She felt his gentle touch on her skin. She heard him whispering 'I love you' in her ear.

He had seen her at the courthouse in Kelab, and that look they shared had been one filled with longing.

Naris had been on Yonah's mind since the rebels helped her escape, but after that look they shared at his trial, Yonah felt herself missing him.

He had beaten Seidon and done something equally or even more horrible to Praha. He had hurt Yonah in the past. Even if all he wanted was to be loved, Naris was a monster. Monsters could only be loved by other monsters.

Yonah looked resolutely at the water. She spoke out loud to give the words more meaning. "I'll never think a nice thing about Naris again. And, if I can, I'll never think of him at all."

"I'm sorry to hear that, my dear."

Chapter Thirty

Yonah's skin prickled at the sound of that voice, that voice she hadn't heard say a word to her in weeks. She turned around to face its owner.

Naris looked well. He was dressed in a casual shirt and pants. His forehead glistened with sweat.

"You were at my trial," he said. "That was very convenient for me."

"In what way?" asked Yonah. He was standing between her and the path up the canyon.

"I told the Guards to follow you back to your hideout."

Yonah's insides twisted. That wasn't possible. "We weren't followed."

"Apparently, it eventually led them to a second hideout where they were able to make the majority of their arrests."

It was all her fault. Thari was right. She had brought nothing but trouble to the rebels. She was the reason Sayzia, Hara, and all the others were in jail.

"I was furious when I found out you had gotten away," Naris continued. "I should have known you would eventually come back here. I didn't expect to see you riding this way just as I was arriving from Kelab."

If only she had come sooner. If only she hadn't been cooped up in Vitora's house.

No, she just didn't need to come here. This errand didn't accomplish anything.

"Come back to the house, Yonah." Naris held his hand out to her. "Come back to me."

"To be your slave?"

"To be my companion. Just as before. Well," he shrugged, "almost. I obviously can't let you wander off on your own anymore. You understand."

"I've never understood."

Naris waited for her explanation.

"I don't understand," Yonah said, "how you can care so little about the freedom of others, how you can claim to love someone but hurt them at the same time. I don't understand what you think love is." Her chest felt like it was going to explode. "I don't understand why I care so much to understand you. I don't know why my life is entwined with yours, but I just want it to end. I don't want to care anymore, not about you."

That soft look in his eyes. She hated it, and she loved it.

He took a few steps towards her. "We're in love, Yonah. You and I make a great romance story."

Yonah shook her head. "Not a very good one."

"We're just in the middle. The end will be very good. They'll paint pictures of our story in new palaces."

Yonah stared dejectedly at him.

"Come with me," he said. "Then we can start to heal from your betrayal."

She swallowed down the bile rising in her throat. He still stood in her way. She shoved the words through her teeth. "Yes, Master."

Naris looked taken aback. Yonah wasn't sure if it was from her formal acknowledgement of his power over her or her giving in so easily. "You can still call me Naris. I'll always be your Naris."

He always insisted on having it both ways; be her master but be treated like her lover; be her husband but treat her like she was his property.

Yonah closed the gap between them, and Naris wrapped his arms around her. He crashed his lips into hers, kissing her aggressively. She didn't have the heart to bother with pretending to kiss him back. Naris noticed, pulled away, and looked at her with a furrowed brow.

"Perhaps close proximity is what it takes to make your heart grow fonder," he said.

She didn't answer, and Naris, taking Yonah's horse by the reins, led the way up to the top of the canyon.

"Do you have word from my sister?" Yonah asked as they climbed, her eyes scanning the ground.

Naris' shoulders stiffened. "They transferred her for questioning."

"Transferred her where?"

Naris turned around to look at Yonah, his expression apologetic. "To the government camp."

The government camp where the slaves that weren't sold to masters were sent. It was rumoured to be the most horrible place in Kelab, where labourers were worked to near-death, barely kept alive until their release.

But Sayzia would never be released. She was a rebel. She would die there.

"I'm sorry, Yonah," Naris said, his voice sincere. "It would have been better for her to die that night in Jalid."

Rage coursed through Yonah, threatening to explode into screams, but she held herself in and continued searching on the ground.

She felt Naris' fingers under her chin, forcing her face to look up to his.

"I'm truly sorry."

All Yonah's efforts were going towards remaining calm and not screaming at Naris for what an imbecile he was.

"You're back to not believing anything I say," Naris said.

When Yonah didn't answer, Naris sighed loudly and started back up the canyon path, his back turned to Yonah. Her eyes went back to the ground.

There was a round rock just a little larger than her hand. Yonah quickly bent over and picked it up. It fell nicely into her palm. She tucked the rock behind her back as she continued walking behind Naris and the horse.

Yonah's chest started to quiver as they came closer to the top of the canyon. She had never attacked anybody before. But it was either her or Naris. It was either enslavement or escape.

Just as Naris and the horse crested the ridge at the top of the canyon, Yonah raised her arm, heart pounding and sweat gliding down her forehead, and struck the rock across the back of Naris' head.

He crumpled silently to the ground like a sack of clothes, weighty but without structure.

Yonah's mouth dropped open in shock as she stared at his lifeless form. His stillness and silence resounded across the empty plain, leaving Yonah feeling extremely alone.

There came a soft moan from Naris, and she breathed again.

She raced to the horse, which had skittered a few feet away, mounted, and broke into a gallop straight for the road to Kirash. Once the horse was at full speed, Yonah glanced over her shoulder and saw Naris on his hands and knees. He was alive. That was good. No, she shouldn't care whether he lived or died.

Yonah pressed the horse onwards and rode into town, straight down the main road to the west end, dismounted, and slapped her horse's rump so it galloped away from her in a random direction. She ensured her scarf covered her face as she strode into the White Stallion.

A few people looked in her direction at her sudden entrance, but it didn't matter if anyone noticed her. Naris would make sure the entire town knew she was nearby soon enough. She needed to find Thari.

He was at the bar talking to Meerha. Yonah walked over to him and grabbed his arm.

"We have to go. Now."

Meerha gasped and whispered, "Yonah, is that you? I've missed you!"

"I've missed you, too," Yonah replied without feeling. "Thari, Naris just arrived from Kelab, and he is in a terrible mood, thanks to me. We have to leave. Did you find horses?"

Thari stood up. "Yes, just outside." He slapped an ora coin on the bar. "Thanks, Meerha."

"Where are you two going? What should I tell Vitora?"

Yonah firmly said, "Nothing," as she and Thari hurried out of the building.

Once outside, Thari led Yonah to two horses tied up at a nearby post.

"Well done, Thari," Yonah said as she mounted the new horse. She watched Thari climb onto his horse with a little less grace. "Do you ride?"

"I've ridden."

"That'll have to do for now." Yonah kicked her horse into a trot and then, as soon as she knew Thari was with her, a gallop.

They rode hard, the Harasan sun beating mercilessly down upon them. Yonah smelled the salt of the sea before she saw the port city of Basee sprawling north and south along the coast.

As soon as she and Thari dismounted, Yonah sent the horses galloping down the street. Thari glared at her.

"I paid good money for those."

"Naris will be looking for me. If anybody tells him they saw two horses running out of town today, he'll follow up."

"What did you do?"

"I'll tell you later," Yonah answered, starting for the bar with a sign hanging over its door that had a picture of a nine-tailed whip on it.

Although she was less known in Basee than in Kirash, Yonah made sure to keep her scarf hooded over her head as they entered the Nine Tails pub. She had been here once before on a mission to sing a song for a musician. It was for this musician she searched.

He was on a raised platform in one corner of the large room, seated on a stool with a guitar over his knee. There were two other men on the stage with him. One played a small flute, and the other's arms and hands glistened in small bells and drums.

Yonah tugged on Thari's arm and led him to the bar. Once seated, her knee bounced impatiently. Naris was searching for her in Kirash by now. She wasn't sure how long it would take him to consider searching in Basee, but once he did, Nine Tails would be the first place he looked.

"You still have some money, yes?" Yonah asked.

"Just a few ora. Why?"

Yonah sighed with frustration.

"You two ordering something?" said a woman behind the bar.

Yonah let Thari order them two drinks so as not to let the barwoman see her face.

"And now we have ten," Thari said, counting the coins in his hand. "Do you mind telling me what the plan is here?"

"That guitarist," Yonah said, pointing to the man named Tolga, "is where Meerha gets all her information from, including anything about Obi."

"Your brother."

"And Obi works on a ship. Hopefully, he can get us out of here and help us rescue Sayzia."

"Does he have access to any resources that can help us attempt a rescue mission?"

Yonah nodded impatiently at Thari. "He has money."

They waited out the musicians' set and watched as Tolga headed straight to the bar for a drink. Yonah slipped off her stool, walked over to the guitarist, and tapped on his shoulder.

He turned around, and his eyebrows slid up his forehead as he registered who stood before him. "Didn't expect to see you here! I thought you were arrested or something."

"Something like that," Yonah replied, "so don't talk so loudly."

"What can I do for you?" Tolga's eyes flicked over Yonah's shoulder. "Is that your friend?"

"Yes, it is. When was the last time my brother Obi made port?"

Tolga scrunched up his face in thought. "That would be about three weeks ago."

"Did he mention anything about when he would be back next?"

"You might have to help me jog my memory."

Yonah turned around and held her hand out to Thari. "Give me the money." Thari slowly placed his small drawstring bag in Yonah's hand. She counted out five ora coins and passed them to Tolga.

"Yonah," he said, his nose scrunching with disdain. "What's this? It's nothing."

"I can give you more once I find my brother."

"You have to make it worth my time to help a rebel."

Yonah dumped the rest of the bag's contents into Tolga's hand. "There's nothing else. Will you tell me?"

"I'll tell you," Tolga replied, slapping two coins on the bar and placing the rest in his pocket. "You can give me the rest once you meet up with your brother. He should be coming tomorrow or the next day."

"He's with the same ship?"

"That's right."

Yonah nodded. "Thank you. Don't tell Meerha you saw us."

"I can't promise that, even if you pay me. She's my one and only."

"My husband was my one and only," Yonah said dryly. "And we kept plenty of secrets from each other."

"And we all know how that turned out," Tolga replied.

Yonah and Thari left the pub and stood on the wide street for a moment.

"Your brother comes tomorrow, and we have absolutely nothing," Thari said.

"Yes."

"What do you propose we do between now and your brother rescuing us?"

Yonah's eyes were on the rooftops. "One of my crazy ideas."

Chapter Thirty-One

She didn't know the streets of Basee the way she knew those of Kirash and Kelab, but Yonah managed to find a way for her and Thari to climb onto the rooftops of the city. Basee was different from the other cities in that it wasn't a sprawling place that went off in all directions; it was a thin strip that ran along the coast nearly as far as the eye could see. It was large but narrow, and there was no avoiding running into others sharing the rooftops.

There weren't as many orphans populating these rooftops as Yonah had seen in Kirash. While they looked suspiciously upon Yonah and Thari, they kept to themselves.

"At least it's summer," Yonah said as she sat down at a walled corner of the rooftop. "It won't get too cold."

Thari gawked at Yonah. "You're being serious right now."

"This is how Sayzia and I survived with our brother when we were younger!"

Shaking his head, Thari sat next to Yonah. They both leaned against the low wall and looked out at the sea.

"Sayzia never mentioned sleeping on rooftops," Thari muttered. "Just that she was homeless for a few years."

"It was how all the kids in Kelab survived. How we hid from the Guard."

"Sayzia's been through a lot, hasn't she? And you, too."

Yonah nodded. "She has. I only know up until we were sold into slavery. How did you two fall in love?"

"What do you mean?"

With a shrug, Yonah replied, "How do you know you love each other? How did it happen?"

Thari stared at the sea as he thought. "It just happened. One day, she was just another person working towards abolition, and the next, I thought everything she said was brilliant and that everything she did was good, and I just wanted to be close to her."

"She's perfect in your eyes."

Thari's gaze turned back towards Yonah. "Yes, and no. She's not perfect, but I can see that everything she does is what she believes in, and I love that about her."

"How isn't she perfect?" Yonah asked, knowing it was a bit of a mean question to ask of her sister's lover.

"Well, you tell me," Thari said with a smile. "You're her sister. You know."

"I'm asking you."

"Are you going to tell on me after we rescue her?"

"I promise I won't."

Thari pursed his lips and narrowed his eyes at Yonah. "She can be very serious. Sometimes, I wish she would pause to laugh. And she's too practical for her own good. Thea was right when she said that Sayzia wouldn't want us taking resources away from the cause to save her."

Yonah nodded solemnly. "I know. She told me to stop trying to keep us together when we were being carted around to different slave markets. I wanted us to be sold to the same master, but she knew that wasn't possible. She told me we wouldn't see each other again."

"She's a realist."

"I can't wait to see her again," Yonah said in a whisper.

A soft smile crept onto Thari's face, and his eyes unfocused as his gaze turned inward. "Yeah."

"YOU TWO LOOK so pitiful out here."

It was Tolga, the musician, who spoke to them. Upon waking up, stiff from the lack of bed pallets, Yonah and Thari came to the busiest section of the port to watch the ships come in, hoping to witness Obi's arrival. They had been there all morning.

Tolga carried a cloth bundle in his hands. He passed it to Yonah. When she unfolded part of the bundle, she saw bread, meat, and cheese piled inside. Her mouth was immediately wet with saliva, and her empty stomach gurgled.

"We don't have any money," Yonah told the musician.

"Consider it a gift. No sign of your brother?"

"No."

"Well, I hope he gets here soon. Rumours have already travelled from

Kirash that you're back in the area."

Yonah resisted the urge to adjust the scarf over her face. "Do any of the rumours suggest I'm in the city?"

"Not yet. But they do suggest that you viciously attacked your master, who's now a bit crazed in his search for you."

Yonah sheepishly looked at Thari. His mouth dropped open. "The rumours are true?" he asked.

"People also assume that Naris will be coming to Basee once he finishes tearing through Kirash," Tolga added. "But you already knew that, didn't you? That's why you're waiting for Obi."

Yonah looked up and down the lengthy docks. "We need Obi to come as soon as possible."

"Stay away from Nine Tails," Tolga said. "And you might try waiting somewhere a little less open. And I'm not bringing you any more food, so make that last."

"Thank you, Tolga," said Yonah, filled with both gratitude and annoyance.

Tolga shrugged. "Give my regards to your brother. And tell him he can pay me the rest of your debt next time he makes port." Tolga returned to Nine Tails: a pub known for its rebel activity. Yonah knew that if Naris came looking for her in Basee, that would be the first place he searched, especially since he knew she had been there before and severely punished her. That punishment was the reason Yonah was required to cover her face to prevent herself from being recognized.

"Your contact is right," Thari said, breaking into Yonah's thoughts. "We shouldn't wait out there, though I'm really more concerned about the Guard harassing us for loitering more than anything else right now."

"Let's take a walk, then," Yonah said.

She and Thari walked up and down the street, one side lined with buildings, the other with ships and boats bobbing on the water's surface. The afternoon wore on, and Yonah's feet started to hurt from standing for so long.

As they were walking past Nine Tails once again, the sight of a particular horse tied to a post outside the pub made Yonah freeze in her tracks.

"That's Naris' horse," she said.

"Great," Thari muttered. "Come on, let's go shopping."

He led the way to a handful of vendor stalls and proceeded to pretend to browse through their wares. Yonah kept one eye on the Nine Tails, waiting to see when Naris emerged from the building.

She saw a face coming down a dock onto the street, a copy of her own, with features that looked better on a masculine face.

Yonah tugged on Thari's arm and ran to her little brother. He noticed her racing towards him, and his face lit up into a bright smile. Without a word, Yonah threw her arms around him and buried her face into his chest. He seemed to grow every time she saw him.

"Yonah!" Obi exclaimed, returning the embrace. "What are you doing here?"

"I need your help," Yonah said, pulling away from her brother without letting go. "Does the offer to stow us away still stand?"

Obi shook his head in confusion. "Who's 'us?'"

Yonah released Obi from her grip and gestured to her companion. "Obi, this is Thari. Thari, this is my little brother Obi."

Thari shook Obi's hand and looked deep into his eyes. "It's good to meet you, Obi."

Yonah added, "He's also Sayzia's–" but then she remembered. Her mouth dropped open. "You don't know!"

"Yonah." Obi's confusion was turning into impatience. "What is going on here? I thought you were in Kelab. Or would have been sold to another master by now."

"Obi." Yonah took her brother's hands in hers. "Sayzia's alive. Our sister's alive. We could all be together again."

Obi's mouth hung open, moving up and down as if trying to form words. Finally, he said, "You told me she died. How could she be alive?"

"It's a long story. The whole thing is a long story, but right now, can you get Thari and me onto your master's ship? Please?"

"Yeah. Yeah, I can help you. We should wait until the ship clears out."

Yonah shook her head. "Naris is in Nine Tails right now. Looking for me."

"Obi." A man dressed in clothing in the style of the island nation just west of Harasa stepped next to them. Yonah recognized him as the captain who had bought her brother all those years ago. "Is this your family?"

"Yes, Captain," Obi replied. "My sister and…her husband."

The captain nodded at each of them. "A pleasure to meet you both. Don't be late, Obi." He started to walk away. "We can't stay long."

"We're leaving in just a few hours," Obi explained to Yonah.

"Even better," Yonah replied. She looked to the Nine Tails. Naris was walking out of the building. She shook her brother's shoulder. "He's coming! He's coming!"

Still unseen by Naris, Yonah and Thari followed Obi down the dock to a massive ship with golden sails. He took them up the gangplank, where two other sailors, both also wearing slave collars, were standing guard.

"This enough to keep you quiet about these two?" Obi asked, holding out a large handful of ora coins to them.

"You got it, O," one of them said, taking the coins.

"Just don't mention us if you get caught," said the other.

Yonah looked to the street. Naris was striding across the street to their dock, his questioning gaze on Yonah. He hadn't recognized her yet, but his suspicions were high.

"I won't," Obi said. "You don't let anybody on here that doesn't belong to the crew."

Yonah glanced once more in Naris' direction. She saw recognition light up his eyes, and he started running.

"Obi!" Yonah said.

Her brother looked down at the dock, saw Naris, and ran to a door on the ship. "Follow me," he said. "And keep up!"

They raced down the steep wooden stairs to not the first nor the second but the third lower deck. Yonah couldn't imagine all of this was inside the ship just from looking at it from the outside.

The deeper into the ship they went, the darker and damper it got. They were definitely below sea level now, which was a thought that unsettled Yonah.

They were in a large room lined with boxes and trunks. Unused ropes were splayed around the place, and a massive piece of fabric the same gold as the sails was bundled in a corner.

Obi ran his hands along the walls of the room. He found the seam he was looking for and pried open a panel to reveal a secret compartment between the vertical wall and the rounded hull of the ship.

"I'll check on you when I can," Obi said, shooing Yonah and Thari inside.

"Thank you," Yonah said, grasping Obi's hand briefly. He nodded and shut the panel, plunging them into complete darkness.

His footsteps swept away from the room. There was just a moment of the ambient sounds of the ship before Yonah could hear shouting from somewhere above them. She started to tremble.

"Naris must have gotten on board," she whispered.

"Let's get away from the entry," Thari suggested. He took Yonah's sleeve, and, together, they sidled along the narrow compartment.

The shouting arose again, and they froze. The voices were closer. Naris was searching the ship himself.

Yonah willed herself not to panic, not to break down into a puddle of tears. If she did, they would most certainly be found, and Naris was furious with her.

A loud bang that Yonah instantly recognized as a nearby door opening. Stomping footsteps.

"Where is she?" Naris screamed. There came another thud and clatter from what Yonah assumed was Naris throwing a crate. "Where are the men she was with! Who are they?"

"Our master can speak with you when he returns."

"I will speak with him! I'll let him know he has one of my slaves stowed on his ship and a couple imbeciles covering for her!"

The shipmates didn't answer. Naris let out one of his exasperated, wordless yells, and Yonah heard his footsteps retreating back to the upper decks.

Thari waited for silence before saying, "He's a charming fellow."

Yonah pressed her shaking hands to her face and gasped as hot tears streamed down her cheeks.

Thari placed his hand on her shoulder. "Yonah, don't worry. He's gone."

"He won't stop." A dreadful sense of hopelessness weighed her down, threatening to pull her to the bottom of the ocean. Naris was single-minded. He would search for Yonah until she belonged to him once more. He said he would always come for her.

"He didn't find us, now," Thari said. "That means this secret compartment works. We might get out of here after all."

Yonah nodded. There wasn't anything she could do right now besides wait and see if they were discovered by Obi's captain. If he found them, he was more than likely to turn them over to the Guard or Naris.

Several minutes later, there came a soft knocking at the wall hiding Yonah and Thari from the rest of the ship.

"Yonah?" It was Obi's voice whispering through the wall.

"We're here."

"Naris has gone back to the deck. He's waiting for Captain Pirung to come back. You just wait here."

"Obi, wait." Yonah shuffled towards the sound of his voice. "Does the captain know about this compartment? Is Naris going to get him to search the ship?"

"I don't know," Obi replied. "The captain doesn't like people pushing onto his ship. I gotta go. The fewer people think you're here, the better."

Yonah placed her hand on the wall as if her brother could feel the touch. She heard his footsteps leave the room and leaned against the hull of the ship behind her.

Neither Yonah nor Thari spoke for a long while. There was nothing to say. All they could do was wait until either they felt the ship leaving port or their hiding spot was revealed, and they were turned in.

With each passing minute, Yonah's trembling slowed until it finally stopped. The tightness in her chest loosened. An inappropriate boredom set in. Still, neither of them spoke. They just waited.

There came distant shouting from above. Yonah looked up as if she were able to see through the levels of the ship to the deck. She turned her focus to her body and felt for the sensation of movement from the ship.

Thari whispered, "I think we're leaving."

A slow smile spread across Yonah's face. "I think you're right." They had escaped Naris. Yonah didn't know what had happened between Naris and the captain, but she was glad it had resulted in them leaving Basee.

It wasn't for a few hours, however, that they finally heard footsteps in the adjacent room. They were brisk and purposeful and stopped at the hidden panel. The panel opened swiftly, letting in lantern light.

As Yonah blinked at the light, she realized it wasn't her brother looking into the secret compartment.

It was the captain.

Chapter Thirty-Two

The captain's face was still, held in a thoughtful expression. His eyes shifted from Yonah to Thari and back again.

"So, Obi did this," he said.

Although it was clear who had let them onto the ship, Yonah didn't confirm the accusation.

"And is it true that annoying man is your master?"

Of all the things Naris had been called, 'annoying' was never one of them. The thought made Yonah snort with laughter, to which her eyes widened in horror.

Captain Pirung narrowed his eyes at Yonah, then suddenly slammed the panel shut and walked away.

"We should go," Thari said.

"Go where? We're on a ship, hopefully in the middle of the ocean."

"We're not in the middle of the ocean. We're along the coast. We can swim to shore."

"I can't swim!" Yonah hissed.

Thari stared with an open mouth at Yonah. "Why can't you swim?"

"What do you mean, 'why can't I swim?' Because nobody taught me! Why can't you ride a horse?"

"I can ride a horse. And riding a horse isn't a life-saving skill."

"Riding horses out of Kirash saved our lives yesterday."

The panel opened again, startling Yonah and Thari into silence.

"Take these two to the brig."

Two shipmates, both wearing slave collars, reached for Yonah and Thari. They were taken to the opposite end of the ship and put into a cell.

As the shipmates and the captain started for the upper decks, Yonah said, "Excuse me? What are you going to do with us?"

"I haven't decided yet." Pirung climbed up the steep stairs.

The tightness was returning to Yonah's chest. Pirung knew that Obi was why they were stowed away on his ship. He would certainly punish Obi, and it was Yonah's fault.

Yonah agonized over her brother's fate while she and Thari bided their time in the cell. The only good news that had come out of that day was that they had escaped from Naris' grasp. For now.

Yonah didn't know what time it was when the sound of a door came from the top of the stairs, and her brother came down at an easy pace.

"Obi!" she cried out, slamming herself against the metal grate that separated her from her brother. She reached for his hands. "Are you alright?"

"I'm fine, I'm fine," Obi said quietly.

"Did the captain hurt you? What's your punishment?"

"He's just taken a couple months' wages from me."

Yonah paused. "What? But you're a slave."

"Ever since Jalid abolished their slave trade, Pirung started paying us regularly. I still have to stay with him until I'm of age, but I'll be well-set for taking care of myself." Obi shrugged. "Two months of wages won't be the end of me."

Yonah wished she could find the words to properly tell Obi how grateful she was to him for helping them escape Naris.

"Now, will you tell me what you mean when you say Sayzia's alive?"

Yonah beamed. "I thought she died in the mountains, but it turns out the rebels saved her. She helped abolish slavery in Jalid and came back to Harasa. She found me and made the rebels help me escape."

"Whoa, escape what?" Obi asked.

"I was on trial for rebel activity in Kelab."

Obi shook his head, trying to wrap his mind around the influx of information. "Then what?"

"There was an ambush. The Guard arrested Sayzia." Yonah looked at Thari. "And Naris told me yesterday that she's been taken to the government camp."

Thari's eyes widened, fear crossing his features.

"That's where you're going?" Obi asked. "To the labour camp?"

"We're going to rescue Sayzia," Thari replied, his voice firm.

Obi said to the man, "And who are you?"

"Thari's from Jalid. He helped with the abolition, and he followed Sayzia to Harasa. He and Sayzia are…" She didn't know what to call them.

"I'm in love with your sister."

Obi's mouth hung agape for a moment as his eyes shifted between

Thari and Yonah. He turned to Yonah. "So, you're running from your master and all the Guards in Harasa?"

"Yes."

He turned to Thari. "Who are you wanted by?"

"Fortunately, nobody around here knows who I am, so nobody."

Obi looked at Yonah again. "And you want to go to the government labour camp to rescue Sayzia. How do you plan on doing that?"

Yonah felt stupid as she said it. "Right now, there is no plan."

"Wow." The disbelief on Obi's face made Yonah want to disappear. "This is a really bad idea."

"It was either this or sit around doing nothing," Yonah explained.

"This is nothing!" Obi snapped. "You have no plan. You have no idea what the labour camp is like. I've seen it, and it is a fortress."

"You've seen it?" Yonah asked with a gasp. "You can help us get in!"

"No, that is the point. I can't get you in because nobody, especially wanted fugitives, gets in!"

"Please, Obi, just tell me everything you know about it!"

"I'm not even supposed to be talking to you right now," Obi said, "let alone helping you scheme."

"Is the camp at a port? Are we stopping there?"

"The ship will be stopping at our planned destination, which is past the labour camp, where Captain Pirung will hand you two over to the Guard."

"You can't let that happen!" Yonah said.

Obi glared at Yonah. "I was never going to!" He lowered his voice to a whisper. "I'll put you two on a rowboat at night and send you to shore."

"Why don't you come with us?" Yonah asked. "Your master will be furious with you for helping us escape."

Obi shook his head. "I'll be fine."

"Help us rescue Sayzia."

Obi's eyes held onto Yonah's. "I don't think you should try that. You should run and hide. I'll try to get you out of here tomorrow night."

"What time is it now?" Being stuck in the darkness of the lowest deck of the ship had hidden Yonah and Thari from daylight and their way of keeping time.

"Dinner time." Obi started to leave.

Yonah called out. "Obi." He stopped at the bottom of the stairs. "Please come with us."

Obi stared at Yonah for a moment, and she saw her baby brother. She saw the little boy who stared wide-eyed with fear as the Guard destroyed their lives. She saw the child who hid his fire so its blaze would not give him away to those that wanted to put it out.

He silently turned and went up the stairs.

Yonah stood at the grate, looking at the stairwell for a long time. Thari sat on the wooden bench behind her and sighed.

"He's not like you and Sayzia," he finally said.

Yonah whipped around to look at Thari. "What do you mean?"

"He lacks your courage."

Yonah shook her head. Her lips pulled down into a frown. "You don't know anything."

Thari shrugged. "Maybe I don't. Do you know if he'll be able to get us out of here?"

"I believe in him."

"Because, if he can't," Thari said, folding his arms over his chest and closing his eyes, "you and I are going to the slave market."

YONAH DIDN'T KNOW how long they waited in their cell. Someone brought food to them not long after Obi left. More food was brought later on, and one more meal after that. But the brig remained dark and damp just the same as when they arrived there.

A door opened, and then came the sounds of soft footsteps from someone trying not to be heard. Yonah gently shook Thari awake.

Whoever was coming down the stairs came without a lantern, and it wasn't until they stood right in front of their cell that Yonah could confirm that it was Obi.

Obi pulled a ring of keys from his pocket and started fumbling with them. Knowing that it was nighttime made the sound of their jangling seem monstrous. He finally tried one in the lock, and the door unlatched.

Yonah and Thari stepped out of the cell and followed Obi up the stairs, past the sleeping forms of his shipmates, and up more stairs to the upper deck. Yonah shivered at the chilly ocean air, although her lungs greedily expanded as they gobbled it down.

"Shouldn't there be other shipmates up here?" asked Thari.

"I paid them off," Obi replied. "They won't be back for an hour."

Yonah asked, "How did you get the keys?"

Obi shook his head. "Never mind." He led them to the edge of the ship and pointed over the railing. "There's your way out."

A rowboat bobbed in the ocean next to the ship. A rope ladder tied to the ship railing was the only way down to it.

"And there's the labour camp." Obi didn't sound very enthused as he said it, but he pointed towards shore, where there stood a massive stone building perched on a cliff face, all angles and hard edges. Its looming presence made Yonah's mouth drop open.

Yonah grabbed her brother's arm. "Obi, are you sure you won't come with us? You'll be in so much trouble with your master."

Obi's face was hard. He was decided. "You're worth it."

"Is Sayzia not worth it, too?" Thari cut in.

Yonah sent a glare in his direction, then placed her hands on Obi's shoulders. "It's hard to make tough decisions. All we can do is our best. Thank you so much for helping us." She squeezed her little brother into a tight hug, her chin just reaching his shoulder.

"I'm sorry, Yonah."

Yonah pulled away, shaking her head but unable to speak. She went to the railing and waited as Thari descended the rope ladder first.

"Will I see you again?" Obi asked. "You'll be able to come back to Basee or Kirash, right?"

"I hope so." But she wasn't safe in Basee or Kirash anymore. She hadn't thought about those places being her only connection to Obi. "I don't know."

Obi's face crumbled, and Yonah's heart broke into a thousand pieces.

"I thought I lost you before," Yonah said. "But we found each other. We can do it again."

"Can the same miracle happen twice?" Obi asked dejectedly.

Yonah shook her head. "It wasn't a miracle. We made it happen." She hugged Obi once more.

"Good luck, Yonah," he said.

"Thanks, Little Bear."

Obi chuckled dryly at the old nickname.

Yonah wobbled down the ladder and joined Thari in the rowboat. She sat across from him and took an oar. Obi pulled the rope ladder back up to the ship, and Yonah and Thari started paddling to shore.

As they worked, Yonah let silent tears fall down her cheeks. Something about this goodbye felt very final. She didn't know if she would find Obi again. As long as she was wanted by the Guard, she couldn't move freely within Harasa, and she couldn't visit her brother at the local pubs.

She had to save Sayzia.

Chapter Thirty-Three

A wave of nausea crashed over Yonah. She pinched her eyes shut, and her throat bubbled wide.

"I think I'm going to be sick," she groaned.

"You can't swim, and you get seasickness," Thari muttered. "We're almost there. Here." Thari took the second oar from Yonah and got to work while Yonah doubled over, cradling her head in her hands.

"How are we going to get inside?" Yonah moaned, keeping her head down. She hoped that focusing on creating a plan would distract her from her nausea.

For a moment, there was nothing but the sound of the ocean waves lapping against the rowboat. Then Thari said, "I think we have to climb up."

Yonah's head zipped upright to stare at the cliff face. It wasn't perfectly vertical, but there was not a single fibre of her being that wanted to attempt that steep climb.

"No," she said. "There has to be another way."

"They put it here because there is no other way," Thari said. "They only have to guard it from one direction."

Yonah returned her head to her hands. "Alright."

"Are you going to make it?" There was sarcasm in Thari's voice. All Yonah's energy was being put towards not vomiting into the ocean.

A few minutes later, Thari said, "It's time."

Yonah looked up and saw that they were against the cliff. The rocks at the bottom were wet from the waves and dried just a few feet up. While there were plenty of crevices and ledges that could be used as hand and footholds, the fact was that they would either be crawling or truly climbing up a cliff face with the risk of plummeting into the ocean if they fell.

"I can't do it," Yonah said, shaking her head. "What if I fall?" She might drown tonight.

"Don't think like that. I'll go first. You go where I go, alright?"

She clenched Thari's arm. "What if I fall? I can't swim."

"Humans can float, Yonah," he explained. "You just lie on your back and kind of flutter your hands every once in a while. Keep your belly button pointed to the sky."

Humans can float. But why did they sink? Yonah's breath sped up.

"Yonah." Thari took her shoulders in his hands and stared at her. "You're not going to fall. That's not an option. If you fall, Sayzia doesn't get saved."

He was right. They were doing this for her sister. Yonah had to get to her, even if it meant making this impossible, death-flirtatious climb.

"Are you ready?" Thari asked.

Yonah nodded. "Yes."

Thari took hold of the side of the rowboat and stepped over to the bottom of the climb. He pushed off, sending the boat careening a little, and settled both feet on the rocky landing. Yonah paddled close to the cliff again and, as Thari started his ascent, climbed out of the rowboat, too.

The cliff face was both wet and sharp beneath Yonah's hands. Her soft-soled shoes slipped on the bottom-most section. She couldn't find a grip to even begin the climb.

"Step there." Thari was pointing to a dry patch.

Yonah followed his direction and was able to push her weight into the spot, rising two feet higher.

Within a few moments, Yonah's forehead was wet with sweat, and her fingers and arms ached from clinging to the rock. Her hands stung from tiny stones and sand biting into them.

The wind blew harder as they climbed. Yonah's scarf kept covering her face, temporarily blinding her. She kept trying to move it from her face, but eventually, she just pulled it from her shoulders and tossed it to the ocean below.

She thought she was going to vomit again, this time from fear. Already over ten feet below her, the black ocean crashed against the rock as if trying to knock Yonah from her perch. She shut her eyes and pressed herself against the cliff.

"You're fine. You're fine. You're fine. You're fine," she whispered to herself over and over in prayer. "You can't just stay here. You have to move. You can't just stay here. You have to move!"

"Yonah, are you alright down there?"

"Yes." Her wavering voice didn't sound very convincing.

"You're doing great. Keep going."

She whispered to herself, "Just keep going. Just like in the gully. Just like in Kelab."

She had scaled buildings and jumped over rooftops before with the threat of falling to her death. This was no different.

Yonah pressed onward, following Thari's path. With her scarf gone, she could see clearly where she placed her hands and feet. They were making good progress. She looked forward to not feeling the stinging sensation in her hands anymore and to resting her tired limbs, but they were doing it.

She was at a point on the cliff face where she was able to move at an inclined crawl rather than a vertical climb. She placed one foot, then one hand, the other foot, the other hand, her first foot–

Her foot slipped, and her chest tipped forward until she smashed her chin on the rock below her. At the same time, Yonah let out a shriek that was quickly cut off by the pain in her chin. She didn't lose any ground, however, and remained on the cliff.

"Yonah!" Thari called out. "Are you alright?"

Yonah blinked away the tears stinging her eyes. "Just slipped. I'm fine."

"We're almost there. There's a window we can go through."

Now was not the time to get frustrated or lose focus. Ignoring the pain in her chin, Yonah found a new spot for her foot and continued her upwards crawl. Soon enough, the cliff started to level out a bit, although Yonah still stayed low. She kept her eyes on the ground and just kept climbing.

She felt a hand on her shoulder, and she looked up. Thari was standing on his two feet, smiling down at her. "You made it."

Yonah realized they were at the top of the cliff. One misstep would send a person careening into the ocean, but they could stand upright.

There was a wide window cut out of the stone of the fortress, void of light, that sat six feet above where Yonah and Thari stood.

"You climb onto my shoulders," Yonah said, "then you pull me up."

"You can take my weight?"

"In my legs, yes. I won't be able to pull you up, though."

Yonah bent over from her hips, knees slightly bent, and placed her hands on the wall for support.

"You're sure about this?" Thari asked.

"Just get on my back to start with, and we'll go from there, alright?"

She felt Thari's foot on her back, but none of his body weight. He hesitated.

"I'm going on three," Thari said. "Ready?"

"Yes."

"One…two…" He trailed off.

"Thari, I handled my fear of drowning to death just now," Yonah snapped. "I need you to figure this out, so we can go get my sister."

"Fine! Three!"

His weight came pressing down on Yonah's back and the muscles in her legs, already weary from their cliff climb, tensed and shook but held. The weight shifted a little as Thari brought his other foot onto Yonah's back.

"How are you doing?" he asked.

"I'm good," she said. Her hands pressing into the wall were helping, too. "I'm going to stand up, and you just walk to my shoulders."

"Well, let me know if I'm hurting you."

"Shut up, Thari, and just get ready. Here I go."

Keeping her hands pressed into the wall, Yonah took small, laboured steps forwards, slowly bringing her body upright as she did so. She felt Thari adjusting his foot placement on her body as she went. Finally, she was upright, and Thari was standing on her shoulders. She looked up and saw he was using the wall for support, too.

"We did it!" Yonah gasped, a smile broadening her mouth.

Thari, now level with the cut-out window, crawled inside. He disappeared for a moment, then emerged headfirst, reaching down for Yonah.

"You're going to be able to lift me?" she asked.

"I trusted you. Now you trust me."

Yonah sprang into the air and grabbed hold of Thari's wrists. He grunted as her weight fell downwards out of her jump. Her body crashed against the wall, but she held on.

"Use your feet on the wall," Thari said, his voice husky from exertion.

Yonah's feet scrambled against the wall, trying to find purchase. She pressed her toes into the stone at the same time as she and Thari pulled against each other. She walked her feet up the wall until she was nearly folded in half, perched in front of Thari and the cut out.

"Let go of this hand," Thari instructed, wiggling his fingers, "and take my arm. One, two, three."

For a moment, Yonah thought she was going to fall backwards to the ground and topple down the cliff, but her hand found Thari's arm, and his hand found hers, and she was a few inches closer to finding safety inside the window.

"Other hand," Thari said. They released and found each other again. "I'm gonna grab your back."

Thari released one of Yonah's arms, took a fistful of her shirt into his hand, and pulled her the rest of the way into the window. Because the walls of the fortress were so thick, there was enough space for the two of them to sit comfortably in the window cut-out. They sat for a while, gasping for breath.

Yonah peered out the window to the steep cliff and the raging ocean. She exhaled in disbelief at their feat. She looked to Thari, who also met her eyes. Although they didn't say anything out loud, something unspoken passed between them that acknowledged that they were proud of themselves and of each other.

Chapter Thirty-Four

"If only that was the hard part," Thari finally said as he and Yonah gazed down at the ocean raging against the cliff face.

"At least nobody's guarding this part of the fortress."

"Yeah, well, what idiot would think to climb up that cliff to get in?"

Yonah turned her mind to the task at hand. "It's nighttime. The prisoners are probably in their cells. They're not likely to make them work through the night, right?"

"Right."

"Naris told me they brought Sayzia here for questioning."

"For torture."

The word sent a shiver through Yonah.

Thari said, "That could be in a special spot, but even if that's the case, they could still return her to her cell every night."

"So, we don't know where she is and we don't know how to get her out," said Yonah. Obi was right. This was a terrible idea.

"We have an advantage," Thari said. "They don't know we're here. And we can keep it that way for a long time."

Yonah frowned. "What do you mean?"

"I suggest we see how large this unwatched area is and see if we can't make this our base for now. Then we can do some reconnaissance for as long as it takes for us to get Sayzia out."

"Are you suggesting," Yonah said, shock and dread rolling through her, "that we spend, what, *days* in here?"

"Maybe it's one day, maybe it's a few. But as long as we stay unnoticed, which I think is possible, given we've been sitting here having this conversation without getting caught, we can gather whatever information and supplies we need to perform our rescue mission."

Yonah's mouth hung open as she imagined living in the fortress for the next few days. "What are we going to eat? Where are we going to sleep?"

"Yonah." Thari leaned close to her. "We currently don't have a plan. My plan is to give ourselves a chance to make a plan that will actually get all three of us out of here in one piece. Now, why don't we just figure out how big this unguarded area is, alright?"

As much as she wished she could come up with a better idea, Yonah realized that Thari's idea to take the slow route truly was the best course of action.

"Alright," she said. "But let's stay together." She turned over from a seated position onto her hands and knees and another wave of nausea sent her head spinning. She groaned and touched her forehead to the ground.

"What?" asked Thari.

"I feel sick again," Yonah groaned.

"Really not a good time."

"Oh, excuse me, I'll just make it stop," she said, making no effort to hide the disdain in her voice.

For a moment, all Yonah could do was squeeze her eyes shut, trying to will the nausea to disappear. The bile in her throat eased, and her roving stomach stilled, although she didn't feel entirely healthy.

"Let's go," she finally said, pulling her head from the floor and crawling from the window well towards the dark hallway.

Yonah and Thari set off in one direction, tiptoeing down the empty hall. Their feet tapped lightly on the stonework that comprised the entire building. Each time they passed a window, Yonah caught another glimpse of the ocean. They peered around the corner and found another empty hallway, not as long as the last one, which ended in a staircase that went up a level on one side, and down a level on the other. There was a door at the upper level. Yonah couldn't see the bottom of the lower stairs.

"My guess is the prisoners are down," whispered Yonah.

"Then we go up?" Thari replied.

Every inch of Yonah longed to race down the stairs and find her sister. She frowned. "For the sake of reconnaissance, we'll go up."

Up the stairs and through the unlocked door took them to an armoury. A row of rifles lined one wall, swords and daggers hung on another wall, and there was a shelf lined with pistols.

Thari grinned. "What do you think? Take some now or later?"

"Later. Definitely. If we're planning on being here a while, we can't start taking weaponry and expect it not to get noticed."

Yonah was about to open the door at the side of the room when she heard a loud snore through it. She held her hand up to Thari to tell him to stop and pressed her ear to the door.

"Someone's sleeping in there," she said.

Thari pressed his ear to the door as well, turning his face away from Yonah's.

"Guards' quarters?" he asked.

"That makes sense." Yonah stood upright. "It wouldn't make sense to put the prisoners next to the armoury."

"What about this door?" Thari started for the third door in the room, which lay across from the door they had entered through.

"I think this might be as far as we should go," Yonah said.

"Everyone's sleeping, except for whoever's on watch," Thari replied. "And they're not going to be posted near the guards' quarters, are they?"

All Yonah could do was sigh in reply. She watched anxiously as Thari first listened at the third door, then reached for the handle.

It wouldn't open.

"What could be through there?" Thari muttered so quietly it was as if he was talking to himself.

"Let's go back," Yonah said.

"We'll check out the lower level."

Despite her trembling insides, Yonah followed Thari back out the door to the stairwell and down to the lower level. There was a door at the bottom of the stairs, but if one took a hairpin turn, there was a short hallway underneath the stairwell. It was down this hallway that Thari and Yonah went to yet another door. It, too, was locked.

An overpowering smell of smoke and heat filled Yonah's nose. "What is that?" She knew she had smelled that scent somewhere before, a long time ago, but she couldn't quite place it.

Thari paused to sniff. "That's a forge. I'm surprised we couldn't smell it upstairs."

"Let's get away," Yonah suggested. She didn't particularly like the smell.

They tried the door at the bottom of the stairs and, upon carefully opening it, saw a multi-storey hallway illuminated with lanterns hanging from the ceiling. Cells lined either side of the hallway, and Yonah could hear the sounds of their inhabitants sleeping. Sayzia was in here somewhere.

A light bobbed at the far end of the hallway, and a red-sashed Guard rounded the corner. Heart pounding, Yonah pulled Thari back into the stairwell.

"Do you think they saw us?" she asked, breathlessly.

"I don't know. Let's go in case they check."

They went back up the stairs, down their unpatrolled hallway, and down the other direction, listening for someone in pursuit. There was nothing but the sound of their own soft footsteps.

There was another split stairway on the other side of the fortress. A listen at the door at the top of the upper stairs confirmed that was where the guards' quarters lay, so Yonah and Thari went downstairs.

There were no doorways at the bottom of this stairwell, only a mess hall. It was immaculately tidy.

"Perfect!" Thari said in an excited whisper. Even Yonah felt her heart lighten at the notion of having found the spot that would sustain them for the next few days, despite her queasy stomach.

"Let's see what we can find." Thari started searching through cupboards and jars.

"Just take a little of everything," Yonah instructed, "so they won't notice."

They took just one piece of flatbread from a covered dish, a few crackers, and a small handful of berries.

"There must be a storeroom around here," Thari muttered.

Yonah scanned the room and pointed to an archway. "I bet that's a kitchen."

As Thari went through the archway, Yonah's eyes landed on another door across the hall. She walked towards it and unlocked the handle. A gust of chilly ocean air brushed Yonah's face as she opened the door.

A small courtyard lay outside the mess hall, landscaped with rocks, pebble paths, desert bushes, and a stagnant fountain.

"Thari," Yonah said, leaning back into the mess hall. She noticed a set of playing cards lying on a nearby table, clearly left mid-game, and two half-drunk cups. The setting made Yonah freeze. She once again scanned the room with just her eyes.

"Thari?" she said again.

"Found the storeroom," Thari replied, appearing in the archway.

Yonah pointed at the cards and cups. "We have to go."

When Thari saw what Yonah pointed to, he nodded. They hastily started for the stairs. The sound of a door opening and closing above them made them stop.

"Hide!" Thari whispered.

Yonah slid under the nearest table with Thari right behind her. Yonah stilled herself and watched as a Guard came down the stairs. She walked past the table where Yonah and Thari hid towards the back of the hall.

Horror weighted Yonah's chest as she realized she had neglected to relock the door to the courtyard. She silently pleaded the Guard wouldn't notice.

The Guard downed whatever was in one of the cups at the back of the hall and took it to the kitchen.

A rough tug on her arm told Yonah to follow Thari from under the table and up the stairs as quickly and quietly as possible. She didn't dare to breathe as she ran upwards. Once back in the upstairs hallway, however, she exhaled in relief.

"I didn't lock the door," she gasped.

"What?"

"The door. To the courtyard," Yonah explained. "That's why there's a Guard there, keeping watch. I forgot to lock it."

"There's a courtyard? Wait." Thari shook his head. "We should hide. I think I saw something just back there." He pointed to the corner of the hall and led the way there. In the corner, a wall spanned from the ceiling to a foot off the floor, about a metre wide.

Thari went down to the floor and crawled on his belly through the hole. "Ha! This is perfect!"

"What is it?" asked Yonah, checking over her shoulder towards the stairs that led down to the mess hall before crouching down and peeking inside.

"I'm not sure, but there's even a couple beds."

Her curiosity piqued, and Yonah slid beneath the wall into the hidden room nestled in the corner of the fortress. It was triangular in shape. On one side, there were two wide wooden planks built into the wall–the 'beds' Thari referred to. There was a small slit of a window on the other side, just wide enough for a small person to slide through.

"How's this for a place to stay?" Thari said proudly.

"Do you think they check this regularly?"

"Besides the mess hall, this whole side of the fortress is unpatrolled. I think we'll be fine here. Now, tell me about this courtyard."

Thari plunked himself onto the lower of the two beds, and Yonah sat next to him. As they ate their morsels—Thari hadn't had the chance to take anything from the storeroom before the Guard arrived—Yonah described the courtyard.

"Maybe we could escape that way," Yonah said. "Then we wouldn't have to go through the prison. And we know there's only one, maybe two Guards there at night."

Thari nodded and pursed his lips in thought. "We distract the Guard and walk out that door and go where? Was there a way out of the courtyard?"

Yonah thought back to the courtyard. "There are windows. Like this one."

Thari stood up and walked to the window. "I could maybe just fit through."

'Maybe' didn't seem too promising to Yonah.

She fought off another wave of nausea.

"So," Thari continued, "we know where they keep the prisoners, we know where the Guards stay, we know where to get weapons, and we might know a way out of the fortress. What we don't know is what cell Sayzia is in and how to get her out."

"And if there's a better way out of the fortress that we know you could fit through," Yonah added, her nausea having subsided.

"The way out might be through the prison," Thari said with a disgruntled sigh.

"Or through the locked door upstairs."

The pair of them sat in silence as they mulled over their predicament.

"Maybe," Yonah said slowly, hesitant to say the words out loud, "we need to wait until daylight to do a search of the prison? To get a better idea of how to get out of here?"

For the first time since their arrival, Thari looked a little shaken at doing something so risky. "You might be right. We don't know enough about this place."

"And then we need to figure out where Sayzia is. We could figure out where the Sayzia goes during the day. It might be easier to break her out from her labour position than from her cell."

Thari nodded, his eyes lighting up. "Almost definitely easier. We'd better get some sleep, then. Morning will be here, soon. I can take the first watch."

Yonah climbed onto the upper bunk to take her turn sleeping. Before she could let herself drift into unconsciousness, however, she said quietly to Thari, "If we're breaking Sayzia out from her labour position, maybe we could help some of the other slaves, too."

Thari didn't answer for a while. Yonah thought he would perhaps just ignore her until he finally said, "Let's figure out one thing at a time."

It wasn't a complete dismissal, so Yonah let it be. Tomorrow would bring them more knowledge and a better idea of what was possible.

Chapter Thirty-Five

Although the wooden planks that served as their beds were far from comfortable, exhaustion quickly carried Yonah off to sleep until Thari woke her up to take a turn at watch. She winced as she shifted, her bones feeling bruised where they contacted the plank.

Yonah alternated between listening for sounds outside from the bottom bunk and lying on the floor so she could peek under the wall. She suffered one more bout of nausea that had her stifling the sound of her retching before daylight started to creep into their hidden room.

She was resting with her back against the wall when she heard a door open. Yonah lay down on her stomach and saw a group of four men and women dressed in the black and red attire of the Guard amble down the stairs at the other end of the hallway, talking and laughing with each other as they went. It was time for their morning meal.

Yonah stayed on the floor with her eyes on the guards' quarters. She watched as dozens of Guards filed down the stairs to the mess hall, which was steadily growing louder. She stood back up and shook Thari awake.

"The Guards are waking up," she whispered. Thari groaned in protest, still half asleep. "Wake up! They'll be taking the prisoners soon."

"Alright," Thari moaned. "I'm waking up."

Yonah lied down on the floor again to watch the stairwell. There wasn't any more movement there.

She felt movement next to her as Thari lay down and shuffled in close to her on the floor, also peeking through the cut-out in the wall. "What are they doing?"

"They went downstairs for breakfast. I think all of them. Or at least most of them."

They watched in silence, listening to the noise from the mess hall. After several minutes, some of them started to come back up the stairs. Some returned to the guards' quarters, while others went down the hallway towards Yonah and Thari. The two of them pressed their bodies sideways against the wall in the hopes of staying out of eyesight.

One of the Guards said, "Do they think we don't know about the kissing corner? I'll shove them in there myself if it means I don't have to watch anymore!"

There was laughter as the group turned the corner. Yonah caught Thari's eye, motioned to their hiding spot, and mouthed, "Here?"

Thari, wearing a frown on his face, gave a slow nod. They wouldn't be able to stay in their hiding spot for long.

After the Guards left the mess hall, the hallway was quiet for a few minutes. Yonah was feeling antsy to leave when she heard a door from afar, then footsteps, then another door.

"That must be the night guards," Thari said, "going to sleep for the day."

"That doesn't leave a lot of time to explore the guards' quarters," Yonah muttered.

"Just during mealtime."

"Well, let's see if we can find out where the prisoners work. And we need to find a different spot to hide if this is the 'kissing corner.'"

"Agreed."

Yonah and Thari had just reached the top of the stairs that led down to the prison when the door at the bottom opened. They threw themselves to the hallway walls and froze as a Guard stepped through, followed by a line of prisoners, all looking dishevelled, overtired, and wearing slave collars. The line walked beneath the stairs, and Yonah heard the tell-tale jangling of keys on a ring and the door to the forge opening.

As each slave walked through the door, Yonah searched their faces for Sayzia.

Once the last slaves and Guards were through the door beneath the stairs, Yonah turned to Thari and said, "I didn't see Sayzia there!"

"That was, what, two dozen prisoners? There must be another spot for the others."

They crept down the stairs and gingerly opened the door to the prison. Sun beams shone in through cells, casting the space in a brighter light. It was void of all life.

Yonah and Thari shared an uneasy glance, then stepped into the prison and closed the door behind them.

Their pace was painfully slow at first. Then, as they realized that they were really alone in the prison, their steps grew more relaxed. They turned corners and peered through doorways, found closets and interrogation rooms. Yonah mapped everything out in her mind as they went.

They realized that there were three entryways to the prison room: the door through which they entered, a door upstairs, and a door at the front of the fortress.

"They must have gone outside," Thari said.

"Yes, but to where? That isn't farmland." Yonah motioned to the desert outside.

"Care to take a look?"

"Not right now. The entrance to this place will be guarded. We need another way out."

"Or a disguise."

Yonah's eyes lit up. "If the changing of the guard works the same way as it did this morning, there should be a period in the evening when the guards' quarters are empty. Meaning, if we took uniforms in the morning–"

"We could return them in the evening, unnoticed," Thari finished. "If we needed to."

"Exactly!"

"We'll watch this evening. In the meantime, why don't we see if we can't scrounge up any more food and maybe a dagger or two?"

Yonah could feel her face twisting into one of unease. Thari said, "Nobody will notice a missing dagger! And it will be nice to be armed in case something happens."

"Like someone visiting the kissing corner?" Yonah asked dryly.

"Let's hope that doesn't happen too often."

They were able to take some more fruit and bread from the storeroom in the mess hall, and they each took a dagger from the weapons room. The third door in the weapons room was still locked, keeping what lay behind it a mystery.

For the rest of the day, they remained in the hidden room, listening for any sounds of doors opening or footsteps coming their way. As the sun began to set, they heard a far-away door and a low rumble of noise that signaled the end of the prisoners' day of labour and their return to their prison cells. Soon after that, the night shift Guards emerged from the guards' quarters, went to the mess hall, then returned to the prison, after which the majority of the Guards went to the mess hall for their evening meal.

"That's the empty guards' quarters," Thari whispered. Several minutes later, some of the Guards started to file back to their sleeping quarters, although many more remained in the mess hall for what Yonah assumed was their free time.

"And no one's raised an alarm over any missing weapons," Yonah said.

"I told you no one would miss them."

"So, during their breakfast tomorrow, we'll sneak into their quarters for extra uniforms, follow them outside, see if we can find Sayzia, then return the uniforms before they come back in the evening and make our plan for finally getting out of here."

"Yeah, I guess that's it," Thari replied with a nod and an exhale.

"So much could go wrong," Yonah muttered.

"Everything could go wrong. But we can't let that stop us."

Yonah sat on the lower of the two beds. "At least, if you had stayed in Kirash, you would have been safe and helping with the rebellion."

"I wanted to come with you," Thari said, shaking his head. "I wanted to help Sayzia."

"I appreciate you coming with me. I wouldn't have gotten this far without you."

Thari shrugged. "I guess we make a good team, after all."

Yonah gave Thari a closed-lipped smile, then looked out the sliver window to the ocean.

"So, what happened between you and Master Naris?" Thari asked. "I mean, I know you were married and got caught helping escapees, but…" He paused, looking at Yonah's wide eyes. "It's just not as simple as that, is it?"

It was such a big question. Yonah's life with Naris seemed so distant now, but the memories of it, the emotional torment, the risk, all of it still haunted her.

"You're right. It's not as simple as it should have been."

Thari waited patiently for her to continue. Yonah wasn't entirely sure she wanted to add more, however. She had never admitted any of her feelings aloud before. She barely admitted them to herself.

"I don't know if it was because he was the first man to show any interest in me, or if it was because we were both so lonely, or what, but…" Yonah hesitated. Thari already knew. That was why he asked. She pressed through the clenched sensation in her chest as she said, "Part of me came to love Naris." She kept her eyes averted, away from her listener. "I didn't want to. I knew nothing could come of it. We were so different. And so similar. He wanted to build a family. I missed mine."

"Were you hoping to see him when you went back to his estate?"

"Honestly, no. I was hoping to put him in the past forever. But he unexpectedly arrived home."

As Yonah recalled striking him with the rock and watching his body fall to the ground, she cringed. She did not know she was capable of violence. She did not know she was capable of hurting him like that.

"Some days, I wished I could be rid of him forever," she said. "And some days, I was glad he was there. I was worried for him when he was under arrest." She looked at Thari. "Isn't that terrible?"

Concern softened Thari's eyes. "It's not terrible. Love can feel uncontrollable."

"I don't know if this is love," Yonah muttered. "It feels too confusing for that."

"Do you hope to see him again?"

Yonah shook her head. "Absolutely not. It's best if I never see him again."

Whenever she saw Naris, Yonah was never quite sure which version of him she might meet and, therefore, which version of herself would emerge. She never knew if she would feel longing or fear.

"Well, then I hope you don't," Thari said. "For your sake."

A relaxed silence filled the room. Glad to have finally faced some of her feelings but ready to move on from the uncomfortable conversation, Yonah said, "I'll take the first watch."

Thari lay down on the lower bed while Yonah settled in for another long night.

She asked, "How did you know you were in love with my sister?"

He spoke without hesitation. "When I realized my old life didn't matter if she couldn't be part of it."

Chapter Thirty-Six

The following morning, Thari shook Yonah awake, and she heard faraway voices. She sat up, and nausea sent her lying back down, pinching her eyes shut, willing the feeling away.

"Yonah," Thari hissed.

"Mhm." She slowly sat up and climbed from the wooden bed.

"It's almost time." Thari was lying on the floor, peeking through the hole.

Yonah leaned against the wall and waited for Thari's signal. He eventually said, "Let's go," and started to crawl into the hallway. Yonah followed, her heart pounding and her skin clammy.

They moved swiftly down the hall to the split stairs, and went up and through the unlocked door to the guards' quarters.

It was empty, just as they had hoped. Rows of bunk beds lined the massive room, all the blankets laid out wrinkle-free over their pallets.

"Where would they keep extra uniforms?" asked Thari.

Yonah strode to a deep wardrobe to the side and opened the double doors wide. "Here." There were shelves lined with immaculately folded piles of black shirts, pants, and red sashes.

Yonah handed a uniform to Thari, who started to dress next to her. She took one for herself and stepped to the other side of the open wardrobe door to change.

The door handle jiggled, sending Yonah and Thari's heads swiveling to the entrance. The door opened a crack, and a voice said in a joking tone, "You tell her not to touch my food, or there'll be trouble!"

Only semi-dressed, Yonah grabbed Thari's wrist and pulled him into the wardrobe with her, pulling the doors nearly shut behind them. Through the crack between the wardrobe doors, Yonah watched a Guard enter the room and walk past. She could hear the Guard rummaging elsewhere in the room, then swift footsteps back in their direction.

When the Guard paused in front of the wardrobe, Yonah's insides began to tremble. Her breathing stopped. The Guard stepped towards the wardrobe and pressed the doors all the way shut, submerging Yonah and Thari into complete darkness. Although Yonah's mouth dropped open, she didn't let herself make a sound.

Only the muffled sound of the guards' quarters door closing, and the moment of silence afterwards told Yonah she could breathe again. Then she realized she was only partially dressed and in close proximity to a man and hastily stepped out of the wardrobe, desperate to get into uniform.

"That was close," Thari said.

"Yes, well, it's not built for two adults to hang around in," Yonah grumbled, keeping her eyes pointed downwards.

Thari snorted with laughter. Yonah looked up at him, finally dressed.

"I meant the Guard almost catching us," he said with a smirk.

Yonah tried to find something to say that would make her feel less stupid but gave up. "Let's just go."

They left the guards' quarters and headed past the mess hall stairs to return to their corner room. From there, they watched the Guards leave the mess hall for the prison, then the night shift as they returned to the guards' quarters. Without a word, Yonah and Thari crawled back into the hallway, armed with their stolen daggers, waited at the top of the stairs for the prisoners to be taken to the room beneath the stairs, and went through the prison to the front door.

Once at the door, they paused.

"They'll wonder why we're late," Yonah said.

"I'll do all the talking. You just keep your head down, so they don't recognize you. We're just late. It happens."

Yonah nodded, hoping that nobody would try to speak to them.

They opened the door and found themselves in an entrance hall. A large door lay across the room from them, which Yonah guessed led to the outside. Stone steps zigzagged up to a second storey door. One Guard was posted at a desk, rummaging through paperwork. He glanced up at Yonah and Thari.

"Better hurry up, you two."

"Yes, sir," Thari replied as he and Yonah walked briskly across the room, pushed the massive door open, and stepped out into the daylight.

Desert lay before them. Empty desert. The only sign of human activity was the road leading from the fortress into the wilderness.

"Are we sure they're out here?" Yonah asked.

"Where else could they have gone?"

"Maybe that locked room above the prison."

Thari shook his head. "They're out here somewhere."

"Doing what? This isn't farmland. Not likely to be good hunting, either."

Thari took Yonah's arm and started walking down the road. As they moved further away from the shelter of the fortress, Yonah turned and looked up at the menacing building.

"Look!" Thari pointed. There was a footpath veering off the road, down which Yonah could see a group of prisoners and Guards walking.

"They're going to see us," Yonah said.

"Yes, they might," Thari replied. They picked up their pace as they started down the path.

A few moments later, Yonah realized what labour these prisoners performed. On a rocky hillside, there was a wooden-framed doorway. The prisoners all carried lanterns and picks.

"They're mining," said Yonah.

"For what?"

Yonah shook her head, unable to provide an answer.

The prisoners filed into the mine, a handful of Guards standing on either side of the entrance. One of them saw Yonah and Thari coming towards them and said, "Slept in, did you?"

Yonah kept her head down as Thari said, "Yes, sorry we're late."

"Just get in there and mind the slaves."

As they followed the last of the prisoners into the mine, Yonah heard a couple of the Guards talking in low voices.

"Are they new?"

"I didn't know we had new recruits."

Yonah started to tremble as she realized that she and Thari were now completely surrounded by Guards, growing further away from escape the deeper into the mine they went.

"Wait!"

Yonah froze. She had been recognized. They had failed. They would be locked up with Sayzia until they died.

"You need a lantern."

Thari swiftly turned back and retrieved a lantern from the outstretched arm of one of the guards. "Wasn't thinking," he muttered, then rejoined Yonah, who felt like she couldn't breathe.

They didn't speak, even as the outside light dimmed to the darkness of the mine. Yonah peered into the face of every prisoner she could, though the darkness made it very difficult to discern any facial features.

The prisoners kept their heads down as Yonah and Thari passed them, some visibly cowering. Their hunched bodies and raised shoulders made Yonah feel a different kind of sickness.

A thud and a crash made Yonah turn her head sharply towards a Guard standing over a prisoner lying on the ground.

"No time to rest, slave!" the Guard snickered, and he used his booted foot to shove the prisoner's shoulder.

Yonah looked around and caught another Guard shaking his head towards the one who had knocked down the prisoner. "Stop harassing them."

The Guard glared at his peer and said with a snarl, "I can do whatever I want."

The two Guards stared at each other for a moment before the second walked away with another shake of his head. The first Guard turned his eyes to Yonah and Thari. "What are you looking at?"

They quickly averted their eyes and walked away, not wanting to draw any unnecessary attention to themselves. Yonah was grateful that the mines were so dark that her scar wasn't so visible on her face.

Many minutes of searching later, Yonah and Thari were no closer to finding Sayzia.

"We need to do something," Yonah said quietly.

"We could pretend we were sent to retrieve her," Thari suggested.

"It's a little late for that. We would have just stayed outside the mine if that was the case."

After a moment's pause, Thari said, "We could ask the prisoners."

Yonah glanced at the prisoners labouring around them, copper collars around their necks, dirt caked onto their skin, bodies weakened from malnourishment. "I guess we could try."

She stepped next to a small woman who was toiling with her pick. "Have you seen the prisoner named Sayzia?"

The woman stared up at Yonah and shook her head.

"Is she here?"

"I don't know her."

Yonah took a step backwards. "Carry on."

She asked a handful of other slaves, but none could tell her where Sayzia was. Hopelessness prevented her from bothering to ask any more people when someone said to her, "Excuse me?"

Yonah held her lantern up to the prisoner who had spoken. It was Thea. Yonah's mouth dropped open, and she quickly hid her astonishment. Thea did a much better job of masking her own surprise.

"What are you doing here?" Thea asked in a hushed whisper. Her eyes flitted over Yonah's uniform.

"We're looking for Sayzia."

"We?" She looked over Yonah's shoulder and saw Thari, who was walking towards them. "Of course. Neglecting your responsibilities to the cause."

"They wouldn't let Yonah help," Thari said. "But, yes, I deserted."

"Have you seen Sayzia?" Yonah asked, impatient with the way the current conversation was going.

"She's in here somewhere," Thea replied. "We got separated this morning. You've come to break her out? Did you know they've got five of us in here?" Thea's voice was tinged with disgust. "But everything else doesn't matter when it's compared to the love of your life."

Thari shook his head. "You didn't even want to help Sayzia, so why are you upset we didn't think to look for you?"

"Because you're being reckless for one person," Thea hissed. "You're going to get caught, and we're going to get punished for it."

"Why did they send you here?" asked Yonah. "You all should have been bought by masters."

"They didn't even take us to the market. Figured we would stir up more unrest wherever we were sent. Better to keep us in a high-security prison."

"There's not much security out here," Thari argued.

"That's right, Thari, it's a good idea to go running in the middle of a desert without food and water."

"Cowardice is holding you back?"

"No, sensibility. I can't help the cause if I'm dead."

"You can't help the cause if you're in here!"

Yonah wrapped her fingers around Thari's arm to tell him to keep his voice down. He and Thea glared at each other.

"I don't know where Sayzia is," Thea finally said before returning to her work.

Yonah watched her for a moment, wishing she could figure out a way to help everyone.

"It's one thing to sneak one person out of here," Thari whispered as if reading Yonah's mind. "It's an entirely different thing to try to break out five."

"But it's the right thing."

"Not if we get ourselves captured in the process."

Yonah glared at Thari. "We know where the weapons are kept. We know where the prisoners are at night. We have disguises."

Thari blinked in surprise. "You're proposing we arm the entire prison?"

"Tonight."

Chapter Thirty-Seven

They managed to stay undetected throughout the day, even as the group returned to the fortress. They hung back as the Guards headed for the mess hall for their evening meal and stowed away into the hidden corner room as soon as they were alone. A few times, Thari said they should abort the plan, and Yonah would have to re-talk him into it, lending an added air of tension between them.

Between the dinner and sleeping hours, a pair of footsteps came towards Yonah and Thari's end of the hallway. Two voices were giggling together. Yonah and Thari exchanged panicked looks as a hand reached through the opening at the bottom.

"This room is occupied!" Thari said.

The voices immediately stopped.

"Who's in there?"

Thari stood in front of the hole to prevent whoever was on the other side from coming any further in. "I said it's occupied."

"Varu, is that you?"

"Uh…"

"Is it just you in there?" Whoever spoke sounded playful. "Come on, I won't tell anyone."

Thari said, "Just a little privacy, please!"

"Alright, alright." The Guard removed themselves from the crawl space. "No need to snap. You enjoy yourself."

Footsteps marked the departure of the two Guards, and Yonah and Thari each released a sigh of relief.

"That was way too close," Thari said.

"Then it's a good thing we'll be leaving soon."

When they were sure everyone was asleep, they took as much food from the storeroom as they could carry, then went to the weapons room and took whatever could fit undetected into their uniforms—mostly daggers and knives.

They were just about to enter the prison when Thari said, "This all seems rushed."

"We already almost got caught in our hiding spot," Yonah replied. "We've already pressed our luck by staying here a few days."

They opened the door into the gloomy prison and split up, passing food provisions and weaponry to the slaves through the bars of the cells with instructions.

"As soon as they let you out of your cell in the morning, you fight, you run, you help the others, you leave."

"Hey! You!"

Yonah whipped her head away from the slave she had just passed a knife to and looked at the Guard that called to her.

"Stop talking to them!" The Guard walked closer to her, lantern in hand. He frowned at her. "Who are you? I don't recognize you."

Yonah kept her head down as she spoke, hoping to keep her scar out of the light. "I was just moved to the night shift."

"Really. And why are you so chatty tonight?"

"No reason."

"I think you and our other new recruit better come with me."

Yonah's chest tightened. "To where?"

"You just follow me." The Guard shouted towards Thari, who was down the hall. "You, there! Come with me."

Thari pretended not to hear, which sent the Guard into a rage.

"You!" he bellowed. "Do not make me come get you!"

A bell chimed through the walls from another part of the fortress, then another, then another. Someone must have noticed the stolen weapons and alerted the fortress. The Guard's eyes widened. He grabbed Yonah's wrist and pulled her closer to him. At such close proximity, she could do nothing to prevent him from looking into her face.

"You," he said breathily. Then he shouted, "Someone get that man! He's an imposter!"

"Thari, run!" Yonah shouted. She watched as two Guards surrounded Thari. He pulled a pistol and a knife from his uniform and readied himself for a fight.

The prisoners surrounding them started to shout and jeer, creating a cacophony of sounds that bounced off the stonework of the walls and ceiling. A pair of hands from a cell pulled one of the Guards near Thari back into the bars. Another set of hands held a knife to the Guard's neck.

"Stop them!" Yonah's captor shouted. One more Guard joined the fray, but the night shift was severely understaffed.

Yonah heard a door open, and several pairs of footsteps headed their way. Reinforcements were arriving.

"Take her downstairs." The Guard shoved Yonah towards the new arrivals. She looked back towards Thari and saw that a few of the prisoners had escaped and were frantically unlocking other cells.

Two Guards grabbed her and dragged her out of the prison and through the door under the stairs. As the burning smell of the forge knocked into Yonah, she caught a glimpse of it beneath a small archway. She was taken down a set of winding stairs, at the bottom of which were three wooden doors. The Guards opened one of the doors, dragged Yonah inside, sat her in a chair in the centre of the unlit room, and began binding her wrists and ankles to it with leather straps.

Yonah tried to break free of the chair, but she was powerless against the two Guards. They quickly finished binding Yonah to the chair, and she watched them step back into the hall and close and lock the door with a resounding clank.

Chapter Thirty-Eight

For a moment, the room was completely dark, but for the sliver of light coming from beneath the door in front of Yonah.

She could hear shouting from above her, but she ultimately had no idea what was happening. She didn't know if Thari was alright, if any of the prisoners were getting away, if someone had managed to get Sayzia out. Once again, she had failed her family.

Yonah's heart raced as she tried to pull free from her bindings. She fought against the panic that was sending her breathing at a faster and faster pace. The bindings kept her in the chair, and her breathing eventually slowed.

Several minutes later, the noise from the prison was still going, but Yonah's eyes were starting to adjust to the darkness. She could make out the shapes of a table to her right and a few chairs of various sizes scattered around the room. In one corner of the room, the soft light from the crack under the door revealed a few obscure shapes on the wall, but nothing more than that.

The noise from the prison was starting to die down, and Yonah felt the atmosphere of the fortress settle. As the building went quiet, so did Yonah's initial terror. That had faded to a quiver that prevented her from relaxing fully.

She wasn't sure how long she waited in the dark room. Long enough that her stomach started to grumble with hunger, and her nausea returned.

With a clanking noise that was deafening after however many minutes of silence, the door to the room opened and let in the glow of lantern light. A short woman flanked by two Guards walked into the room.

"Oh dear, they've tied you up." The woman said to the Guards, "Unbind her. Search her if you must."

The Guards began by running their hands along Yonah's limbs and torso, removing the blades she had concealed in her uniform as they went. Once satisfied with their search, they unbuckled the leather that bound Yonah's wrists and ankles.

Now that the room was lit, Yonah could tell she was in a torture chamber. Panic returned as she took in the blades of various sizes and shapes that hung on the wall, the tongs and tweezers, the mallets and nails. Yonah didn't want to imagine the kind of harm these tools could inflict.

A horrible thought struck Yonah as she recalled that Naris had told her Sayzia had been brought here for interrogation. She imagined her sister strapped into this very chair.

"You are the fugitive known as Yonah, correct?"

Yonah hadn't noticed the woman's stare. The woman had cropped hair and wily pale brown eyes. Her face was all sharp angles, from her thin jaw to her pointed nose.

Yonah knew there was no point in trying to deny her identity. The scar on her lip prevented that. She nodded in affirmation.

"You must be looking for your sister, Sayzia."

Yonah didn't respond. That was one connection she could try to deny.

"It will please you to hear," the woman continued, "that she was among the prisoners that escaped during tonight's commotion."

If that was true, she had finally done something right for her siblings.

"Speaking of which," the woman placed her hands on the arms of the chair Yonah sat in, bringing her face-to-face with Yonah, "how did you manage that? We know you had an accomplice."

Despite her trembling insides, Yonah remained silent. The interrogator sighed and stood upright.

"You do realize where we are right now," she said, gesturing to the room. "I can make you answer my questions one way or another."

Yonah's eyes shifted to the tools on the wall.

"Who is your accomplice?"

Did he escape, too? Or was he also in an interrogation room?

"Yonah…"

She couldn't risk giving anything away if he was still here.

The woman strolled over to the wall, her hand raised, poised to grab whatever struck her fancy. She moved along the wall as if she were shopping for food and not in pursuit of a torture device.

"Who are you working with?"

She remembered the burning sensation as Naris pressed a knife to her lip and sawed through it.

"He's just a friend," she said.

The woman continued eyeing the tools on the wall. "From a rebel group?"

"It doesn't exist anymore. Most of them were arrested by the Guard."

"Where was this?"

"Why does that matter?"

The woman took a plain knife from the wall and turned around. "I'll be asking the questions, Yonah. Where were your friends arrested?"

"Kirash." Something in Yonah told her to lie, to keep Thari and the others as far from this as possible.

"And what is your accomplice's connection to your sister?"

"Nothing. He was just helping me."

"Oh, Yonah," the woman sighed. She went to one of the lanterns hanging from the wall, opened its small door, and held the knife up to the flame. "I know you're lying."

Yonah shook her head. "I'm not."

"There haven't been any arrests in Kirash this entire season. And either your accomplice knows Sayzia, or you're also here for the rebels who recently arrived from Kelab. I know you were there at the time of a massive arrest." The woman held the now hot knife up. "Would you like to try again?"

Sweat was gathering on Yonah's face. "Yes, those are the rebels I was with, but I didn't know they were here. I just came for my sister." She was speaking very quickly.

"Then your accomplice knows her." The woman stepped close to Yonah and held the knife so close that Yonah could feel its heat. "What is his name?"

If Thari had escaped with Sayzia, giving his name to the authorities would only make it easier to find them again.

Despite her visibly shaking body, Yonah resolutely kept her mouth shut. Her interrogator's eyes went from a cool, inquiring look to fiery annoyance. The woman pressed the flat edge of the knife to Yonah's neck.

With a terrifying hissing sound, searing heat burned at her skin. Yonah couldn't help but emit a closed-lipped whine as she quickly withdrew from the heat, pressing her body deeper into the chair. The hot knife had only been to her skin for a second at most, but the pain of it left her gritting her teeth as she tried not to yelp out loud.

"What is your accomplice's name?"

Tears filled Yonah's eyes. There was no way out of this. She would either hurt Thari and Sayzia's chances at survival or send herself to a painful death.

The interrogator bent over so she could look into Yonah's face. Her brows were furrowed, and her eyes inquisitive. "Do you break so easily?"

Yonah turned hatred-filled eyes up to the woman. She would not break. Love for her sister would stop that.

"Oh, not quite," the interrogator said with a little giddiness in her voice. "Your sister wasn't easy, either. She put up a good long fight." She returned to the open lantern to reheat the knife. "But they always eventually tell me what I need to know, your sister included."

Sayzia knew more about the rebellion than Yonah. She would have provided far more useful information. Yonah couldn't figure out what they wanted from her.

"So, let's try again." The woman brought the reheated knife close to Yonah's neck. Yonah leaned away, but the chair back stopped her from going very far. Every centimetre of her skin was screaming for the heat to go away. "What is your accomplice's name?"

"Leave me alone."

The blistering heat returned. This time, Yonah couldn't help but yell. She tried to pull away again but was trapped in the chair. Her pain and rage took over and Yonah's hands went to the interrogator's wrist. She wrenched the weapon from her interrogator's hand, sustaining a cut on one hand that her adrenaline helped her to ignore, leaped out of the chair, and ran straight for the door.

The two Guards standing at the door easily stopped her attempted escape with a swift punch to the gut that sent Yonah to the floor, releasing the knife and holding her stomach. Nausea sent the world spinning again as she folded herself into a ball.

"Bind her."

She was lifted from the floor and placed into the chair, where the leather straps were again put to use to restrain her arms. Yonah was still recovering from the blow to her stomach. She could feel the gash on her right palm burning.

"Your sister didn't try anything like that," the woman said. She picked the knife up from the floor and set it on the table at the side of the room. "She just quietly took her punishment."

"Punishment for what?" Yonah gasped.

"For betraying the government."

The familiar flame that burned within Yonah found new life. "What kind of government tortures and enslaves its people?"

"One that understands the importance of discipline and consequences." The woman removed a tiny, serrated blade from the wall. "And doing what's best for the greater good."

Although the new weapon sent a shiver of fear through Yonah, her most prominent feeling at the moment was the urge to vomit from the numbing pain in her stomach.

"Yonah, do you remember what it was like when your husband split your lip?"

Yonah's skin prickled at the memory. It had been the first time Naris hurt her. He had accused her of rebel activity when she had really been searching for her brother, but she never told him the truth about that.

She remembered the feel of the blade ripping through her skin, of Naris towering over her, of her panic as she tried to writhe away, of warm blood flowing down her chin.

The tiny blade was suddenly pressed against Yonah's lip.

"What is the name of your accomplice, and where is he going with Sayzia?"

She had survived this once before; she could surely survive it again. Admittedly, the estate healer had stitched her up afterwards, but she could survive the pain of it. She knew it.

The corner of the interrogator's mouth crept just a few centimetres upwards, and she applied pressure to the blade, splitting Yonah's scarred lip open once more.

At first, Yonah pressed her eyes shut as tears burst forth as if the pain would leave her alone if she placed herself in darkness. She whimpered in pain as she felt the serrated edge of the knife saw through the tough skin of her scar. Her fists clenched. Her entire body clenched.

Then she opened her eyes and met with her torturer's face. As the woman registered Yonah's look, an expression of admiration lit up her face.

"Now, that is more like your sister."

Yonah pulled her face away from the knife and said in a low voice and with clenched teeth, "Stop talking about her."

"Why? Does it bother you to think about all the things I've done to her? Do you, perhaps, blame yourself for that?"

Yonah tried to keep her face still, but it seemed this woman was very skilled in the art of reading people because her lips curled into a disgustingly coy smile.

"Maybe I'll finish this," the woman used the knife to tap on Yonah's partially cut lip, sending Yonah into a recoil, "another time. Instead, I'll show you how I got what I needed from your sister."

If Sayzia could survive whatever was coming, so could Yonah.

Unless this woman was lying about her sister being alive. About her having escaped.

No, she was being tortured for information on who Sayzia was with and where she was going. Sayzia was safe for now. As long as Yonah could keep her mouth shut.

"Now, I started with some light burns with Sayzia, as well," the woman said in a tone that belonged to someone instructing someone on how to bake, not what torture techniques they'd been using. "And while I waited for them to blister a little bit, I used..." Her hand drifted along the wall as she searched for the tool. "This!" she said brightly, plucking a pair of tweezers.

Yonah willed her quivering lip to still, both at wanting to appear fearless and the fact that it hurt her cut lip for it to move so much.

The woman took Yonah's fingers and laid them flat on the armrest. "You," she said to one of the Guards. "Hold her down."

The Guard came over and pressed Yonah's hand flat, immobilizing it. The woman used the tweezers to grab hold of one of Yonah's fingernails.

"This can be a little tricky at first," the woman muttered. Keeping hold of Yonah's fingernail, she started to wiggle the tweezers. The tug at her nail was distinctly uncomfortable, but Yonah knew a far worse pain was coming.

The tweezers slipped from Yonah's nail, and she let out a sigh of relief. The woman grinned. "I know, the anticipation is worse than the pain."

Yonah felt her nose wrinkle with disgust, but all she did otherwise was still herself for the next bout of pain.

The tweezers were back on her nail, and the interrogator started to tug. Yonah clenched her teeth, closed her eyes, tried to keep her breathing steady.

Her nail gave way and tore from the nailbed. Yonah let out an exclamation of pain. She looked down at her nail and saw half of it was still attached to her finger, but it was oozing blood.

"And the best part," said the woman, "is that there are nine more to go."

She started to lower the tweezers to the next finger on Yonah's hand, but Yonah lifted her legs and gave the woman a powerful kick to her hips. The woman stumbled backwards, falling into the second Guard's arms. The Guard holding Yonah's hand down gave her another punch to the stomach that sent her gagging.

"Yonah," the woman sighed. "We can move you to the table if you like."

She didn't have anything to say. This woman would do what she wanted with her.

"Will you be good, or do we have to restrain you further?"

Yonah sent the woman her dirtiest glare. The woman bent over to bring herself level with Yonah's face and watched her like she was an animal in a cage.

"Move her."

The two Guards undid the leather straps around her wrists, then dragged her to the table at the side of the room. They placed her on the table, not bothering to be gentle with her, and proceeded to strap her arms at her sides and her ankles below.

"There's a head strap, too, Yonah," the woman said. "Do we need to use that as well?"

"Use your best judgment," Yonah snarled, wincing as her lips touched together with the 'b' and the 'm' in her sentence.

The woman rested her hands on the table as she leaned over Yonah. She whispered, "I will break you. Just like I broke your sister."

Sayzia was alive. Sayzia had survived this. She could, too.

For the next several minutes, the woman plucked at each nail on Yonah's right hand. Yonah writhed away from the pain, but it stayed with her no matter what she did, no matter how she tried to distract herself. When the job was done, her whole hand felt like it was on fire. A slow wave of tears dribbled from her eyes to the table.

The interrogator paused and watched Yonah in silence. Yonah turned her face away from the woman, but she grabbed Yonah's chin and forced her head towards her.

"Who's your accomplice?"

All Yonah was thinking about was that she could work through five more fingernails. It would be terrible and enraging, but she would survive. She would not break.

As if hearing Yonah's thoughts, the woman said, "Perhaps we'll move on to something else. What did I do to Sayzia after the nails?" She picked up the first knife she had used to burn Yonah's neck. It had cooled by now. "Unless you're ready to talk?"

Her lip had been re-split, her neck burned, half of her nails ripped from their beds, and she had cut her palm in an attempted escape, but, no, Yonah wasn't ready to talk. Every second she made her interrogator waste in here was another second closer to safety for Sayzia and Thari. She slowly shook her head.

"That's fine." The woman brought the knife's edge to Yonah's neck and gently dragged it along the burn. Sharp pain atop a throbbing one. Yonah exhaled to stop herself from crying out.

"Aren't you worried," Yonah said, though it was a struggle to keep her voice even, "you'll hit a fatal vein?"

"Oh, I know exactly how to kill you, Yonah. But don't worry. I'm strictly prohibited from doing that. A good government doesn't kill its citizens."

"Just tortures them."

"This is a last resort. We don't want to hurt you."

A laugh that sounded more like a cough escaped Yonah's lips.

"Why are you laughing?" The woman's voice was gentle.

"Ever since I was ten years old the government's been doing nothing but hurting my family and me."

"If you're referring to the labour program–"

"I'm referring to enslavement laws dressed up as a source of social and economic protection for the country when, really, it's just a way to keep the upper class pacified and the rest of us distracted while Althu tries to stay in power."

"My goodness, you've been reading a lot, haven't you? With fancy words like that, you'd think you were university-educated."

"I would have been if it weren't for people like you."

"I'm just a cog in the machine, Yonah."

"You're willingly enabling this corruption. Partially because you're a sadist, but that's a different kind of problem." She looked at the two Guards standing at the door. "You're part of the problem, too."

"Don't engage with them," the woman said sharply.

"Afraid that they'll realize if all the Guards in Harasa joined the rebellion, they could help overthrow this government?"

"Is that your plan? Try to turn the Guards into rebels?"

"I have no plan. I was just here to rescue my sister, and I was successful. That's it."

"Then what is your sister's plan?"

"Probably find a way to rebuild the rebel group."

"In Kelab?"

"Your guess is as good as mine. I haven't had a chance to chat with her in a while, you see."

"Yonah, I need you to be a little more helpful if you want to leave this room with your limbs intact."

"You need me in good enough shape to labour after this, though, right?"

"Accidents can happen. Knives slip. Prisoners try to attack their captors."

"I'm bound to a table."

"President Althu doesn't know that."

Yonah ignored the terrifying implications the woman was making and said, "So you report directly to the president?"

"That's none of your concern."

Keep her talking. The longer they spoke, the less torture.

"Then you must be in charge here," Yonah said.

The woman didn't answer as she removed a coil of rope from the wall. She uncoiled it as she walked back to the table and threaded it through a pair of holes Yonah hadn't noticed before. Yonah quickly realized that she was about to be strangled.

One of the Guards crawled under the table and Yonah felt the two ends of the rope move as he took hold of them.

"So, Yonah, you've probably figured out how this works by now. I ask you a question, and you either answer me, or the rope gets pulled. You have all the power."

Yonah's fear drowned out any disdain she felt at the woman's ridiculous statement.

"What is your accomplice's name?"

She steeled herself.

The woman tapped on the table, and the rope went tight around Yonah's neck. Immediately, she couldn't breathe. The pressure of the rope was crushing her windpipe, and the fibres cut into her burnt and cut skin. Her limbs tried to rip through their bindings, but there was nothing Yonah could do but panic as her lungs scrambled for air. Yet a few more tears crept from her eyes.

Another tap on the table and the rope was released. Yonah gasped for air, which caught on her injured windpipe, and she coughed.

For the first time since the interrogation had started, Yonah wasn't sure she could survive this.

"Who's your accomplice?"

As she continued to gasp for breath, Yonah considered how many times she could go through the suffocation, how much longer each time would get, how long until she would give an answer.

The tap on the table. She had waited too long to provide an answer. The rope went taut. Her eyes bulged in panic. She pulled at the leather bindings around her wrists and ankles. The rope scratched her skin. Her neck hurt. Her lungs cried out in protest. The woman was watching her. So calm. Unfeeling.

This was longer than last time. Yonah's panic grew in strength, and every inch of her body was fighting against the restraints, searching for a way out, fighting impending death.

Yonah didn't hear the tap on the table that signaled for the Guard to release the rope. She coughed weakly this time as air rushed down her throat.

"The name of your accomplice, Yonah."

A fresh bout of tears erupted as desperation swallowed her up. Yonah shook her head. She didn't quite know what she was trying to say with that gesture. Stop? I won't betray my friend?

The woman smirked and tapped on the table again.

Yonah's tears continued as the little breath in her was trapped by the rope bearing down on her throat. Even though, emotionally, she was already exhausted, her body was just beginning its instinctive fight to live.

Pressure was building in her head. Her eyes were going to pop out. Surely, someone was hitting her across the head. And the pain in her neck just kept coming. Burning lungs. Pounding head. Still no air. She was going to die.

She heard a slam from across the room, and the rope released. Her breath came ragged, and it hurt her throat to breathe.

There was yelling. A gunshot. A scream. The sound was far away. Yonah closed her tear-filled eyes. Another gunshot. And another. All she could think about was how much everything hurt.

Someone was yelling at her from right above her. She lazily looked up and saw a face she knew she should recognize. Slightly curly hair. A trim, shaped beard. Golden-brown eyes.

What was meant to be a whimper came out as a low gargle as Yonah realized that Naris stood over her, desperation in his eyes. She knew that, at least right now, he wouldn't continue this torture. Right now, it was over.

Chapter Thirty-Nine

"Yonah, can you hear me?" Naris' eyes were panicked as he looked down at her.

She nodded slowly, too tired to look at him.

He was moving her body. Yonah grimaced at the movement.

"Can you walk? Did she hurt your legs at all?"

She couldn't answer. Naris sat her up on the table and wrapped one of her arms around his shoulders and took her by the waist.

"Hold onto me," he said and slid her off the table to the floor.

Where there had been the interrogator and the two Guards, there were now three bodies crumpled on the floor, pools of blood puddling around them. Yonah looked at Naris to confirm that he had done this.

"Hold on," he said. They started walking. It took all of Yonah's strength to stay upright, but she knew it was the only way out. Naris took much of her weight by holding her waist.

They went up the stairs, past the prison door, up to the armoury, through the door that had always remained locked for Yonah and Thari. It was an office. Another door took them to a sunny hallway. There was a pair of Guards there who came towards Naris and Yonah at a brisk walk.

"This woman is my slave, and I've come to take her home. Nareeb had no business holding her without informing me."

"We can't just let you leave."

Naris revealed his pistol and shoved the barrel underneath the chin of the Guard who had spoken. "The Harasan courts recognize this woman as my slave. I am taking her home." He lowered the gun from the Guard's chin and started down the hallway at such a quick pace he was practically dragging Yonah along with him.

Through another door took them to the top of the stairs in the entrance hall, and, within a few moments, they were outside, where one of Naris' horses waited for them. Naris helped Yonah onto the horse, then climbed on behind her. She leaned back against his chest and closed her eyes. Naris forced the reins into her hands. She felt him kick the horse into a gallop, and they raced away from the fortress.

YONAH DIDN'T REMEMBER much about the next twenty-four hours. All she knew was that she and Naris rode for hours at breakneck speed. She knew they stopped at an inn to sleep, but she passed out the moment Naris laid her on the bed.

In the early hours of the morning, just as the black night sky was turning grey with light, abdominal pain woke Yonah from her deep slumber. She groaned and shifted beneath the bed sheet.

Naris was at her side in moments, clasping her uninjured hand in his. "Yonah," he whispered. "What's wrong?"

She couldn't speak for her injured throat. Yonah shoved the bedsheet away and looked down. Thick clots of blood soiled the otherwise white sheet. Realization hit Yonah, and a mixture of grief, relief, and confusion swirled inside her, each vying for position as her main emotion.

"Is that normal?" Naris asked. "I know women have bleeds but..."

Yonah squeezed Naris' hand. "I think..." Her voice was a hoarse whisper. Speaking was a great effort. "I think I was pregnant."

Naris mouthed the word, then glanced down at the blood. "But not anymore?"

Yonah shook her head. She hadn't had a lunar bleed since before she was arrested for rebel activity.

Naris' eyes glistened with tears he refused to let fall. "What did they do to you?"

Not wanting to think about it, Yonah closed her eyes and waited for the cramping to dissipate.

Within the hour, she and Naris were back on the road. Today, she sat side-saddle. For the hours they rode, Yonah and Naris were quiet. Although sleep was out of the question on horseback, Yonah tried to close her eyes and rest as much as she could. Naris' arms on both sides of her helped to keep her upright on the horse.

Naris asked her if she needed to stop for a rest or if they could press on and finish the ride to Vaha. They pushed for another while, and long after the sun had set, the white peaks of the palace materialized.

Naris helped Yonah up the stairs to her old bedroom and into bed. Yonah tried to sleep, but a few minutes later, Daza, the estate healer, was tending to her. He cooled her forehead, examined her neck, stitched her lip, wrapped the fingers on her right hand, and gave her a medicinal tea. When he finally left Yonah's bedside, she closed her eyes and tried to sleep.

"Will she be alright?" she heard Naris ask in a whisper.

"I think so, Master Naris," the healer replied. "Her recovery may be a very long time, though."

"That's fine. She's safe now."

THE FOLLOWING DAY, one of the household slaves–not Praha–brought food up to Yonah. Daza came in to check on her again and, after he finished examining Yonah, handed her a letter.

"Praha has been holding onto this for you," he said quietly. "She asked me to bring it to you as soon as possible."

Despite her weakened state, Yonah felt her heart pump just a little harder. "How is she?" she croaked.

Daza hesitated, then said, "She's managing."

Yonah wanted to ask more about her friend, but between the pain in her throat and the fact that Praha wasn't here, she let it be. She unfolded the letter, and a small note fell from it. The note read:

Some time after Naris took you to Kelab, a letter addressed only to you arrived from an estate southwest of Vaha. The letter was just an order form, but a note at the bottom specially requested that you reply. I replied, and soon I was writing back and forth to a man named Sharinn, the brother to ex-Minister Hara.

I'm not sorry for helping you with the rebellion. I am sorry I can't see you. I just haven't found the strength yet.

Praha

As she folded the note and turned to the letter, Yonah quickly glanced upwards. Daza had left the room.

Yonah,

I hope that this letter will find you someday soon. My name is Sharinn OBura. You knew my sister as Minister Hara.

Shortly after you met, my sister informed me of your alliance. I am grateful she did because it wasn't long after that that she was arrested and enslaved. I know she currently works on an estate in the southern part of Harasa.

I wanted to contact you to let you know that you still have an ally at our estate. Since Hara was arrested, our family no longer holds any political power (of course, President Althu would never let the sibling of a rebel become a minister in his government!), but we still have friends among our country's politicians.

If you are ever able, you are more than welcome to come to our family estate. Just wait at the entrance to the maze and tell anyone who asks that you're the new gardener.

Good luck and good health,
Sharinn

Yonah tucked the letter and Praha's note into her pocket and fell back into her pillows, exhausted. It was nice to know there was still someone she could turn to for help with the rebellion. She just didn't know how or when she could get to the OBura estate. She needed to heal first, and the Guards were most definitely looking for her and Naris after their escape from the labour camp.

Yonah closed her eyes and fell back to sleep.

Chapter Forty

Around noontime, Naris brought in a tray and sat in a chair next to the bed. He silently set Yonah up with lunch—broth and a small bowl of berries—then sat and watched as Yonah slowly sipped at the broth.

Although the silence was weighted with everything that had happened since Yonah's arrest, Yonah was content not to speak, partly for her sore throat and partly for not wanting to address the past horrible weeks.

Naris finally broke the silence. "I know you're not well, but," his soft eyes bore into Yonah's, "how are you feeling today?"

Thinking about the interrogation sent Yonah's body shaking. She held up her bandaged right hand to look at it. "Uh…" Her voice was not her own. It belonged to an elderly woman. She turned her gaze back to Naris, who, seeing her distress, reached for her hand but paused. Yonah stared at his hand, frozen mid-reach. She cradled her hands at her chest and shifted her eyes to her tray, not wanting to see the hurt she knew would be filling Naris' eyes. "I'm better than yesterday."

"I'm sorry I couldn't have come sooner," Naris muttered. "Did you do what you set out to do?"

Yonah looked up at him, perplexed for a moment, then remembering that he was the one who told her Sayzia was at the labour camp.

"I think so," she replied. "Or so that woman told me." The woman who smirked every time Yonah showed any emotion. "You killed them."

Naris pursed his lips. "Yes. I…was angry."

"At me?"

Naris shook his head. "At them. For hurting you."

It seemed no matter what wrongs Yonah inflicted on Naris, be they imagined or real, he would always try to protect her from any others who wished to harm her.

"You'll be arrested again," she said. And, without a master, she would likely be sent back to the labour camp. She was sure the government didn't want to risk her attempting any further rebel activity on another estate. The thought sent a thrill of panic through Yonah that she had to breathe out.

"Yes, well, they'll certainly try."

Yonah gave a questioning look to Naris but didn't say anything.

"We're leaving tomorrow," he said.

"Leaving? You're going to run?"

"I'm not going to prison, and I'm certainly not going to let them turn me into a slave. That would be the end of me."

Yonah looked at Naris with scorn. "Now that you're at risk of enslavement, you're against it?" She folded her arms across her chest to further illustrate her disbelief at his hypocrisy.

"We won't be together if we're arrested," Naris said.

Yonah shook her head, already too exhausted to pursue this conversation that was quickly turning into a heated argument. "Where will we go?"

"I had originally hoped to find someplace north near Kejal's estate, but I think that's where they'll look first. So, we're heading south."

Away from the OBura estate. Beyond Kelab. "With no destination in mind?"

"Maybe Modeef."

That was the country south of Harasa. Yonah had no intention of going there. But if she and Naris were heading south, they would pass near Kelab, and Yonah could either get away from him or convince him to join the rebellion.

"We'll find someplace where they can't find us, and we can just be happy together," he said.

It was unlikely that she would be able to convince him to join the rebellion. All Naris wanted was to live his fairy tale life with Yonah, albeit an altered one. He didn't really care about the politics of the country or the wellbeing of his fellow human beings. But Yonah would have a little time to try to convince him.

"We leave tomorrow?" she asked.

"Yes. It will be just you and me again."

Things were never simple when it was just Yonah and Naris.

Epilogue

Under the cover of night's darkness, Sayzia and Thari collapsed onto the fountain in the middle of the town square and took their first drink of water in over a day. They made no effort to keep their clothes dry as they sloshed life onto their faces and into their mouths.

Some of the other escapees had made it to town as well. A few had perished in the desert, too weak to fight the elements.

Thea stumbled over and drank from the fountain, then lowered herself to the ground. She glanced up at Sayzia and Thari, who were sitting at the fountain's edge, holding hands.

"I haven't said thank you yet," Thea said.

Thari didn't acknowledge the sentiment. "I'm sorry we left Yonah."

Sayzia's eyes were on the horizon in the direction from which they came. Thari couldn't know it, but she was imagining Yonah locked in a cell, working the mine and the forge, or worse yet, trapped in an interrogation room just as she had been.

"We have to find cover," Thea said. Sayzia was grateful for the interruption of her thoughts. She couldn't get lost thinking about something she couldn't change.

They left the fountain just as more escapees arrived and found an empty alleyway to hide in for the rest of the night. There was no plan-making at the moment. The three of them simply curled up next to each other and fell asleep, exhausted from their dangerous trek through the desert. It wasn't until the following morning that they began to move beyond mere survival and could begin thinking about next steps.

"Should we go back to Kelab?" Thea asked.

"Who do we know there, now?" asked Sayzia.

Thari said, "Nobody. Dani and Ravi are in Kirash with another abolitionist group."

"How did that happen?" Sayzia asked.

"Yonah brought us to them."

"Do we go there then?" said Thea.

Sayzia shook her head. "There needs to be a movement in Kelab. That's where the politics is. But we should get word to the Kirash group so we can start working together. Thari, you'll go there to let them know what's happened and set up a communication line we can use between Kirash and Kelab."

"But Sayzia," Thari took Sayzia's hand. Her nailbeds had already hardened after her interrogation. "I just found you again."

"You can join us in Kelab when you're done in Kirash," Sayzia replied firmly. "You're the only one of us who knows how to find the Kirash group."

"Just come with me," he pleaded. "We can go together."

"You'll join us after," Sayzia said. She gave Thari's hand a squeeze. "We'll be alright."

At nightfall, Sayzia, Thari, and Thea emerged from their hiding place.

Some of the other escapees had the same idea. The three of them quickly spoke to as many of the escapees as possible to let them know that if they wanted to help with abolishing the Harasan slave act, they were welcome to join them in Kelab. Some people were very interested in helping, some didn't know where else to go, and others declined, saying they wanted to go home to their families.

A small group was forming in the square, waiting to depart for the capital. Sayzia and Thari stood apart from them as they said their goodbyes.

"I'll see you soon," Thari said. He clutched Sayzia's hands.

"Thank you for rescuing us."

Thari shook his head. "It was all for you, Sayzia. I shouldn't have, but I deserted the cause just to save you."

Sayzia smiled wryly. "I should never leave you and my sister alone together. You're both too passionate." Her face fell as she thought of Yonah.

"We can go get her," Thari said. "I know a way in. It does require a boat and a little stupidity."

"We can't right now," Sayzia said softly. "But if we can get rid of the slavery act, then Yonah will be safe."

Although part of him wished that Sayzia was ready to perform a rescue mission for Yonah, Thari nodded in understanding. The abolitionists were soon to be in a much better position than prior to the breakout.

"I love you," he said. "Be safe."

"I love you, Thari. I can't wait to see you again."

They shared a soft but long kiss and separated. Sayzia joined Thea and the others headed for Kelab, and Thari went north, back to Kirash.

Acknowledgements

Despite the term "independent author," producing a book isn't a solo job. I have these people to thank for helping me create a book I can be proud of:

Thank you to Alix, Jenneth, Karlee, and Madison for beta reading this manuscript. I received exceptional feedback from you all.

A big thank you goes to Mandi from Stoneridge Books. She is wonderful to work with, and I am extremely grateful that she was able to provide the cover design and interior formatting for this book.

Thank you to my friends and family who, over the past couple years, have asked me how this book was coming along, and when the next launch was going to happen. Frankly, your interest feeds my artistic ego.

And endless thanks to my husband for being so supportive of my writing and this project. Not everyone is as lucky as I am to have someone in their corner helping them chase their dreams.

About the Author

A Burden of Love is Heather's second novel. Her passion for reading, writing, and learning more about the human condition led to her earning a Bachelor of Arts in English with a History minor at the University of Saskatchewan. When she's not writing, Heather is working as a group fitness and music instructor, or volunteering in her local performing arts community. She resides in Saskatoon, Canada with her husband, child, and dog. You can learn more about Heather and her upcoming projects at www.heatherhataley.com.

Printed in the USA
CPSIA information can be obtained
at www.ICGtesting.com
LVHW092117090923
757631LV00001B/87

9 781777 797324